THE

TEMPLAR'S REVENGE

A James Acton Thriller

By J. Robert Kennedy

James Acton Thrillers

The Protocol	*Amazon Burning*
Brass Monkey	*The Riddle*
Broken Dove	*Blood Relics*
The Templar's Relic	*Sins of the Titanic*
Flags of Sin	*Saint Peter's Soldiers*
The Arab Fall	*The Thirteenth Legion*
The Circle of Eight	*Raging Sun*
The Venice Code	*Wages of Sin*
Pompeii's Ghosts	*Wrath of the Gods*

The Templar's Revenge

Special Agent Dylan Kane Thrillers

Rogue Operator	*Death to America*
Containment Failure	*Black Widow*
Cold Warriors	*The Agenda*

Delta Force Unleashed Thrillers

Payback
Infidels
The Lazarus Moment
Kill Chain
Forgotten

Detective Shakespeare Mysteries

Depraved Difference
Tick Tock
The Redeemer

Zander Varga, Vampire Detective

The Turned

THE

TEMPLAR'S REVENGE

A James Acton Thriller

J. ROBERT KENNEDY

ISBN-10: 978-1548349349

ISBN-13: 1548349348

First Edition

10 9 8 7 6 5 4 3 2 1

For Manchester.

THE

TEMPLAR'S REVENGE

A James Acton Thriller

"Saladin ordered that they should be beheaded, choosing to have them dead rather than in prison. With him was a whole band of scholars and Sufis and a certain number of devout men and ascetics, each begged to be allowed to kill one of them, and drew his sword and rolled back his sleeve. Saladin, his face joyful, was sitting on his dais, the unbelievers showed black despair."

Imad ed-Din
Saladin's secretary, on the execution of captured Templar Knights
Circa 1187

"Non nobis, Domine, non nobis, sed Nomini tuo da gloriam."
"Not unto us, O Lord, not unto us, but unto thy Name give glory."

Motto of the Knights Templar

PREFACE

Around 1119 AD, nine men traveled to the Holy Land as part of the First Crusade. Led by a nobleman, Hugues de Payens, they approached King Baldwin II of the Kingdom of Jerusalem, and received permission to form their order, the Poor Fellow-Soldiers of Christ and of the Temple of Solomon. Their headquarters was established at the Temple Mount, and for almost two centuries, they fulfilled their duty to protect pilgrims on their journey to the Holy Land, and much more.

From humble beginnings, these nine founded what would become a force of over 20,000, with over 2,000 knights. Their power and influence stretched from the Holy Land to Christendom, their accumulated wealth enough to rival kings. The first international bankers, they held vast amounts of real estate, and were answerable only to the Pope.

All of which would lead to their betrayal.

And downfall.

But as skilled warriors and tacticians, with such wealth at their disposal, could such a group truly be destroyed?

Would those who survived the purge, truly lay down their arms while those who had betrayed them continued on, unpunished?

After eight centuries, this group continues to fascinate, leaving millions still to question what became of the Knights Templar.

Saint-Pierre-la-Mer, France

Present Day

Simone Chartrand gripped the wheel tightly with both hands. He had trained for these situations, yet had never been in one before. It was exhilarating and terrifying at the same time, and though part of him enjoyed the adrenaline rush, he would trade it all for the leisurely drive to the chateau originally planned.

But it would appear Pierre Ridefort, his employer's son, had other plans for his passengers.

"Weapons?"

He glanced in his rearview mirror at his passengers, two professors his employer had flown over for a purpose he wasn't privy to. "I've got a Glock in my shoulder holster, spare mags in the glove compartment."

"Can we call someone?" asked the woman.

Chartrand shook his head. "I've already tried, but I'm getting no answer. It's as if the lines are down."

"No cellphones at the chateau?"

"No, Monsieur Ridefort always considered them insecure. In fact, he has jammers so they can't be used on the grounds."

Archaeology Professor James Acton's eyes narrowed. "A little paranoid, isn't he?"

"With good reason, evidently," said his wife, Archaeology Professor Laura Palmer.

Chartrand pressed on the accelerator, taking the next corner hard, as he tried to put more distance between them and the vehicle following them. "Sorry about that."

Acton collected himself in the back seat. "Don't apologize. Just get us to the chateau."

Chartrand gasped as he saw something ahead. He reached forward and hit the cruise control as a loud bang preceded the splintering of the windshield.

And the end of his life.

Outside Hattin, Kingdom of Jerusalem
July 4, 1187 AD

Raymond glanced over his shoulder at his master and friend, the grief on the man's face matching his own. It was a massacre. There was no other word to describe it. They had marched into battle against the forces of Sultan Salah ad-Din, commonly known among the Christian population as Saladin, 20,000 strong, including 1500 knights on horseback.

And they were no more.

Saladin's forces were larger in number, but that wasn't why they had lost. His master, Sir Guy of Ridefort, had been privy to the disastrous planning sessions by their leaders, leaders so filled with distrust of each other, that those ultimately in charge did the opposite of what their political rivals recommended, seemingly even if it were obvious the advice was correct.

And it had led to their downfall.

Almost every man was dead or dying, and now a long line of their brothers, their fellow soldiers, all devout members of the Poor Fellow-Soldiers of Christ and of the Temple of Solomon, all members of the Knights Templar, were being shown no quarter. While the nobles had been shown mercy, for kings did not kill kings, the local converts to Christianity were slaughtered, and the European Christians that had survived, prepared for sale in the slave markets.

But the Templar and Hospitaller Knights were beheaded one by one, as Saladin watched on from an elevated platform, smiling and laughing with his court. Eager leaders of their blasphemous Muslim religion stood in line for the opportunity to behead one of these brave men, proving to Raymond they were the bloodthirsty savages his clergy had warned him of. He couldn't imagine a Christian clergyman eagerly beheading an infidel, yet here, hidden among the rock-strewn hills, he and Sir Guy watched the depravity enthusiastically endorsed and participated in, by men who claimed to hold their god above all else.

What god would want innocent men who had surrendered, to be slaughtered?

He had heard it told that the Muslims worshiped the same god as he did, yet he found that impossible to believe. But if they did, they had corrupted His teachings, as had the Jews who had once overrun this land and murdered his Lord, Jesus Christ.

A tear rolled down his cheek as he saw the venerated True Cross hoisted over the heads of the cheering mob of soldiers, their shouts of Allahu Akbar echoing between the hills that had hemmed in the Crusader army, ultimately dooming it.

"We must do something, your honor."

Sir Guy tore his eyes away from the torturous sight below to look at his sergeant. "And what would you propose we do? Rush down there and take on thirty-thousand men, just the two of us?"

"But it's the True Cross! Those heathens will destroy it!"

"Which is why we must keep our heads. We are but two, with no hope of retrieving it. If there is ever any hope of rescuing that upon

5

which our Savior sacrificed Himself for our sins, then we must know what they do with it."

"But what if they destroy it here, today?"

Sir Guy shook his head. "No, I don't think Saladin will do that. He will destroy it for his people to see, to prove their victory over us to those he needs to sustain his armies. He will take it to a city and destroy it publicly. We must determine where that is, and where in that city he is holding it. Only then can we act."

"But we are still only two."

Sir Guy reached out and grabbed Raymond's shoulder with a smile. "You are mistaken, my friend. We are at least three." His eyes turned to the Heavens. "We have God on our side, and with Him, nothing can stop us."

Raymond nodded, not saying anything, instead turning to watch another of their friends beheaded by the horde below.

If God is on our side, who was on theirs that could defeat us so soundly?

Saint-Pierre-la-Mer, France

Four years ago

Jacques Ridefort sat on his couch, watching the horrifying events unfold at the Vatican, tens of thousands of Muslims having charged the gates of the holy city, overwhelming the small, mostly symbolic force. What had already been a stressful situation for him and his son was now even more so. The loss of the Vatican was an unfathomable occurrence, yet here it was, on his television screen, playing out for the world to see.

It wouldn't last.

The Italian government was already promising swift action, with many nations already pledging troops. Some commentators were calling for the army to kill everyone in sight, others calling for calm.

He feared who would win the day.

But these calamitous events weren't his primary concern. It was the discovery of the crypt holding four Templar Knights that had led to the discovery of a scroll containing a passage from the Koran that occupied his thoughts. It wasn't the Koranic fragment that concerned him—he couldn't care less, his opinion on Islam one of disdain. It was the bodies of the knights themselves. For they were family, and with their discovery, they were no longer at peace, and someone, perhaps someone of importance, would eventually wonder why they were there.

And that was something he wasn't certain the world was ready to know.

"They've identified them!"

He looked up as his son, Pierre, barely twenty, rushed into the room, holding up his iPad. "It's on the BBC website."

Jacques frowned. "So soon?" He sighed. "Well, if our documents are accurate, then the sarcophagi were engraved with their names, so I guess we shouldn't be surprised."

"Oh, I think you will be."

Jacques' eyes narrowed. "What do you mean?"

"They've identified them as Sir John of Ridefort, Rodney of Ridefort, and get this." There was a dramatic pause. "Hugues de Payens and Godfrey de Saint-Omer."

Jacques' jaw dropped slightly as he leaned forward. "They don't know about the nameplates!"

Pierre shook his head. "Evidently. But why would they get two right, and two wrong?"

Jacques chewed his cheek for a moment. "I don't know. But this does complicate things."

"Does it? They've desecrated the bodies of our ancestors, whether they have their names right or not. We need to do something!"

Jacques stared at his son. "And what would you have us do? Reveal ourselves to the world, and risk that which we have protected for so long?"

His son sighed, dropping into a chair across from his father. "Why not? What our family has done for eight centuries is, well, cool! We're actually Templars. Who else can say that? Why shouldn't we go public with who we are, and what we do? It's not like we have to tell everyone where the artifact is. But shouldn't we get some credit for what we've done? For what we've sacrificed?"

His father shook his head. The boy was impetuous, obsessed with things his generation seemed uniquely cursed with. Instant gratification, recognition without effort, fame, fortune, adulation. It made him fear for the future of what remained of the Order. Jacques was the current Grand Master of the Knights Templar, his family carrying on the traditions in their own small way, handed down for almost 800 years in anonymity, hidden from the world. As far as he could tell from reading the journals of those who had come before him, none had ever questioned their duty, though he was certain those accounts were whitewashed to a point. All boys had their problems, though over time, they became men, eventually realized what that meant, and became responsible adults.

But this generation was different.

His son showed no signs of maturing, instead growing increasingly obsessed with the fact he was a Templar, and how "cool" that was, how important that was, and how it entitled him to a glory that was being denied him unfairly.

But he was young.

And he should have another twenty years before it would be his turn to lead.

Should.

Yet he wouldn't. Jacques was dying. Pancreatic cancer. He had perhaps a year or two left, unless the aggressive treatment he was undergoing worked, and even then, the chances of him being alive in five years were slim to none. That meant Pierre would be taking over.

It was terrifying.

Should he go public, that which they had protected for so long might be lost to zealots hell-bent on possessing it, or worse, on destroying it. And that had to be his focus, not concerns over whether his ancestors were treated with respect, now that they had been discovered.

"Well?"

He gazed at his son, still staring at him impatiently. He hadn't told him about the cancer, and his son was so self-absorbed, he hadn't noticed that his father was wasting away before his eyes. He frowned. "We must protect it at all costs, and cannot risk public disclosure, not now." He returned his attention to the television screen. "For now, we need to ensure the dignity of our ancestors is preserved."

His son growled in frustration. "And how are we supposed to do that?"

Jacques pointed at the screen, footage playing from earlier of a hasty helicopter evacuation from the university where the bodies had been taken, showing a man and a woman escaping just in time, a man and woman he recognized from the inquiry after the events in London a year ago.

Professors James Acton and Laura Palmer.

"Perhaps *they* can help us."

Pierre peered at the screen. "Who are they?"

"Two professors brought in by the Vatican, if we are to believe the news." Jacques sighed. "But I think we will have to wait for things to calm down."

Damascus, Ayyubid Sultanate

August 1, 1187 AD

Raymond stood at the rear of the gathered crowd, his fist pumping the air in sync with those around him, though his lips were sealed with a frown, his face stained with tears.

For it was a gut-wrenching sight.

The True Cross, a spear lancing its top, was paraded upside down through the crowd, while the filth spat at it and threw their sandals, with Saladin, standing on a platform at the head of the Citadel, grinning as the holiest of relics was desecrated. His religious leaders and advisors flanked him, praising their cursed Allah, giddy with their recent success, and Saladin's own audacious display, dragging the True Cross behind his horse as he entered the city.

Saladin silenced the crowd with a raised hand, and spoke to the masses, his words repeated by others so those in the back could hear.

And what Raymond heard enraged him.

He reached for his sword, hidden under the traditional robes of the Bedouin they had disguised themselves as, but felt a steadying hand on his wrist. He glanced over at Sir Guy, who gently shook his head, his eyes imploring him for calm. Raymond sighed, returning his attention to the speech that had those surrounding them in near rapture.

These infidels worshiped this man as if he were a messiah, and it was clear to Raymond that Saladin relished in their adoration. And as he droned on about their great victory, and those yet to come, Raymond tuned him out, instead focusing on the True Cross as it continued to be disrespected, before Saladin's guards finally seized it and carried it inside the building, perhaps the last time mortals would ever see it.

For if his understanding of Arabic was accurate, and it was, tomorrow, it was to be burned.

St. Paul's University

St. Paul, Maryland

Present Day

"With this memorial, we honor their memories, and the contributions they made to the world in which they thrived for too short a time. I know I, for one, shall never forget any of them, for they touched my life in ways they could never know. I know those of you who were here at the time will remember Robbie Andrews. He was a brilliant student, but also a funny guy."

Professor James Acton smiled at the thought of his protégé, desperately clinging to the happy memories of those days, rather than giving into the horror. "You could never get those darned earphones off his head, always listening to his iPod wherever he went."

"I can't live without my tunes!" shouted someone from the gathered crowd of friends and family, of students and faculty current and old, eliciting urgently needed laughs.

Acton tossed his head back, jabbing a finger in the direction of the comment. "That's *exactly* what he would always say. In fact, he said that very thing to me moments before he died." Acton's voice grew subdued, and his chest ached as he sucked in a deep breath and held it, his wife, Professor Laura Palmer, stepping forward and squeezing his hand. He nodded at her with a slight smile, tears filling his eyes.

"Robbie was the bravest boy I ever met. He sacrificed—" Acton gripped the podium, and his best friend and boss, Dean Gregory Milton, stepped up beside him, gripping Acton's shoulder. "He sacrificed himself to try and save me. And he succeeded. Thanks to his heroic actions, I was able to survive." A tear rolled down his cheek, and his chin dropped to his chest as he battled his survivor's guilt, something he thought he had put long behind him.

He looked at Robbie's parents, sitting in the front row, both with tears running down their cheeks. He stared out at the crowd, surprised to see he wasn't alone in his grief as he saw face after face in anguish, some he recognized, many he didn't.

St. Paul's was a small university, a tight-knit university, and the massacre that had taken his entire archaeological team had affected it deeply. Though few of the students that attended the school today were here at the time, all had heard the stories, and some now worked the very dig site in Peru where his students had perished—massacred by men he now considered friends, all members of America's elite Delta Force.

They had been manipulated by a corrupt President, fed false intel naming him and his students as terrorists, then sent in to execute them, all in an attempt to recover an archaeological artifact they had found. A crystal skull. He shivered at the thought, then smiled as he remembered young Robbie had done the same when holding it. He drew in a quick breath then sighed.

"Sometimes I miss the old days when men weren't supposed to cry." He wiped his cheeks clean as some in the audience chuckled.

15

Laura handed him a bright pink handkerchief. Acton held it up for the audience to see. "A manly choice." He dried his cheeks and handed it back as the chuckles turned into outright laughter, the crowd desperate for relief.

"So, that's enough of my reminiscing. We're not here to dwell on the events of that day, but to celebrate their lives, and the legacy they left behind. That's why I was so thrilled to find out about this memorial in their honor, and I am touched that so many turned out today to remember them. Thank you, and God bless."

He stepped back, and the crowd rose from their seats, a roaring ovation ensuing as those gathered fed off of each other's energy, desperate to dispel the negative emotions so many were feeling. Acton exchanged handshakes with those gathered on stage, then stepped down to pay his respects to the relatives in the front row. It was a whirlwind of tears and laughter, each parent and loved one with a story to tell, a memory to share, all of which Acton at once rejoiced and mourned in. It was painful yet cathartic, emotions he had suppressed for years returning to the surface, though with the benefit of time to temper them.

He exchanged a final hug with Robbie's mother when he spotted four men in suits walking away from him. Four men that appeared very familiar, all well-built, one large and black, one short and Asian, one with a shaved head, the last with civilian hair and a dangerous, confident bearing.

Atlas, Niner, Red, and Dawson.

All members of the Delta Force unit he now considered his friends.

And responsible for the massacre now commemorated.

"Excuse me for a moment." He gently pushed through the crowd, Laura noticing.

"What is it?"

He said nothing, but raised his hand, pointing over the crowd toward the four men who were approaching a black SUV. Acton finally freed himself of the crowd, breaking out into a jog as a key fob was held out and pressed, the lights on the SUV flashing, the alarm chirping.

"Hey, guys!"

All four turned, smiles spreading on their faces as Acton came to a halt in front of them. "Leaving without saying hello?"

Command Sergeant Major Burt "Big Dog" Dawson extended a hand and Acton shook it, the others doing the same, Sergeant Carl "Niner" Sung pushing Acton aside as he rushed toward Laura and picked her up in a bear hug.

"How's my favorite British archaeology professor?"

She laughed, pushing him away as regular hugs were exchanged with the others. "That's rather specific, isn't it?"

"Hey, I know a lot of professors, and I love them all."

Laura turned to Dawson. "I'm surprised to see you guys here."

Dawson nodded, his face becoming grim. "You weren't supposed to see us."

Acton gestured toward the massive Atlas. "He's kind of hard to miss."

Niner smacked Sergeant Leon "Atlas" James' shoulder. "I told you we should have left Hulk back at the hotel."

Atlas dropped his chin, smacking his fists together at the knuckles. "Atlas sad."

Acton chuckled at the Hulk imitation. "Well, we saw you. I assume you're here for the memorial and not to see us?"

Dawson smiled slightly. "Professor, at least one of us has been here every year to pay our respects. We all lost that day, and in the days that followed, but none more than your students." He stared over Acton's shoulder at the newly erected monument. "I intend to be here every year that I'm able."

Acton's head bobbed slowly. "I understand." He paused, staring at each of them. "You guys know I don't blame you."

Laura took Acton's arm, her eyes filled with tears. "None of us do. You were lied to. We know that."

Dawson grunted. "True, and that does make it easier, but *I* killed those students, and I'll have to live with that."

Niner shook his head. "*We* killed those students, and I shot the guards. It doesn't matter who pulled the trigger, we were all there."

Atlas' impossibly deep voice rumbled in agreement. "The tiny man is right. We're a team, but I know BD'll never let us share in the blame."

Dawson gave Atlas an appreciative look when his phone rang. He answered it. "On our way." He shoved the phone back in his pocket. "We've gotta go." He quickly shook Acton's hand then gave Laura a hug.

"Say hi to Maggie for me."

Dawson smiled. "Will do."

Goodbyes were exchanged with the others, then they piled into their SUV. Dawson put the window down. "Try to stay out of trouble, Professors. We won't be able to help you this time."

Acton laughed, placing a hand on his chest. "What, us get into trouble?"

Niner laughed. "Doc, that golden horseshoe up your ass is tipped the wrong way." He pulled from the curb and Acton waved at their friends as they drove away. Milton walked up to them.

"Is that who I think it was?"

Acton nodded. "You should have said hi."

Milton frowned, absentmindedly rubbing his back. "I'm not sure I'd be as forgiving as you two have been."

Acton smiled slightly. He understood his friend's reluctance. One of the men from Bravo Team, who Dawson led, had shot Milton twice, leaving him for dead. He had survived, but had been wheelchair bound for over a year. He could now walk again, though still had problems with endurance.

But he was walking.

"Back to my place for some drinks?"

Acton exchanged a glance with Laura who grinned. "Absolutely! But don't forget, we've got an early flight in the morning."

Milton paused for a moment. "Wait, I remember, just give me a second."

Acton winked at Laura. "It must suck getting old."

Milton faux glared at him. "I'm what, four years older than you?"

"Yeah, but most of those years have been behind a desk." Acton reached out and rubbed Milton's protruding stomach then poked it. Milton tried a poor imitation of the Pillsbury Doughboy. Acton gave him a look. "Never do that again."

Milton laughed. "Trust me, that sounded far better in my head." He snapped his fingers. "South of France. Someone claims to know who your four Templars are that were found under the Vatican."

Laura patted him on the cheek, delivering her congratulations as though Milton were a baby. "There's the good boy! I knew you'd remember!"

Milton frowned. "Did I mention it was BYOB?"

Acton shrugged. "No problem." He tilted his head lazily toward Laura. "Don't worry. He'll have forgotten by the time we get there."

Damascus, Ayyubid Sultanate

August 1, 1187 AD

Raymond inched forward, his torch bright but still, little air moving in the tunnels underneath Damascus. Built for the most part centuries ago by the Romans, these tunnels moved water from the Barada River throughout the city and beyond, irrigating the fertile lands surrounding the burgeoning population.

And it stank.

Though the water flowed, centuries of creatures great and small had made their way inside, living and dying within the confined walls. It was overwhelming, and on any other day, Raymond may have complained, though not today. Not tonight. Tonight, he and his master, Sir Guy, led a small force on a mission perhaps more critical than any of them had undertaken before.

A mission to rescue the True Cross.

Saladin had promised to burn it publicly tomorrow, leaving tonight their only chance. After witnessing the desecration by the gathered hordes celebrating Saladin's victory, they had retreated to the safety of a secret Templar residence, finding only eight men able to fight, another half a dozen who had escaped the slaughter, too sick to help, despite their willingness. They chose five, leaving the others to execute the rest of Sir Guy's plan, a plan at once foolhardy and brilliant in its simplicity.

The problem with it, was that it required everything—*everything*—to go right.

But this was the True Cross, and surely, with God on their side, they would prevail.

And so far, they had.

The tunnels were a forgotten feature of the ancient city, something that just was, like the streets under one's feet. They had always been there, and always would be, and few paid them any mind.

Which meant they were unguarded.

Gaining entry had been easy, and one of their guides knew them like the back of his hand, this the easiest way to move about as a Christian in a Muslim-controlled city. Yet these tunnels would only get them so far. Once inside the Citadel, they had no idea what to expect.

Their guide, Gerard, raised a hand, bringing them to a halt. Raymond's heart pounded from the excitement of what was to come, and the stifling stench and oppressive humidity that made breathing difficult in their heavy armor. Gerard pointed up, and Raymond stepped forward carefully, peering at an access point above them. Sir Guy hooked a rope ladder to the bars that covered the hole, then pulled himself up. Raymond positioned himself underneath, gripping his master's boots as Sir Guy stood on his shoulders, balancing himself.

Gerard handed up a heavy hammer wrapped in thick cloth, and a metal chisel, as the others tied off the long, narrow boat they had brought with them. Raymond stared up, his view mostly blocked, little if any light overhead, and nothing but the sounds of their own heavy breathing. Sir Guy quickly went to work, carefully and deliberately hammering at the ancient stone holding the bars in place. It sounded impossibly loud in their confined space, but the cloth produced a dull thud, and if Sir Guy's placement of the chisel were judicious yet efficient, they might gain entry undetected.

Though only if the room over their heads were unoccupied.

And they wouldn't know that until they were either discovered, or they gained entry. Another thud, a sharp retort from the chisel hitting the rock responding. And still no shouts of discovery. Sir Guy pulled on one of the bars, crumbled stone splashing at Raymond's feet, then a gasp of victory as it came loose. He handed it down and Gerard took it, carefully placing it in the water at their feet so it wouldn't make a sound.

Sir Guy pushed up on his toes, poking his head through the opening, glancing around. He reached down, his hand opening and closing.

"Torch," hissed Raymond.

Gerard placed one in Sir Guy's hand, and it was quickly shoved through the hole, Raymond slowly spinning in place, giving his master a full view of what awaited them. The torch was handed down.

"It's clear. Let's make quick work of this." Several quick, heavier raps, and another bar was passed down, followed by another. By the fourth, the tools were returned, and the pressure on Raymond's shoulders eased. He shoved his palms under Sir Guy's heels and pushed, grunting from the effort as he heaved his master through the hole above. He quickly followed, using the rope ladder hooked to the last remaining bar, Sir Guy pulling him through.

Raymond rolled to his feet then helped the others as Sir Guy stepped away. They spread out, daggers drawn, for if it came to swords, it would mean they were discovered. And dead. Raymond advanced to Sir Guy's position, and with his eyes adjusted, could see they were inside the outer wall of the Citadel.

Sir Guy pointed to the far end, a guard tower with torches revealing two men. He glanced over his shoulder to see the same not two hundred paces from where they crouched. A boisterous celebration had masked the sounds of their entry, Sir Guy's suggestion that they come before most fell asleep, so far proving wise.

The Muslims' overconfident merriment would prove their downfall.

Sir Guy moved forward, hugging the building lining the entire rear of the walled Citadel, then stopped under a window. He rose to his full height and peered through the bars, then crouched down again as the others gathered. "Those godless bastards! The cross is inside, on the floor of the room, surrounded by their shoes and covered in garbage."

Raymond's belly filled with rage as he rose to take a look. Two of Saladin's men were marching around the True Cross, wearing Templar tunics. The room roared with laughter as the men grabbed at their necks, then collapsed to the floor as if their throats had been slit.

And it gave him an idea.

He lowered himself and turned to Sir Guy. "Sir, I had a thought."

"Yes?"

"We have no hope of remaining out here undiscovered, and we cannot go inside and fight that many."

"Agreed."

"But, what if we just walked in and took it?"

Sir Guy's eyebrows rose, and Gerard smacked him on the shoulder. "Have you been drinking?"

Sir Guy smiled slightly and exchanged a knowing glance with Raymond—alcohol never passed his sergeant's lips.

Raymond pressed on. "They are mocking us in there, pretending to be soldiers. We both speak fluent Arabic. I say we take advantage of their overconfidence."

A smile spread across Sir Guy's face. "Brilliant idea." He pointed at the others. "You will cover our rear. If we are caught, leave so you might try again. But if we succeed, it will be up to you to hold them off so we may escape with the True Cross. Understood?"

Everyone nodded, and pride surged through Raymond as he realized these men were accepting their orders, knowing they would likely die in the next few minutes.

Sir Guy turned to Raymond. "Ready?"

"Yes."

"I suggest the stereotypical drunken Christian knight routine."

Raymond agreed. "I shall try my best, your honor."

Sir Guy smiled then pointed farther along the wall. "Let's hope that door is unlocked." He crouched past the window, then rose, straightening his armor and clipping his chainmail ventail across his mouth to hide his European features. Raymond did the same as the others took up position on either side of the door.

Sir Guy gripped the handle and paused before opening it and stepping boldly inside. He stomped his feet heavily while lifting his knees high, his arms at shoulder height, his elbows bent as he did an exaggerated march into the room, Raymond imitating him as best he could as Sir Guy shouted in Arabic that he surrendered.

The entire room froze, turning as the two men marched toward the True Cross. Someone laughed. Then another. Then the entire room erupted as Sir Guy reached the cross and knelt beside it, his hands pressed against his heart, begging the mighty soldiers of Allah for mercy. Raymond knelt on the other side of the blessed artifact, doing his own impression of the weak and pathetic Crusader, the drunken soldier bit already abandoned.

The gathered enemy, scores strong, cheered and threw food at them. Sir Guy gestured animatedly at the cross, reaching over and picking it up, Raymond grabbing the other side.

"What have you done to our precious relic?" cried Sir Guy as he hoisted it to his shoulder. "We must rescue it from the infidels!" His voice was one of exaggeration, the audience buying his charade, none suspicious as Sir Guy marched deeper into the throng with Raymond, and farther from the door.

He made an abrupt turn, his knees still high as he aimed them toward the door at the far end of the room. They marched forward, Sir Guy continuing his entreaties for mercy as they neared the door. He whipped his hand in the air, about to say something, when his glove hooked on his ventail, tearing it free.

Revealing his face.

The crowd continued to revel in the display. But not those who could see his face. Raymond stared, wide-eyed, as they continued toward the door, no one reacting at first, unable to believe their eyes.

Then someone pointed. "Christians!"

The room fell silent, and Sir Guy bolted for the door. Raymond followed, stumbling, as those gathered fell silent. An angry roar filled his ears as those leisurely draped upon pillows and silks struggled to their feet. Sir Guy burst through the door, Raymond following as Gerard pulled the door closed behind them, sliding his sword through the hooks as those on the other side yanked on the door.

"Let's move!" hissed Sir Guy as they rushed back toward the entry to the tunnel. Sir Guy dropped to his knees, shoving the foot of the cross through the hole. The crossbar slammed on the surrounding stone—there was no way it could fit through.

"What do we do?" cried Raymond.

"We do what we must." Sir Guy drew his sword and swung, hacking the bottom of the cross off at the crossbar. Raymond gasped, a wave of nausea sweeping over him as Sir Guy dropped the hacked off piece through the hole, then angled the remaining section through the opening. The door broke open, dozens of angry Saracens spilling out.

"Everyone in the hole. We can hold them off better down there."

Sir Guy dropped first, followed by Raymond. He helped his master load the two pieces of the cross into the small boat as the others climbed down, one by one.

There was a cry overhead, then one of their own dropped unceremoniously into the water. He gripped his side, wincing as he was helped to his feet.

"Leave me. I'll hold them as long as I can."

Gerard gripped his shoulder. "Go with God, my brother."

Infidels began to drop into the tunnel, and their wounded hero sliced them open, one by one, as Raymond and the others escaped. Gerard pulled a small horn from his belt, and sounded three rapid notes, repeating them three times. Within moments, the rope they had played out behind the boat became taut, then the craft surged away from them.

"Forgive me!" cried their hero, the sound of a knight's armor collapsing into the water signaling the death of another of their order.

Sir Guy sprinted after the boat, Raymond on his heels, the others close behind as the echoes of dozens if not more of their enemy filled the tunnel. The oppressive heat and humidity strained Raymond's lungs, and they burned from the effort, their heavy armor inhibiting their movements as the horde of enemy soldiers, unencumbered, closed in. Raymond glanced over his shoulder, their enemy only paces away, their only saving grace the narrowness of the tunnel.

The Templar at the rear spun, swinging his sword and slicing open the belly of the nearest. The heathen cried out, their advance brought to a momentary halt, and the knight pressed his advantage, thrusting forward with his blade, more of his prey crying out as Raymond and the others put as much distance as they could between them and those who would surely slaughter them in the most gruesome of ways.

They rounded a bend, the torches of their enemy gone, what little light they had from openings above them, spaced far apart, a lone torch in the prow of the boat showing the progress of their precious victory.

For this was the most ingenious part of the plan, provided by Gerard, who had advised them he had done this many times before, and was sufficiently equipped should Sir Guy choose to avail himself of his proposal. By using the boat to carry the cross, it assured that should they all fall protecting it, those at the other end would still succeed in the mission.

"Here they come!"

Raymond checked over his shoulder to see Gerard spinning on his heel, a crescent of light rounding the last bend, revealing the seething mass of flesh. Raymond resisted the urge to stop and help, as there was nothing he could do. Only one could fight at a time, and the more distance they put between themselves and the enemy, the more likely at least Sir Guy would survive. For it was his life that he cared about, and his alone.

He had served by his master's side for over twenty years, and hoped to serve another twenty, though should he fall tonight, saving his master and the True Cross, he would die content that he had done so as not only a Templar, but as a good Christian, serving his Lord. For tonight, unless something should go disastrously wrong, the True Cross would be rescued and returned to Christian hands, saved from those who would desecrate and destroy it.

Sir Guy cursed.

Raymond looked ahead to see the boat lying on its side, the torch askew. Sir Guy pressed ahead faster than before as Gerard continued to battle behind them, the two remaining men on his heels breathing heavily. They reached the boat to find it caught on stones that had collapsed in from overhead, the rope taut as those at the other end battled to free it with no success. Raymond helped Sir Guy free the boat, battling against those at the other end, it finally loose and skimming along the water once again.

Sir Guy stood for a moment, hands on knees, gasping for breath, the others leaning against the walls, doing the same. "I remember there were several other blockages like this. At least one of us must survive to ensure it gets through, otherwise all of this will have been for naught."

Raymond nodded as he sucked in lungsful of air. "It should be you, your honor. You are the most senior among us."

"Yet I am not the youngest nor the fastest." He looked at the two who remained, easily ten years their junior. "One of you should go."

Both shook their heads. "No, your honor. The youngest should stay to fight. The longer we delay them, the more likely it is that you'll get away."

Gerard cried out in the distance, finally felled by the overwhelming numbers. Sir Guy rose, stretching out his arms.

"Then remove this armor. I can't run fast enough in this."

Raymond quickly removed the restrictive and heavy protection, each piece splashing loudly as the horde closed in. Finally free to move, Sir Guy turned to Raymond.

"Let me help you."

Raymond shook his head as the torches of their enemy neared. "There's no time." He pointed after the boat in the distance. "Go! I will be right behind you. I've always been faster than you, old friend." He smiled, and Sir Guy slapped him on his shoulder.

"I shall see you at the other end." Sir Guy sprinted after the boat, Raymond turning to the others, one already preparing to face the enemy. "Good luck, my brothers."

He rushed after Sir Guy, the other on his heels, their lone comrade left to face certain death. Raymond could see the silhouette of Sir Guy a good distance ahead, making excellent time, as the torch from the boat continued in the distance before turning out of sight. And though he could no longer see the boat that contained that for which they had already sacrificed so much, as long as he couldn't see its torch, then neither could those who pursued them.

Swords clashed, but this time he didn't look back. There was no point. Instead, he ran, working at his armor, freeing himself of what he could. He rounded the bend and saw Sir Guy in the distance, working to free the boat once again as their young companion continued to battle behind them. Sir Guy waved, the boat surging forward once more, and he stood, catching his breath as they caught up.

As soon as Raymond reached him, he began removing his sergeant's armor. "Sir, you should go."

Sir Guy shook his head. "No, one of us must make it, and should fatigue overtake me, then you must be as swift of foot as I know you can be."

Raymond decided arguing would be pointless, and stood, arms outstretched, as his master removed the armor, a task he had never performed before, this the work of servants. Yet though Raymond had never before seen his master perform such a task, he did so deftly, soon freeing him of enough armor to make good time.

Sir Guy turned to the final man. "Keep up with us as best you can, and know that should you fall, you have earned yourself a place in the Kingdom of Heaven, at our Lord Jesus Christ's side."

The young man bowed slightly, humbled by Sir Guy's words. "I shall do my best, Sir Guy."

Sir Guy grabbed Raymond by the arm. "Let's go, quickly now!" They all sprinted after the boat, the young man in his armor quickly falling behind, the sounds of his friend still fighting giving Raymond some hope that they might just make it.

He had no idea where they were or how far they had come. Though it felt like they had been running for hours, it had only been minutes, and with their armor, they hadn't gone far. "How much farther?"

"Not much," gasped the young man behind them, part of the Templar's spy network within the Muslim city. "Only a few hundred paces."

Raymond smiled, his energy renewed, and as they rounded another bend, he saw the boat ahead, its torch raised then doused in the water, a gentle blue glow replacing the warm yellow of the flame. It was the moon, shining off the water of the river.

Sir Guy reached the others first, the True Cross already removed and lashed to a raft prepared for this very occasion. Sir Guy stretched out his hands, and two of the men stripped him down to his undergarments, two more doing the same for Raymond.

"Quickly, we have little time," hissed one of the men, urging Sir Guy and Raymond into the water. They both stepped in and grabbed a corner of the raft. Their contact pointed to their left, down the river. "Clear the city limits, and there will be others waiting for you on the left bank."

"Thank you, my friend."

The man clasped Sir Guy's hand. "Go with God, brother."

Sir Guy kicked with his legs, Raymond joining him, as the others climbed into a boat and paddled in the opposite direction, a torch lit on their prow in the hopes they would draw the enemy with them. Raymond continued to kick, his legs already exhausted, the water thankfully cool and calm.

There was a loud splash behind them, and Raymond checked over his shoulder, his chest tightening as he saw the young man, the last of their party, struggling from the water, his sword still lunging forward as the Muslims poured from the opening like vermin.

"Focus on your task."

Raymond turned to Sir Guy, his face in the moonlight calm and reassuring, though creased with the pain he shared at the thought of yet another brother of the Order dying at the hands of those without God in their hearts. As the sounds of the desperate struggle faded behind them, a final cry signaling an end for their young companion, they slowly made their way down the river, unnoticed by the boats that bobbed lazily nearby, and eventually cleared the city limits.

A torch on shore had them kicking desperately toward it, the river not as calm here. Raymond's legs were like dead weights attached to his hips. His entire body was numb, and where it wasn't, his muscles screamed in agony. Sir Guy pressed forward without complaint, giving no indication he was in any discomfort.

They finally reached the shore, and strong hands grabbed Raymond, hauling him to his feet, leaving him no time to see if they belonged to those friendly to the cause, or Saracens eager to claim their prize.

"Sir Guy, you have done it!"

Sir Guy grunted, nearly collapsing to the ground, two of those waiting for them catching him under the arms and helping him farther ashore. The two pieces of the True Cross were gently lifted from the raft and carried toward a nearby horse-drawn wagon. "We must hurry. They could search here at any time."

Raymond allowed himself to be hoisted upon a horse, his master at his side, both slumped over their saddles, every ounce of energy they might have once had, spent.

Sir Guy reached out and clasped his shoulder. "You did well."

Raymond grunted. "I did nothing. It was Gerard and his men that gave us victory."

Sir Guy nodded, his eyes drooping. "We won't be victorious until we reach Jerusalem."

Milton Residence

St. Paul, Maryland

Present Day

"So you're meeting Hugh in France?" asked Sandra Milton as she sat, glass of chardonnay in hand.

Laura Palmer shook her head, taking a sip of her own. "Spain. We're going to France tomorrow, then when our business there is done, we'll meet up with Hugh and his son in Spain for a few days."

James Acton took a swig of his Moosehead Lager. "I'm looking forward to meeting the kid. Hugh never really talked that much about him, what with the estrangement and all, but now they really seem to be patching things up."

Sandra sighed. "I'll never understand how parents can use their children as pawns against each other."

Acton nodded. "Me neither, but that wasn't the case here."

Laura put her glass down, curling her feet up under her. "I feel bad for him, really. He's so alone." They all fell silent as they thought of Kinti, the Amazon woman that their friend, Interpol Agent Hugh Reading, had fallen hard for in the jungle, and then had die in his arms only days later.

It had changed him.

Acton feared he would forever push away any chance at love and happiness, at least from the female companionship side of things. It hadn't helped that his former partner from Scotland Yard and best friend had deserted him, then died horribly soon after they were reunited.

But with his son reentering his life over the past couple of years, perhaps some of his solitude would end, and Acton was determined to do whatever it took to facilitate that. He had a feeling all he could do on this mini-vacation would be to make the boy's old man look cool.

"Perhaps Spencer will help change that," he finally said, breaking the silence.

Sandra leaned forward, changing the subject. "So, France?"

Laura nodded. "Yes. That's business, though I always love spending time in the south. I love the architecture and history."

Acton agreed. "Apparently we're going to be staying at a chateau for the night, owned by our host."

"Oooh, money."

Milton gave his wife a look. "If that's what floats your boat, you married the wrong guy."

She sighed, taking another drink. "Don't I know it. I thought professors were supposed to be rich." She elbowed him. "Especially deans."

Milton rolled his eyes. "Well, you can always divorce me and marry her." He tipped his beer toward Laura.

Laura raised her left hand, displaying her wedding band. "Sorry, I'm taken." She glanced at Acton. "Buuuut, if things don't work out with him, we'll talk."

Acton's eyebrows shot up. "Hey, who says we need to get divorced? I'm sure there're a few places we could move to that would let me have two wives."

Laura laughed. "You'd like that, wouldn't you!"

He shrugged. "I think one is probably trouble enough." He avoided her swing, Milton raising his hands in surrender for all males everywhere.

"Careful, buddy, you can't win this one."

"I'm beginning to realize it." He leaned in to give Laura a kiss when she turned her head, presenting her cheek.

"That's all you get for now."

He pecked it. "I'll take what I can get." He leaned back, spreading his arms and legs. "I, on the other hand, am offering all *this* for your viewing pleasure."

Laura eyed him. "Been there. Done that."

"Yeah, you know it." He raised a fist for a bump with Milton, who recoiled after a look from his wife.

Laura tilted her head further forward. "I didn't mean it that way."

Acton grabbed at his heart with both hands. "You wound me, woman. And here I thought everything was perfect."

Sandra rolled her eyes. "Ugh, newlyweds."

Acton grinned. "We're not that new."

"Newer than us."

"So, what you're saying is—"

"None of your damned business," interrupted Milton, blushing slightly. "Why don't you tell my lovely wife what fool's errand you're on this time?"

Acton laughed, draining his beer, Milton reaching into the cooler and introducing a fresh soldier to the battlefield.

Sandra's eyes narrowed. "Fool's errand?"

Acton flipped Milton the bird then turned to Sandra. "It's a fool's errand we can't ignore any longer."

"Any longer?"

"Well, this story starts a few years ago, at the Vatican."

Sandra's eyes narrowed. "When the Muslims stormed it?"

Acton nodded. "Exactly. What you don't know is what happened after those events."

Jerusalem, Kingdom of Jerusalem
September 20, 1187 AD

Raymond lay on his stomach, peering out over the rise at the holiest of cities below. It had been his home longer than any other, and the surge of faith he experienced every time he saw it after being away, never diminished. Yet today, though the fervor was still there, it was almost overwhelmed by the fear he felt for his beloved Jerusalem.

They had managed to outflank Saladin's massive army, the numbers humbling, numbers he knew weighed heavily on his master and the others. He glanced at Sir Guy, lying beside him. "What should we do?"

Sir Guy drew a slow breath, pursing his lips. "I fear Jerusalem will fall."

"Surely not!"

Sir Guy shook his head. "With over twenty-thousand lost at Hattin, there are barely enough soldiers to keep the peace, let alone defend against thirty-thousand battle-hardened heathens."

"But surely God will not let it fall!"

"He has before, and I fear He shall again."

Sir Guy glanced back at the wagon carrying the True Cross. They had traveled for weeks, sticking to the back trails to avoid the Muslim scourge, and Raymond only recently felt his former self after their exhausting experience in the tunnels under Damascus.

"We cannot let the True Cross fall into their hands yet again."

39

Raymond stole a look at their precious cargo and nodded. "Then what shall we do?"

"Hide it."

"Where?"

"There are caves to the south. We'll hide it there then go help our brothers defend Jerusalem."

"And should we die?"

Sir Guy frowned. "Then the cross will remain protected from these animals until such time as God sees fit to reveal it once again."

Sir Guy crawled back from the ledge, Raymond and the others following, then they mounted their steeds. The pace was excruciatingly slow, what with the wagon and its delicate cargo, already reverently lashed together in one piece, a proper repair having to wait for more skilled hands.

It was nearly nightfall before they reached the caves to which Sir Guy had referred. As if he knew exactly where he was going, Raymond's master led them into one of the openings along the rock face, a torch in hand, confidently navigating the passageways within.

Finally, after more minutes than Raymond cared to contemplate, and after more twists and turns than he could ever hope to remember, Sir Guy came to a halt. He pointed into a large alcove, several cloth-covered piles revealed by the flame.

"Place it there."

The others, carrying the True Cross, complied. Sir Guy yanked a cloth from one of the already present bundles, revealing a cache of weapons and armor. He carefully covered the cross with it, then bowed his head, the others following suit. A prayer was offered, then a salute.

Sir Guy headed back the way they had come, Raymond completely lost once again, relieved when he finally caught sight of the dusk sky, the sun low on the horizon. Sir Guy pointed to two of the men. "Unhook the horses. We'll be leaving the wagon here. Take only what is precious to you, as we must be swift." He swung onto his horse as the others went to work. Raymond mounted his own, then leaned closer to his master.

"Sir, it is critical you survive, otherwise I fear none of us will find the True Cross inside."

Sir Guy smiled at him. "You couldn't keep track?"

Raymond lowered his eyes, a wave of shame sweeping over him. "No, I'm afraid I was lost within moments of entering."

Sir Guy leaned in. "Good. That is the point. But not to worry, the senior members of the Order know the way in, and I will now share it with you." He leaned in closer. "At each point in your path where there is a choice of which way to go, look up at the ceiling. Above each path will be numbers. They will appear random, but simply follow, in order, the year in which our Order was officially recognized by the Pope."

Raymond's eyes widened. "1129?"

"Yes. Follow the tunnels in sequence, labeled one, then one, then two, then nine, then repeat. You will be lead directly to the chambers. There you will find the True Cross, along with weapons, gold, and supplies, should anything go wrong." He slapped Raymond on the back. "Just remember to reverse the numbers on your way out!"

Raymond smiled. "You knew this day might come."

Sir Guy shook his head. "No, the Grand Masters did, long ago. This was set up years ago in case something went wrong. I doubt anyone thought it would be used to hide the True Cross." Sir Guy glanced over at the others, their work done. "Good. Let us make all haste. The cover of darkness should shield us from Saladin's men, but it will also hide our identities from our archers. Let us pray their aims are not true tonight."

The return to Jerusalem took little time now that they were unencumbered by the wagon. Peering over the same hill they had earlier, they could see scouting parties from Saladin's army, but the bulk of his forces appeared to have not yet arrived, or he had set up camp out of sight of the city. Whatever the reason, it meant they at least had a chance of reaching the gates of the city.

Raymond watched as four men on horseback galloped by below, another group following close behind. "They certainly are bold."

Sir Guy grunted. "Indeed. But I think that is their purpose. To ride openly, arrogantly, to show the defenders of the city that they have no fear." He rose, returning to the horses. "And why should they? They will win the day. All we can hope is that in the end, the slaughter will be merciful."

Raymond mounted his horse and followed his master down the hillside and onto the plateau below. Sir Guy raised a fist, bringing everyone to a halt, watching the horsemen charge past once again.

"Now." He urged his steed forward, Raymond following, and they were soon at a full gallop for the front gates. Raymond checked to his left to see the Muslims turn toward them, their approach not to go unnoticed. As they neared the gates, he could see the ramparts manned, torches lighting the entire wall, the gates well lit. Sir Guy slowed as they approached, holding his empty hands out to his sides.

"Do as I do," he ordered, Raymond extending his arms as did the others. "Open the gates! I am Sir Guy of Ridefort of the Knights Templar. We come with news for the King!"

A voice called from above. "Sir Guy, is that you?"

Sir Guy tilted his head back, searching for the source of the voice. "Bertrand? Never would I have thought I'd be so happy to hear the voice of a lowly Hospitaller!"

Raymond grinned at the joviality in his master's voice, and sighed with relief at the laughter from overhead.

"Open the gates!"

Within moments, the mighty gates opened as the hoof beats of their pursuers grew louder. Sir Guy urged his horse forward as a volley of arrows loosed overhead, their sound unmistakable as they sailed toward their enemy. The tips thudded as they reached their destination, several cries and the unfortunate screams of innocent horses signaling success. Raymond took one last glance over his shoulder as the gates closed, to see a single horseman left standing, his arms stretched wide, as if inviting death.

Raymond hoped the crazed man's wish would be granted.

Bertrand greeted Sir Guy with a thumping hug. "We thought you had all died at Hattin. I'm relieved to see there were survivors of your order." He glanced at Raymond and the others. "Please tell me there are more."

Sir Guy shook his head, closing his eyes for a moment. "I'm afraid the news is as bad as you have heard. My sergeant and I only survived because we had been scouting an alternate route. By the time we returned, the battle was lost." He lowered his chin, closing his eyes. "We watched as our brothers were humiliated then beheaded." He shook his head. "It was a sight I pray never to see again."

Bertrand made the sign of the cross. "And what of *it?*"

"The True Cross?"

"Yes."

"Seized by Saladin with a promise to burn it."

"That unholy bastard!" Bertrand spat on the ground as Raymond turned away, covering his surprise at his master's incomplete truth.

"Indeed. Let us pray it is merely a rumor and not the truth." Sir Guy urged his horse forward. "I wish you and your brothers well, Sir Bertrand, and may God deliver us from the evil about to befall us all."

Raymond wasn't listening anymore, the reply lost among his own thoughts. Surely, those within these walls would be buoyed by the news the cross was safe and no longer in the hands of the evil responsible for its brief desecration. Surely, these terrified souls—for they were terrified, he could see it in the eyes of those still out at this ungodly hour—surely they would take solace in the knowledge.

Yet Sir Guy had denied them that, had lied *as* a knight, and *to* a knight, both of which were sacrilege. Raymond chewed on his cheek as they made their way toward the Temple Mount, the headquarters of the Templars in Jerusalem.

Did he lie?

In reality, he hadn't. What he had said was the truth. Saladin *had* seized it. He *had* promised to burn it. Those were truths. And Sir Guy hadn't said it was still lost.

He shook his head slightly as he stared at the back of his master, a clever, pious man. He represented the ideals of the Christian knight, of a Templar. He had seen far too many rise through the ranks to become obsessed with the wealth and power that being a Templar *could* yield.

That would never be his fate, and though his master had power, he didn't covet it. He merely wielded it for the good of the Kingdom of Heaven on Earth. In all the years Raymond had known his master, the man had never changed. He was still the kind, good-hearted soul that had taken him on as his squire, then sponsored him for entry into the Order.

Sir Guy dismounted, handing his horse to a valet. He made for the stairs, turning to the others. "Wait here. I must see the Grand Master at once." He rushed out of sight as Raymond stretched, wondering if the Grand Master had been allowed to return to Jerusalem by Saladin, the only Templar spared what had befallen the others.

Kings don't kill kings.

Shouts erupted, then cries, causing Raymond and the others to look about, wondering what was happening.

"They're here!" shouted someone sprinting past. "The Muslims are here!"

Raymond mounted his horse and raced back to the gates, hopping off and climbing the ramparts, finding Bertrand staring in the distance.

"Where?" asked Raymond as he peered into the darkness, the torchlight making it difficult to see.

But before Bertrand could answer, Raymond gasped.

"Oh my God!"

Ridefort Residence

Saint-Pierre-la-Mer, France

Present Day

"What do you intend to tell them?"

Jacques Ridefort regarded his son, their relationship beyond strained, the outright hostility displayed almost every day heartbreaking. Even the discovery his father was dying of cancer hadn't been enough to soften the tirades. If anything, Jacques now had the distinct impression that his son looked forward to the day his father died, and was even determined to hasten it should he be given the opportunity.

For once he was dead, any debate over the future of their charge would be put to rest. It had taken several years to get to this point, his reaching out to Professor James Acton proving futile until he had finally been forced to give him concrete evidence. He had hoped the man's natural curiosity would have won out, but it hadn't.

Acton was a stubborn man.

Or he thought you were some conspiracy nut.

Yet Acton was now coming, along with his equally qualified wife. And a duty to his family's past had morphed during that time into one that could change its future. No longer was he concerned with having his ancestors' remains properly identified and honored. Now he was concerned with the very future of an oath sworn 800 years earlier.

"Well?"

47

He frowned at his son. "I intend to tell them everything."

"You're insane. And what if they tell somebody? Every zealot on the planet will descend upon this place, demanding to see it. Every damned fanatic out there will try to destroy it. We're only a few people. How can we possibly guard it against that many?"

"I don't believe we'll have to."

His son's eyes narrowed. "What do you mean?"

"I mean, I believe the oath has been fulfilled."

Pierre's jaw dropped. "You don't mean—"

"Yes, yes I do."

His son leaped to his feet. "You can't do this! You don't have any right! My entire life has been spent preparing for the day when I assume the honor, and now you would deny me it? You hate me, don't you? You truly do hate your own son!" Pierre threw up his hands. "I wish mother were still here. Maybe she could talk some sense into you."

Jacques frowned at the mention of his late wife, dead almost ten years now from a diving accident. "She would support me in this, as you should."

"What, you think my own mother would hate me enough to throw away my entire life on your maniacal whims?"

"You seem to be operating under the false assumption that what this family has committed to for over eight centuries, was meant to bring honor to us. It wasn't, and it isn't. We swore to protect it, and *return* it, when the time was right." He stared at his son. "And the time is now right."

"How can it possibly be right? There hasn't been three generations of peace."

"I feel there has."

Pierre pulled at his shoulder-length hair. "Are you insane? Muslims invaded the Vatican just a few years ago!"

His father shook his head. "No, rioters who happened to be Muslim, stormed the Vatican. It was hardly as if a nation invaded. Rome and the Vatican have known peace since the end of World War Two. That's over seventy years. It is time."

His son dismissed his conclusion with a wave of his hand. "No. Absolutely not. I'm going to talk to the others. Surely they can't agree."

Jacques smiled slightly. "I've already spoken to the family. Some agree, some don't. But they all agree it is my decision to make."

Pierre jabbed a finger at him. "I'm going to stop you from doing this. I swear to God, I'm going to stop you!" Pierre stormed from the room, leaving Jacques exhausted.

He was now constantly weak, the cancer overwhelming him. He had weeks to live at best, and even if he doubted whether his family's oath had been fulfilled, he couldn't risk letting his son take his place, not with his state of mind. He would corrupt everything they had stood for all these centuries, and Jacques feared he would use it for personal gain.

The Rideforts had led quiet lives for centuries, and though wealthy, they did not flaunt it. The chateau had been handed down for generations, and the first-born son had led the family, every generation having had a son to carry on the tradition.

Though none had a son such as Pierre.

It was a sad, ignominious end to eight centuries of honorable duty, all forced to a perhaps hasty conclusion by one bad seed. He wondered if he had more time, even just a decade, would his son truly embrace the ideals of what it meant to be a Templar? Would it change how he now felt? Would he still feel that three generations of peace had truly passed?

Yet it didn't matter.

His mind was made up, the decision made.

Whether young Pierre agreed, or not.

Jerusalem, Kingdom of Jerusalem

October 1187 AD

Twelve days.

Only twelve days.

Raymond still couldn't fathom the swiftness of their defeat. Though defeat had been inevitable, he had imagined they would hold on for months, perhaps even long enough for help to arrive from Christendom.

But no help could arrive in just twelve days.

Yet despite the humiliating defeat, Sir Guy seemed pleased with the outcome. Casualties had been kept to a minimum, and in magnanimous gestures designed to make Christianity appear the lesser religion, Saladin and his generals were allowing tens of thousands to leave, unscathed, if they paid a ransom. The Templars, among the richest in the land, had been included in the reprieve this time, unlike at Hattin, where they were singled out and slaughtered mercilessly.

Raymond found himself in the caravan of Templars, their belongings on carts, including much of their riches, part of a mass of citizenry now leaving the holy city under the watchful eye of their conquerors. When they had arrived, Sir Guy had met with the acting Grand Master. He had sworn them all to secrecy, issuing a secret edict that they alone should protect the True Cross and return it to Jerusalem when it once again was in Christian hands, and, should that ultimately not come to pass, to Rome should they feel it would be safer there.

It had surprised Raymond, and he could tell it had his master as well. As the group of them, only six in number, discussed their new responsibility over the days that followed, they realized the honor bestowed upon them was great, and the responsibility even greater. To be the protectors of the True Cross was an incredible burden to place upon six men, who, due to the secrecy of their duty, couldn't directly draw upon the help of others.

With the city encircled the very night of their arrival, they had been forced to wait out the siege, and with their numbers few, had been isolated from the battle, the Grand Master himself saying their lives couldn't be risked. They had heeded that order for the first several days, but by the fourth, they had all snuck out at night to help those in need, their hearts unable to bear the suffering around them.

And now they were still six, with two carts, three horses each, and no servants, their secret too great to risk bringing in others, especially those who were not knights. Their plan was simple, laid out by Sir Guy earlier in the day. They would leave with the caravan, and once out of sight of the city and Saladin's men, they would break from the others, retrieve the cross, then make for Christendom by sea and await news on Jerusalem.

As they slowly wound their way toward the city gates, Raymond's heart ached at those left behind, pleading for the money to pay the ransom demanded by Saladin for their safe passage. The wealth his brotherhood carried in their wagons was enough to pay the ransom for all, but what many didn't understand, was that it wasn't theirs to give.

It was the collateral that backed the paper used for their banking system, a first in Christendom and the Holy Lands. If someone in France wanted to travel to Jerusalem on a pilgrimage, rather than risk his wealth, he merely gave his money to a Templar office in France, in exchange for a note, then turned it in when he arrived. Their treasure here backed those notes. Certainly there were excess funds, as they, among other things, charged fees for this service, but again, it wasn't theirs to give.

"Please, M'lord, can you help us? At least my daughter. Please, if she stays, the Muslim heathens will certainly have their way with her!"

Raymond's chest tightened as Sir Guy stared down at the desperate mother, her young daughter gripping her side. It was a pathetic, heart-wrenching sight, seen dozens of times already this morning. But it was the brilliant blue eyes, the striking blonde hair, that made this one different. *She* would command a high price on the slave markets.

And it wouldn't be as a servant.

She would be sold into sexual slavery to some wealthy Muslim, her body ravaged for years to come until they tired of her and sold her to another. It sickened his stomach, and he reached for his purse when Sir Guy spoke.

"How many are you?"

The woman's eyes widened. "Myself and my daughter, and my husband and two sons."

"So five?"

"Yes, M'lord."

Sir Guy reached into his purse, extracting several coins, then leaned over, handing them to the woman. "Tell no one."

She sealed her mouth, her eyes wide with gratitude as she nodded. Unable to resist, she reached up and squeezed his boot in its stirrup. "Bless you, M'lord."

Sir Guy ignored her, urging his horse slightly faster, when someone cried out behind them. "The Templars are paying the ransom!"

Shouts erupted from either side of the caravan, the mass of desperate souls surging forward, their outstretched hands clasping at empty air as those relegated by their station to a life of perpetual slavery, begged for salvation. When coins failed to appear, the crowd turned quickly on those they thought had been their benefactors, attacking the carts.

"Swords!" cried the commander in charge, the scores of Templar Knights drawing their weapons and charging forward with their horses, pushing the crowds aside and protecting all that was left of the Order in Jerusalem. Blades were swung and jabbed, though most only in an effort to keep the masses at bay, few daring to tempt fate, yet some desperate enough to rather die by the sword of a Christian knight today, than at the hand of a slave master years from now.

Raymond's mount was alongside Sir Guy's, along with the other four in their tiny entourage, boots the chosen method of repelling those surrounding them. Shouts in Arabic were followed by a large group of Saladin's men surging into the square, creating a barrier between the caravan and those relegated to the fringe of society, terrified to challenge their new Muslim masters lest their future be made far worse.

"Forward!" ordered the commander, and Raymond turned his mount toward the gates, the caravan once again moving, a large gap in the line formed by the riot allowing them to move faster in an effort to catch up. They soon reached the gates, and Raymond looked up to see the flag of Saladin's armies flying from the ramparts, and his mouth filled with bile as they passed through.

One day, we shall return, and rid this land of the Muslim vermin.

They cleared the gates, and Raymond breathed a deep sigh of relief, the air tasting like freedom, the fact they had been allowed to leave in peace one he still marveled at, though whether they could trust Saladin to keep his word of safe passage back to Christendom, was questionable.

"We have a problem."

Raymond glanced over at Sir Guy, then turned to see what he was looking at. Hundreds, if not thousands, of Saladin's men were accompanying the caravan on either side, all well-provisioned, no evidence they had any intention of leaving their side anytime soon.

Which meant they wouldn't be able to leave the caravan to retrieve the True Cross.

"What shall we do?"

Sir Guy frowned, shaking his head. "I fear there is little we can do. We will continue with the caravan as long as we are forced to, then when a chance presents itself, we will return and fulfill our duty."

"And should there be no chance?"

Sir Guy stared at him. "Then we will *make* a chance."

Milton Residence

St. Paul, Maryland

Present Day

"Yes, I remember the tomb with the four Templar Knights, of course," said Sandra Milton, Acton and Laura having quickly recapped what had happened a few years ago. "But I never actually heard what happened afterward. Everyone was so absorbed with that thing from the Koran that was found with them, then, of course, the reconstruction and the trials." She sighed, shaking her head. "Unbelievable that there is so much hate in the world."

"Church."

Milton's eyes narrowed as he stared at his friend. "Church?"

Laura rolled her eyes. "He's been binge watching Breaking Bad."

"Ahh, that explains a few things. Just don't shave your head, Heisenberg."

Acton ran his fingers through his thick head of hair. "I *have* been tossing around the idea…"

Laura looked at him, aghast. "Don't you dare!" She reached over and let her fingers flow through his locks. "This head of hair is one of the things that attracted me to you."

Acton's eyebrows bobbed up and down suggestively. "You mean when you had a crush on me for years, keeping National Geographic under your pillow, the page with my picture dog-eared so you could quickly find it in your hour of need?"

She pulled her hand away, frowning. "I'm beginning to wonder if I was a fool."

"Wonder no longer."

Acton flicked a bottle cap at Milton. "And here I thought you were my friend." He turned to Sandra. "What you didn't hear was that the Vatican stopped all work on the tomb, instead resealing it to protect what might still be inside. Remember, it was opened from the ceiling by accident during construction, so they had the elements to worry about, not just the crazies."

"But I thought they took the bodies out?"

"They did. The remains were moved to Sapienza University, and remain there."

"And they know who they are?"

"Yes, each sarcophagus had an engraved nameplate that identified them, but now there's some question as to the identities."

Sandra's eyes narrowed. "What? The nameplates were what, fake?"

Acton shook his head. "We're not sure. A few years ago, somebody I assumed was a quack sent me an email, telling me that he knew who the four knights were, and that two of them weren't who we thought."

"Which ones?"

"Hugues de Payens and Godfrey de Saint-Omer. They were two founding members of the Knights Templar, and their bodies had been missing for almost a millennia. Two of the sarcophagi were clearly labeled with their names, the dates of birth and death matching what we knew about them."

"So what makes him think they're wrong?"

Acton took a drink. "Well, he said he had proof, but never offered it up, so I ignored it. You have to realize that once you get a little bit of celebrity, the nutbars can come out of the woodwork. I trash most of the emails I get, otherwise I'd never get anything done."

"So what changed your mind?"

Acton exchanged a glance with Laura, her cheeks slightly flushed from the wine. "It was an email he sent a few months ago that finally had details I couldn't ignore. Or rather, I could easily have verified."

"What?"

Acton put his beer down. "He said the nameplates on the sarcophagi were fake. He said that Sir John of Ridefort and his sergeant, Raymond, were accurate, but the other two were fake. All four were supposed to be fake, the original nameplates covered over, and he claimed that the other two must have come off over time. He claimed that if the tomb had indeed been sealed, then the remains of those two nameplates must still be inside."

Sandra leaned forward, her wine forgotten. "And? Were they?"

Acton's head bobbed. "Yes."

Alexandria, Ayyubid Sultanate

March 1188 AD

They had never been given the chance. Saladin's forces were too great along the entire route to risk the six of them getting killed before retrieving the cross.

They were now in Alexandria, resigned to their fate of deportation from the Holy Land. Raymond was at once excited and disappointed. He hadn't been in Europe for so long, he could barely remember what it was like. He doubted they would remain there, certainly not long enough for him to return home, though simply being surrounded by Christians, without the constant fear of betrayal from one of the untold Muslim minions, would be a welcome reprieve, however brief.

As he led his steed toward the boats awaiting the wealthy Templars, he noticed large piles of oars near the shore, guarded by soldiers loyal to the governor of Alexandria. Sir Guy noticed as well.

"I wonder what that's about?"

Raymond stared at the boats in the harbor, his eyebrows rising. He pointed at the empty oarports visible in most. "It looks like they belong to them."

Sir Guy shook his head and flagged down one of the guards. He rushed over, bowing to the knight.

"Yes, your honor?"

Sir Guy gestured toward the oars. "Explain this."

"Sir, the Italian captains refused to pay the taxes they owed, so the governor ordered their oars seized until they do."

Sir Guy chuckled, exchanging a smile with Raymond. "Clever. And I take it they have not?"

"Oh, they have sir, but now they continue to refuse the second condition."

"Which is?"

"Free passage for the refugees, your honor."

Sir Guy dismissed the soldier, who hurried back to his post.

Raymond stared at the throngs lined up to board the ships. "With so many Christians leaving, I wonder if there will be any desire to return."

Sir Guy grunted. "We'll be back. And in force. Of that, I can guarantee."

"And if you're wrong?"

Sir Guy's mouth curled into half a smile as he stared at his sergeant. "When have I ever been wrong?"

Raymond opened his mouth to spew out a list of relevant responses, then snapped it shut. "Never that I can recall."

Sir Guy roared with laughter, slapping Raymond on the back. "Ahh, you're a loyal servant and a good friend. I'm glad I rescued you all those years ago. I don't know what my life would have been like without you."

Raymond shrugged. "Definitely shorter."

Sir Guy laughed again, the others joining in. "You've definitely saved my pathetic behind on more than one occasion."

"And you mine, your honor."

"Then perhaps we are even." Sir Guy's face clouded over as they approached their boat. He turned and took in the masses behind them, and those lining the docks, desperate for safe passage. "It is a wretched land, isn't it?"

Raymond noted oars now being carried toward the water, agreement apparently reached with the captains. "Aye, it is. But there is no place I would rather be."

Sir Guy smiled slightly, nodding. "For me as well. I only wish my son were here to share it."

Raymond smiled at the thought of the boy neither had seen in over a decade. "He will be of age soon. Perhaps he will choose to join his father then."

Sir Guy frowned. "Join a father one probably barely remembers, if at all?" He sighed. "I fear even I wouldn't come." He stared up the coastline, into a distance farther than any man could see. "It would, however, be fortuitous timing should he join us upon our return, for I fear we will need all the trustworthy help we can get if we are to succeed in our mission."

Milton Residence

St. Paul, Maryland

Present Day

"I contacted the team examining the remains, and they confirmed they had found shattered shards that when reassembled, were nameplates of two knights. They had assumed they were left over from two other sarcophagi that were moved at some point in the past, though there was no evidence to support that."

Sandra Milton was thoroughly engrossed, as was her husband, despite having heard the details before. "Then what happened?"

"Well, it took some time, but the Vatican gave them permission to reenter the tomb, and they found that the other two sarcophagi had fake nameplates as well. And when they removed them, the names underneath matched those provided by this mysterious person in the south of France."

"Who were they?"

Acton shrugged. "We don't know, and he refuses to tell us. He insists on telling us in person."

"But what do the history books say?"

Acton shook his head. "Nothing. Sir John of Ridefort is a footnote in history, Raymond has no mention that we can find, and the other two appear to be relations of Ridefort, the dates suggesting perhaps a father and son. We're assuming three generations of the same family, but why they are there, is anyone's guess."

Sandra shook her head in amazement. "I should have gone into archaeology. This all sounds so fascinating."

Acton grinned. "It's never too late to go back to school. But if you're going to sleep with your professor, you'll need to get Greg's permission first."

Sandra took her husband's hand. "I don't sleep with the help. I sleep with their boss."

Milton gave a toothy grin. "It's good to be the king."

Acton leaned forward and clinked bottles with Milton. "Word."

Laura threw her head back. "I wish I could torch that bloody Netflix account."

Acton emptied his bottle. "That, my dear, is grounds for divorce in some jurisdictions."

"Uh huh, don't make me test that in Maryland."

Acton took her hand and kissed it, then checked her watch. "Ugh, getting late. We better head home and pack, otherwise I'm going to want another, and a hangover at thirty-thousand feet doesn't sound appealing."

Sandra finished her wine. "What, no private jet this time?"

Acton rose, the rest following. "Oh, we're getting a private jet, just not Laura's this time."

"You mean 'ours.'"

Acton smiled, giving a slight shrug, still not used to the fact that by marrying Laura, he was now incredibly wealthy. Her brother had sold his tech company for hundreds of millions before he died, and had left it all to her. "Sorry, still getting used to being one of the uber-rich. I don't know if I ever will."

Milton led them toward the front door. "Well, just don't go all snob on us, otherwise I'm not sure if we'll be able to continue being friends. Unless you buy me expensive gifts, then I'm perfectly willing to remain your friend."

Acton laughed as he slipped his shoes on. "I'll keep it in mind." Hugs were exchanged, and Acton followed Laura to their car, yawning. She glanced at him.

"Don't you start. If you yawn, then I'm going to start, then we'll get nothing done tonight."

He smiled. "Empathy, babe, empathy."

She took the wheel, her one glass of wine far less than his three beers. They waved goodbye as they pulled out of the driveway, the Miltons closing the door. "Do you think we're actually going to learn anything useful tomorrow?"

Acton shrugged. "No idea. But aren't you curious?"

"Of course I'm curious, I just think we should be careful. We don't know who this person is. For all we know, he could be one of those nutbars you're always talking about."

"I'm sure we'll be perfectly safe."

Laura brought their car to a halt at a stop sign, giving him a look. "Umm, how much did you have to drink? You do know who we are, right?"

"The happiest, most handsome and beautiful couple in the world? The 'it' couple of archaeology?"

"You *have* had too much."

Acton winked. "Yes, you're right, we should be careful, but I have to know why these four knights, unknown to history, were worthy enough to be buried, with full honors, under the very church that later condemned their Order, one just months before their brothers would have been arrested."

Laura sighed, pulling away from the stop sign. "You're right, of course. I just have a bad feeling about this for some reason. I couldn't find anything on Google about him, which is really weird."

"He's a private citizen who shuns technology. No big deal. Hell, if you Googled me, you wouldn't find me on social media."

"No, I'd just find thousands of hits about your exploits across the globe."

"Maybe I'm a bad example."

"I'd say you're the *worst* example."

Laura waved a hand, dismissing the debate. "It doesn't matter. We'll meet this guy, deal with whatever happens, then meet up with Hugh in Spain. *That's* what I'm actually looking forward to."

Acton squeezed her leg. "Me too."

"Bullshit."

He grinned. "You know me so well."

Acre, Kingdom of Jerusalem
July 13, 1191 AD

Sir Guy rose, raising his glass for all to see, a smile on his face, this the happiest Raymond could recall ever seeing his master. For it was a joyous day, a day neither had ever hoped to see. It was the day an unexpected reunion had taken place.

"To my son, John! Heir to all that I have, which is nothing but my brothers, and that which the Order provides!"

"All hail, John!" cried the others as glasses were raised in salute, young John grinning at his father's side, his cheeks flushed from excitement. News had reached them only days before of Sir Guy's nephew's arrival in the Holy Land, bearing an unspecified gift. He had reached them yesterday, on the very day the Christian forces had retaken the city of Acre, a banquet in his nephew's honor already planned, all excited at the prospect of news from home.

But true joy had never before been expressed by all the souls Raymond had encountered in his years, as that when Sir Guy's nephew presented his gift.

"This is John."

Sir Guy had bowed at the young man standing slightly to the rear of his nephew.

"John of Ridefort."

Raymond suspected he had figured it out before Sir Guy, goosebumps racing up his arms and back as his master's jaw dropped slightly.

"John…of Ridefort. My…my son?"

His nephew beamed. "Your son."

Sir Guy stepped forward slowly, examining the young man as his eyes gleamed, his head slowly bobbing, pleased at what he saw. He grabbed the boy by the shoulders. "My son!" he cried to the knights surrounding them, a roar of approval erupting from those gathered, led by Raymond with a fist pumping the air. Sir Guy embraced the boy, hugging him hard, and Raymond smiled as a tear streaked his master's cheek before he pushed the young boy away, still gripping his shoulders. "You've got your mother's eyes, lad."

"And his father's nose!" shouted someone from the side.

Sir Guy turned the boy's head with a finger to his chin, and joined the laughter. "Aye, he does. Careful with that, boy, some Saracen is liable to slice it off in battle!"

More roars of laughter had followed, the reunion a happy one, Raymond impressed with the young man, and thrilled for his master. He couldn't recall him being this happy, and he prayed the joy would fill his master's heart for the rest of his days. Yet the evening hadn't been all pleasant, word of Sir Guy's wife's death devastating to all who knew him, his master often talking fondly of the woman he hadn't seen in over a decade. She had been a loyal spouse, had delivered him a son, and now his son was here, of his own volition, to join the Crusade against the unholy Muslims.

And not a moment too soon.

For tomorrow, they were to depart into dangerous territory, and retrieve what they hoped remained hidden, so many years before.

Pierre Ridefort Residence

Saint-Pierre-la-Mer, France

Present Day

Pierre Ridefort shoved the door aside, striding into the center of the great room of his home, rented two years ago after he could no longer bear to live under the same roof as his father. For what was the point? For generations, the Rideforts had lived in the chateau, and for good reason. They were indoctrinated into the Order from birth, taught the ways of the Templars, schooled in the art of war, strategy, and the technology of the day. He was as well-trained as any soldier, with the equivalent of several degrees in ancient studies and religion. He knew his history, he knew what the Templars represented, and from birth, he had been trained to protect his family's birthright.

His birthright.

But now there was no point.

His father was going to return that which they had protected for eight centuries. Yet what had at first been anger, fury at his father's decision, had turned into determination. He was convinced his father was wrong, and was doing this merely out of spite.

So he had taken a vow of his own.

To take that which was his, and continue his family's duty. He had hoped his father would die before the actions planned tomorrow would be necessary, but it was too late. His father was still alive, and Professor

Acton was arriving tomorrow, no doubt to take their charge and return it to the Vatican.

He looked around the room at the men he had brought into his confidence. Four he had grown up with and trusted with his own life. Until two years ago, they had no idea who he really was, or what his family represented. He had shared with them everything, including what it was the Rideforts had been protecting for so many years, and all had been stunned, and even more willing to help him once they knew the truth.

Yet they weren't soldiers, and soldiers guarded the chateau. All modern Templars, the Ridefort family not a single line, but dozens strong at any given time, the lineage handed down by the males of the family concentrated in the area, all sworn to continue the family's duty. It was a tight-knit group, though through the generations, some lines had split off, no longer interested in maintaining their vows, which was permitted so long as they kept the family secret.

And all had.

At this moment, he had two uncles, both part of the Order, with sons of their own. They and at least a dozen cousins of varying degrees of separation guarded the chateau at all times, and unlike the knights of old, not only were modern Templars adept with the sword and bow, as well as hand to hand combat, they were thoroughly versed in all forms of modern weaponry.

It would be a fight he and four friends couldn't win.

Hence the other four men in the room.

Hired mercenaries.

Men he didn't trust with the true purpose, yet men he required to get them in and out stealthily, with hopefully minimal casualties.

He sat, his friend Albert bringing him a beer. He took a long drag then sighed, holding up the glass to acknowledge the room.

"Has he changed his mind?"

Pierre shook his head at Albert. "No, he's a stubborn old fool. He's even more determined today, I think, than he ever has been."

"Perhaps because he knows he's about to die."

Pierre shrugged. "Perhaps."

"And your uncles?"

Pierre batted away the suggestion. "They're as stubborn as he is. They don't even really agree with him, but they're so bound by duty and honor, they refuse to go against him." He cursed. "Ridiculous these Templars."

"Templars?" The leader of the guns-for-hire, Johann Schmidt, leaned forward. "Did you say Templars?"

"Forget I said anything."

Schmidt exchanged looks with his men, then returned his attention to Pierre. "Just what have you gotten us into?"

"Nothing more than I've already told you. Your job is to get us in and get us out, with minimal casualties. We'll do the rest."

Schmidt frowned. "And as I've said to you before, some of your family will die, unless they drop their weapons like cowards." He leaned back in his chair, crossing one leg over the other. "You said they were Templars, something that sounds like bullshit to me. But let's assume they *think* they're Templars, and they fight like Templars should, they will *not* drop their weapons and run. They *will* fight, and my men and I will kill them. Is that what you really want?"

Pierre's chest tightened. No, it wasn't what he wanted. This was his family. His friends. People he had grown up with his entire life. He loved every one of them—except for his father.

But none of that mattered.

All that mattered was the continuation of what the family had dedicated itself to for over 800 years, a continuation that would allow him to share in the glory that his father and grandfather, and countless generations before them, had enjoyed. "You've already been paid. What do you care?"

Schmidt shrugged. "I don't care. We'll go in, take care of business, and leave. Whether we kill nobody or everybody, I'll sleep like a baby tomorrow night, because I didn't know any of them. You'll have to live with the consequences."

Pierre frowned, his cheeks burning. "I don't see that we have an alternative."

Schmidt smiled. "That's why you hired us."

Pierre's eyes narrowed. "What do you mean?"

"I mean, your father is almost dead, correct?"

"Yes."

"And if he dies before he does whatever the hell it is you don't want him to do, then you win, correct?"

"Yes."

"Then it seems to be we simply have to stop him from doing it."

Pierre slammed his beer on the table, the golden liquid sloshing over the sides of the glass. "What the hell do you think we're doing here? Tomorrow we stop him!"

"No, tomorrow you take what's yours. If you simply stop him, then nature can take its course."

Pierre grabbed at his forehead, massaging his temples. "You're driving me nuts! What the hell are you talking about?"

"Forget the chateau, forget your father, forget your damned legacy or whatever it is. Just stop the meeting."

Pierre froze, then slowly removed his hand from his head, sitting up straight. "Stop the meeting…"

"Exactly. Let's just kill this professor, then the meeting will never happen, your father will have to make alternate arrangements, and he'll die before he has a chance. Your family survives, you take over doing whatever the hell it is that they do, and nobody you care about has to die except some inconsequential teacher who stuck his nose where it didn't belong."

A smile spread slowly across Pierre's face. He looked at his friends, all appearing to like the idea of not going into battle against Templar knights. He nodded at Schmidt. "Now *that* sounds like a plan."

Outside Acre, Kingdom of Jerusalem

July 1191 AD

Raymond awoke with a gasp then rolled to his side as the long curved blade plunged into his bedroll. "Alarm!" he cried, alerting the others as he leaped to his feet, sword in hand, swinging in a wide arc and nearly decapitating his would-be assassin. Young John struggled to his feet as Raymond put himself between their attackers and the boy.

"Father!"

Raymond glanced to his right and cried out, Sir Guy gripping his stomach, his breaths rapid as he tried to hold his innards inside, his stomach sliced open. Raymond roared with rage as he surged forward, the others now awake and joining the fight.

John rushed to his father's side, pressing against the wound with his blanket, when Raymond heard the galloping hooves of more bandits approaching. He thrust forward, burying his blade deep into his master's assailant as he shouted over his shoulder. "Run, John! Run!"

John stared at him for a moment.

"Run!"

John looked back at his father who reached up a bloody hand, clasping it around the young boy's neck. "Go, my son. Someone must survive." The hand dropped with a thud to Sir Guy's chest.

"Father!" The anguish in the young man's voice was apparent, and cut at Raymond's heart like a dagger as he and the others continued to battle the half-dozen that had surprised them in their sleep. He glanced over at the body of one of their lookouts slumped by a nearby rock, an arrow embedded in his chest, another with his throat slit, apparently taken by surprise from behind.

"John, you must go! Now!"

John rose, giving Raymond one last, desperate look, then determination spread across his face as the reinforcements arrived. He retrieved his sword and rushed forward, joining those that remained.

Raymond glanced at him as they readied themselves. "You're too much like your father."

John grunted. "I do believe that's the nicest thing you've ever said to me."

Raymond laughed as those on horseback leaped from their steeds, rushing forward. "Let us pray it is not the last!" The four men surged toward the enemy, swords raised high, outnumbered three to one

But they were knights, Templars, with God on their side, and the knowledge that should they lose, the True Cross would be lost forever. Failure tonight was not an option.

Raymond dropped his sword down hard, cleaving his target's shoulder in two as blades clashed on either side. He kicked forward, freeing his sword from the man's torso as he watched with envy the young bones of John make quick work of two of their attackers.

The enemy's numbers quickly dwindled, leaving the final three to beat a hasty retreat, Raymond and the others giving pursuit. He turned to John. "Remain with your father! We'll be back!"

John nodded, and Raymond dug his heels into the commandeered horse's sides, not knowing at that moment the peril he had just left the young man to face alone.

Béziers Cap d'Agde Airport

Portiragnes, France

Present Day

"Professors, I am your driver, Simone Chartrand. Monsieur Ridefort extends his apologies that he could not meet you personally, but circumstances that prevented his coming, will be explained when we arrive at the chateau."

Acton nodded at the driver as Laura climbed into the back seat of the Mercedes-Maybach S600. "No problem." He followed his wife in and the door shut, their luggage loaded into the trunk with a slight jostling of the car. Moments later, they were underway, Acton sinking into the sumptuous leather of the overstuffed seats, trying to figure out which was more comfortable—the Maybach or the Learjet.

He took Laura's hand, and they drove in silence, each looking out their respective windows, enjoying the view as the sun slowly set in the west, the lights of the towns twinkling on, Acton's favorite time of day about to begin.

He sighed.

Laura squeezed his hand. "What?"

"I love this area."

"We could move here."

He frowned. "I love Maryland too. I don't think I could ever leave my students."

Laura smiled. "I did. Sort of."

His head lolled to the side so he could gaze at her. "Yes, but you'd do anything to be closer to me."

She gave him a look. "Un-huh. So you're saying you wouldn't have moved to London?"

"Nope, I'm a selfish sonofabitch."

She gave him a playful slap. "Don't worry, there was no way I was making you move there. Things just were never the same after the inquiries. Too many whispered questions. You don't have the tabloid press like we do in the UK. It's so ridiculous, it should be illegal."

"They wouldn't do it if it didn't sell."

"True, which is what is really depressing about it." She sighed. "No, I have no regrets about moving in with you, and I'm blessed that I get to continue with the dig in Egypt, and guest lecture from time to time." She stared out the window again. "But a summer home here might be nice."

Acton smiled. "Hey, if you're buyin', I'm tryin'."

She elbowed him. "*We.*"

"I know, I know."

The car sped up slightly. Acton glanced at the rearview mirror, catching the driver checking a little too frequently. "Problem?"

"I think we're being followed." Acton spun in his seat to look out the rear window, the traffic light with no one doing anything suspicious behind them.

"Which one?"

"Two cars back. He's been with us since the airport."

"He could just be heading in the same direction."

"Perhaps, but I've been told to expect trouble."

Acton tensed, exchanging a nervous glance with Laura. "Trouble?"

"Monsieur Ridefort's son is not pleased with your meeting tonight."

Laura's eyes narrowed. "And his own son would actually do something…violent?"

The chauffeur shrugged. "I don't know. I know they haven't been getting along for years now, yet tonight is the first I have heard of genuine trouble. My orders are to get you to the chateau at all costs."

At all costs.

Acton frowned, this no longer sounding like a peaceful, curiosity-satisfying meeting anymore. "How much farther?"

The driver tapped the navigation console. "Fifteen minutes." Acton peered through the rear window, the distance growing between the cars behind them now that their driver had accelerated.

The second car pulled out to pass.

Shit!

"Okay, I think you might be right."

"I'll get you to buckle up, please."

Laura grabbed for her seatbelt, buckling in as Acton did the same. She grabbed his hand again as she checked the rear window. "I *knew* I had a bad feeling about this trip."

Acton grinned. "Then why didn't you say something?"

She shook her head, smacking him gently on the cheek. "You're so bad sometimes."

"That's why you love me." He leaned forward. "What's our status?"

"The car is armored with bullet resistant glass. We've got run-flat tires and a full tank of gas. Unless they've got some heavy duty hardware, they're not stopping us."

"Weapons?"

"I've got a Glock in my shoulder holster, spare mags in the glove compartment."

"Can we call someone?"

"I've already tried, but I'm getting no answer. It's as if the lines are down."

"No cellphones at the chateau?"

"No, Monsieur Ridefort always considered them insecure. In fact, he has jammers so they can't be used on the grounds."

Acton's eyes narrowed. "A little paranoid, isn't he?"

"With good reason, evidently," said Laura.

The chauffeur took a corner hard, the tires protesting as Acton was shoved into the door. "Sorry about that."

"Don't apologize. Just get us to the chateau."

Suddenly the driver gasped, then there was a loud bang and the windshield splintered. Laura screamed and Acton turned to find her covered in blood. His heart hammered as he reached for her. "Are you okay?"

She shook out a nod as the car drifted slightly. Two loud beeps were heard from the dash, and the car straightened itself as Acton finally realized what had happened.

"Holy shit!" He unbuckled his seatbelt and climbed forward. A sizeable chunk of the driver's face was missing, a well-placed round from a high-powered rifle having removed him from the equation.

"James!" Acton looked to see where Laura was pointing, the road curving ahead, a sharp drop-off to their left. He battled with the seatbelt, finally succeeding. He reached for the steering wheel when it turned itself.

"What the hell?"

"What?"

He pulled the Glock from the chauffeur's holster and handed it to Laura. "The car's driving itself!"

"That's handy. But how long will it keep doing it?"

Acton shook his head as he pulled the driver from his seat and into the back with them, the car continuing to steer on its own.

"Should we just sit back here and stay down?"

"Hell no, these systems are designed to shut off if something tricky is detected. And I think you have to keep touching the steering wheel or something."

Laura handed him the weapon. "Then I better drive." She scrambled over the center console and settled into the seat, adjusting it and the mirrors so she could stay as low as possible.

"How much farther?"

She glanced at the nav system. "Ten minutes."

Acton peered through the rear window, their tail now on their bumper. "Why isn't he doing anything?"

"He might be wondering what the bloody hell is going on. They just took out the driver and the car kept going as if nothing happened."

"Maybe we should leave them guessing."

Laura glanced at him. "What do you mean?"

"Don't speed up. Just let the car do its thing, as long as we're still heading toward the chateau."

"You still want to go there? Shouldn't we look for police?"

Acton glanced out the window. "I have no idea where the police are, but I do know that apparently we'll be safe at Ridefort's place, and it's nine minutes from here."

"Okay, let's do this your way. But if we get killed, we're going to have words."

Acton grinned at her then looked at the map. "Sharp turn ahead. Better get ready to take over." Laura nodded, her hands hovering over the wheel. "If we survive this, remind me to buy one of these when we get home."

Pierre Ridefort sat in the passenger seat, Schmidt driving, two of his men in the back. "What the hell is going on? Who's driving?"

Schmidt shook his head. "I don't know. My sniper reported a kill, but the car kept going as if nothing happened."

"Well, have him shoot whoever's driving now!"

"He doesn't have a shot anymore. We're long past his position."

Pierre's chest ached, their plan falling apart. If they didn't stop this American professor from meeting with his father, he'd have to take matters further, which meant members of his family could, and probably would, die. "Then let's take out the damned car."

They rounded a sharp turn, a turn Pierre was painfully familiar with. "We're going to be home in five minutes. If we're going to do anything, we've got to do it now."

Schmidt opened the sunroof, snapping his fingers. One of his men stood in the back seat, hauling with him the biggest machine gun Pierre had ever seen. And when it opened fire, the loudest.

The car ahead finally reacted.

"Get down!" Acton dropped to the floor behind the front seats, pushing their poor chauffeur's body between him and the bullets now tearing at the car. He glanced forward and saw Laura crouched down, the car surging forward as she hammered on the gas.

"Seven minutes!"

"We're not going to make it, not with that kind of firepower." He scrambled forward and opened the glove box, retrieving the spare magazines. "Just keep us heading in the right direction."

He gave her shoulder a quick squeeze, then slithered back to the rear of the car, the bullet resistant glass now a patchwork of splinters he had no doubt would eventually give. Laura made another sharp turn, giving them a momentary reprieve, and Acton took advantage. He lowered the passenger side rear window, not wanting to risk a lucky angle shot making it through to Laura, and positioned himself with the Glock extended out the window, his wrong hand gripping it tightly.

He waited for the car to reappear in the rear window, then opened fire, carefully switching angles with each shot, but it was too dark, and the window too damaged, to tell if he was even coming close. The car swerved and slowed. And he smiled.

"Let's move!"

Laura hammered on the gas as she sat up slightly, their attackers thrown off the pace, at least for a moment. "Five minutes!"

"The bastard shot me!"

Schmidt glanced over his shoulder at his man, Pierre doing the same, almost butting heads. "Did your vest catch it?"

"Yeah, but still. He's one hell of a shot."

"Bullshit, he just got lucky. Now get your ass back up there and finish him off."

The man didn't look happy about it, but one glare from Schmidt had him back in position, the weapon soon belching lead as Pierre stared out the window and up the hill they were now climbing, the chateau silhouetted against the dusk sky, no lights evident. His family had always kept a low profile, rarely leaving the walls when he was a child, and lighting their home in all its glory would merely attract tourists.

And that couldn't be tolerated.

They owned the land around the chateau, giving them enough of a buffer that the erected fence with razor wire kept out all but the most curious, and their security system detected them quickly enough. There were few incursions, their family's secret never in any real danger of being revealed.

And should an actual thief breach the walls, it was likely he would never be seen again, his uncles telling tales of a crypt below, that contained the remains of dozens who had managed the unlikely feat over the centuries.

The thought of what would happen to his brethren should their plan here fail, sent shivers up his spine. Would they be buried beneath the castle? He assumed they would, as all Rideforts had been for centuries.

And what of him?

What would happen to him should he die tonight, his attempt at reclaiming the family honor a failure? Would he be buried with honor, or would he be disposed of as a thief, relegated to the crypt his uncles told of?

The very idea disturbed him.

He was a Ridefort. He had never wavered in his commitment to his family name. It was his father he was in a dispute with, a father who would be dead within days, and who had no right to end what had been his family's duty for centuries. He slammed a fist into the dash.

Why don't you just die, already?

Schmidt glanced at him as bullets continued to rain down on the car ahead, now swerving from side to side, someone returning the occasional volley that would have Schmidt's man ducking back inside every once and a while.

"This isn't going to work." Schmidt surged forward, slamming into the back of the Maybach as it slowed for a sharp turn. Its rear end kicked out, but the driver managed to regain control, pulling away from them as Pierre lowered his hands, raised moments before to cover his face from the expected impact of the airbags.

Schmidt chuckled at him. "We modified the car. Your movies have been lying to you."

Pierre shook his head, pointing at the gates to the chateau. "We're too late."

"Or are we?"

The Maybach came to a halt, the driver turning it hard so that it blocked the road, centuries-old walls lining either side.

"What happened?"

"Automatic fuel cutoff in a rear-end collision."

Pierre smiled.

Acton jumped out the passenger side, the driver side exposed. Laura crawled over the seats as he fired two rounds at their pursuers. The door opened, and Laura spilled out onto the cobblestone road. The gates were only a couple of hundred feet away, but it might as well have been a thousand miles. The road climbed at an angle high enough that they would be completely exposed if they were to try and reach the gate.

"Stay down, behind a tire."

Laura nodded, taking up position behind the front tire, Acton at the rear. Gunfire erupted from several sources, the armored plating on the car beaten, the metallic pings and thuds filling the evening air. Acton lay flat on his stomach then rolled slightly to his side, peering under the car and back at their attackers. He took aim and fired, hitting someone in the shin. A cry rang out, and a body crumpled to the ground as his target continued to scream in agony.

Suddenly the area was bathed in light, and Acton rolled back behind the tire, searching for the source. The main gate of the chateau was lit up, searchlights aimed down the road at them. He heard machinery, the glare of the lights changing as the gates opened. The sound of at least one engine approached their position, and Acton heard their pursuers' vehicle roar back to life, beating a hasty retreat.

"Are you okay?" asked someone in French, Laura responding in the affirmative. Silhouettes rushed toward them, and Acton debated whether to aim their lone weapon at the new arrivals, deciding against it. He lowered it to his side as a hand reached out for him.

"Professor Acton?"

He nodded, taking the hand, the man hauling him to his feet.

"And Professor Palmer, I presume?"

Laura stood. "Yes. And you are?"

"Bernard Ridefort. You're here to see my brother." He gently pressed on Acton's back. "Hurry, let's get inside in case they return."

Acton took Laura's hand and followed Bernard up the road toward the gates, two vehicles from the chateau continuing to block the road, half a dozen men in tactical gear covering their backs. They stepped through the gates, the vehicles returning, and Acton didn't breathe easy until the gates slammed shut.

A man appeared in the large, columned entrance, Acton surprised to see him in a wheelchair, the very definition of frailty. "Professors Palmer and Acton, I am Sir Jacques of Ridefort, Templar Knight, and guardian of that upon which He made his ultimate sacrifice."

Al 'Ayadiyeh

Outside Acre, Kingdom of Jerusalem

August 20, 1191 AD

Raymond covered his nose and mouth, the stench of death overwhelming. In all his years, he had seen nothing like it, and he prayed he never would again. Yes, at the battle of Hattin four years earlier, more had died, yet that was different. Those were soldiers, every one.

But not today.

The slaughter ordered by King Richard included women and children, their only crime being Muslim. The moral high ground occupied by the Christian Crusaders had been lost with one barbaric act, and he was ashamed to be associated with it, despite not participating.

For he had a far more important task than to partake in the atrocities committed this day. He had to find Sir John, his master's son. Nothing had gone according to plan.

Nothing.

After the banquet upon John's arrival, they were to have departed for the caves outside Jerusalem, but had been waylaid. King Richard himself made an appearance at the banquet under the guise of welcoming the son of a prized knight, though in reality, probably seeking some place to drink and be merry with those who would shower him with adulation.

King Richard had invited Sir Guy and his son to court, an offer no one would refuse. It had delayed their departure, though it had provided Raymond and Sir Guy time to continue the training of his son begun by Sir Guy's nephew during their two-year journey to the holy land.

And now, with his beloved master dead, murdered in the night by what turned out to be Bedouin slavers, his sole responsibility was to his master's son, a son he had left behind in a foolish pursuit, a son who hadn't been seen in weeks.

A son he had lost hope of ever seeing again.

It had been a challenge to find their camp again in the dark, and when they finally had, John was gone, evidence of a half-dozen horses left in the sand, though no new blood. Young John had either escaped into the night, or been captured by whoever had arrived after they left. Either way, their search had proven fruitless, the winds quickly erasing any trail left in the sands.

They were only three now, and had split up to search the slave markets for Sir Guy's heir. He had yet to hear back from the others, though if they had failed as he had, there would be nothing to report. And as he surveyed the massacre before him, he felt the loss of this one young man more than that of the thousands of innocents that lay before him now.

And it racked him with guilt.

Then he saw something. Several knights ahead, beckoning at someone deep within the bodies. He urged his horse forward, peering out over the corpses, to see someone kneeling among the carnage. Someone wearing the tunic King Richard himself had gifted him.

He urged his mount forward, racing toward the others, then jumping to the ground and rushing toward what could only be his master's son.

"Sir John, thank the good Lord you are all right!" He grabbed the boy by the shoulder, spinning him around to confirm it was indeed him. "When we found your father's encampment, and you were gone, we feared the worst."

John didn't say anything, instead focusing on the bodies of several young children at his feet. He placed his palm on one young boy's chest, tears streaking his face.

"Sir, we must leave at once. Saladin's army is coming, and there will be no quarter for those he finds, not after this."

John moved aside the young boy's robe, revealing a long tube with a strap around his neck. He gently removed it then touched the boy's forehead. "I will take care of this for you now."

"Sir John, we must hurry!"

John finally stood, staring at four young boys, three horrifyingly young, then wiped the back of his hand across his tear-stained face. He turned to Raymond. "Why do you call me 'Sir John?'"

Raymond placed a hand on John's shoulder. "For you are the eldest, and with your father's death, you inherit his wealth, his title, and, should you accept it, my loyalty."

John nodded, saying nothing, instead slinging the tube he had retrieved over his shoulder as Raymond summoned the others to bring a horse. They both mounted their skittish beasts, the earth already vibrating from the pounding hooves of thousands of Saladin's soldiers closing in on their position, hell-bent on revenge.

Ridefort Residence

Saint-Pierre-la-Mer, France

Present Day

Acton's eyes narrowed as he processed what had just been said. "You're a Templar?" There was no hiding the skepticism in his voice, and if it weren't for the fact there were men on the other side of the wall with guns, he would have turned on his heel and walked back to the airport. But that fact, and something about the man himself, gave him pause.

"Yes."

"That's preposterous." Laura was the one who voiced his opinion for him, smiling her thanks to someone who appeared with a bowl of water and towels to wash herself of the chauffeur's blood. It struck Acton as something straight out of medieval times.

The old man smiled, a shallow, weak effort. "I understand your skepticism, but if you will permit me, I shall prove it to you."

Acton glanced about, at least a dozen heavily armed men in sight, how many more weren't, he had no idea. They appeared serious enough, and had a bearing that suggested they knew what they were doing, as opposed to some of the thugs he had encountered over the years.

And leaving at the moment wasn't an option he cared to exercise, or test.

"Very well."

Jacques Ridefort motioned toward the door, and a young man appeared from the shadows, pushing his wheelchair inside. Laura handed back the towel then she and Acton followed, holding hands, the guards remaining outside.

"Don't worry, you're perfectly safe here."

Acton exchanged a glance with Laura, and he could tell she was no more comforted by their host's words than he was. Then his eyes widened. As they moved deeper into the chateau, he noticed the suits of armor, the flags and shields, the swords and other weapons of ancient warfare. All perfectly preserved, all in remarkable condition. And all suggesting at least an association with the Templars. "You have an impressive collection."

Jacques glanced over his shoulder. "Preserved from a time when duty and honor meant something. Not like today, when they are just hollow words spoken by hollow people."

Acton grunted. "I've met a few people who embody those very words."

Jacques nodded. "Yes, there are some, but they are too few these days. After the Templars were arrested and the Order dismantled, a few of us went into hiding, eventually settling in this very castle, quietly living out our lives and fulfilling our oath."

"But I thought the Templars were eventually pardoned and allowed to live out their lives in peace?" Acton phrased it as a question, yet knew the answer full well.

"Yes, they were, but not as Templars. We, the Rideforts, refused to give up our titles, refused to give up the Order."

Acton's eyes narrowed. "Please tell me you're not about to claim you have the missing Templar treasure here."

Jacques laughed, then coughed for a few moments. "I assure you, we have money, but not *the* treasure. That is another story entirely."

Acton paused, his jaw dropping slightly. "You mean you know where it is?"

Jacques waved a finger at him. "We're not here to discuss the matters of man, we're here to discuss something far more serious."

Laura squeezed his hand tighter. "Are you referring to what you said? That you are the 'guardian of that upon which He made his ultimate sacrifice.' Are you referring to the True Cross?"

The frail man signaled for his attendant to turn him around. He stared at Laura then at Acton. "You know of it?"

Acton nodded. "Everyone knows of it. The True Cross is the cross upon which Jesus Christ was crucified. It was discarded by the Romans along with the two crosses the thieves were crucified on, and rediscovered in the fourth century by St. Helena, along with the sign nailed to it that said 'Hic est rex Iudaeorum.'"

"Here is the king of the Jews," whispered Laura, her hand now gripping his tightly. "Are you saying you have it here?"

Jacques didn't answer. "Tell me more."

Acton smiled, realizing this was a test, perhaps a test of their worthiness to see it. A test he was determined to pass. "Over the centuries, slivers of it were given to various places of worship or important families, and when the first Crusaders arrived, they tortured the Greek Orthodox priests who had hidden it in Jerusalem. They finally gave up the location, and the fragment that remained was incorporated into a large golden, bejeweled cross, that was then carried by the Crusader armies into battle until Hattin in 1187."

Jacques smiled. "You know your history well, Professor. And what happened in Hattin?"

"The Crusaders were massacred, over twenty thousand of them captured or killed, including over one hundred Templar Knights who were beheaded. The cross was lost to Saladin's forces, then never seen again."

"And that, Professor Acton, is the only fact in which you are mistaken."

Acton's eyes narrowed. "If you're referring to the reported sightings in Damascus, those were never confirmed."

"I guess it depends on who you believe, though it is of no matter. I can confirm it did indeed make it to Damascus, was desecrated by the Muslim hordes, and then was rescued by a small force of Templars, led by my family."

Rome, The Papal States

1215 AD

Raymond's old bones ached with every movement of his horse. He was far older than a knight should be, though the past twenty years had seen few battles, merely unwavering duty. A decision had been made all those years ago that the Holy Land was no place for the True Cross, not while much of it was controlled by the Muslims.

The Order remained strong, and the Grand Master's commandment that they protect the True Cross at all costs, and in secrecy, remained. It was an order they had heeded to this day.

Yet they were old.

Raymond knew he was not long for this earth, and their two companions were no better. Sir John was relatively young compared to them, yet was showing his age. It would be Sir John's son that would carry on their duty, his new master having married before taking his vows.

Raymond had remained alone, already having taken his vow of celibacy, though some of the others already had families before joining the Order. These children were the future of their tiny cadre of Christian soldiers, protecting the True Cross now for over twenty years. Twenty years of unrelenting violence in the Holy Land, and twenty years of treachery and intrigue throughout Europe.

The True Cross did not belong to any one man. In consultation with the Grand Master, they had decided it must remain secretly under the protection of the Templars, until such time as three generations had passed with peace in either the Holy Land, or the Holy See. Should one of these sacred locations see peace long enough for those who had warred with each other to be dead and buried, then all the ancient hatreds would be gone, and the True Cross could be returned to mankind, with no more wars for it to be desecrated by.

And with the next generation now preparing to take their place, they could honestly say peace had not yet been achieved, and their task would carry on, Raymond feared perhaps for centuries.

They were in Rome with the blessing of the current Grand Master, a man Raymond respected tremendously, and who had renewed their orders of keeping the True Cross' location secret even from him. After it had been retrieved from the caves, they had gone into hiding in plain sight, making sure they remained in Christian strongholds certain to remain so long enough for them to have time to escape upon a Templar boat, should any enemy arrive at their walls.

And the enemy had arrived, and they had fled across the sea with their precious cargo, to reunite with Sir John's family, a family they hadn't seen in over five years, Sir John sending them back to Christendom years ago, his son to be trained in the knightly arts.

Today was a pilgrimage of sorts, Sir John insisting they pass through Rome and see the Vatican before their final journey home. Raymond spotted the basilica first, his heart leaping at the grandeur of it.

"Look."

Sir John followed Raymond's gaze, his jaw dropping slightly at the sight of Saint Peter's Basilica. Despite spending most of his life in the Holy Land, standing upon the very spot Jesus Christ himself had been crucified, walking through the streets of the town He had been born in, and praying on the ground where He had been buried before His resurrection, he was still in awe.

For this was glorious.

While the monuments in Jerusalem were sacred ground, they were old and scarred from over a millennia of conflict. Yet here, it was as if the entire Vatican shone in a brilliant white, untouched by the evils of man.

"And I say also unto thee, that thou art Peter, and upon this rock I will build my church; and the gates of hell shall not prevail against it."

A smile creased Raymond's weathered face as he looked at his friend. "Your Latin remains excellent, I see."

Sir John chuckled. "With you drumming it into my head for twenty years, it better be."

"Well, someone had to teach you some culture. The heathen child I met at Acre was in desperate need of teaching beyond the sword."

Sir John nodded. "What was it you always said? 'Wisdom wields more power than the sword?'"

Raymond tore his eyes away from the holy site, and regarded Sir John. "Correct. But do you believe it?"

Sir John's eyes stared into the distance for a moment before he returned his gaze to Raymond. "Absolutely, but"—he held up a finger—"not for years."

"With age comes wisdom."

"Then you are the wisest man I know."

Raymond frowned. "And apparently little respect."

They both roared with laughter and urged their steeds on. A shout rang out, then more. Raymond spun in his saddle to see what the commotion was, and Sir John gasped. A cart had broken loose, and was rolling down the cobblestone road they now occupied.

Sir John leaped from his horse, leaving Raymond for a moment to wonder what was happening, when he spotted a group of children playing in the path of the cart, ignorant of the danger. Sir John shouted at them, pointing at the cart. The children turned toward him, staring at him, rather than where he was pointing.

The roar of the wood wheels on the ancient stone echoed through the street, the children finally realizing the danger they were in. They scattered, but not all, one tiny girl crying in the road, frozen from terror. Raymond struggled from his horse, urging his decrepit body forward, as his younger master waved at the girl to move.

Yet she didn't.

Raymond watched in horror as the cart, laden with heavy bags of flour, bore down on his master, Sir John diving at the girl, knocking her to the ground and shielding her with his body. Raymond cried out as the wheel of the cart slammed into his master, riding up his back and over his body, the rear wheel repeating the tortuous act.

Sir John gasped then collapsed, the young girl continuing her screams, his sacrifice succeeding in saving the child. A woman ran over, crying, and pried the tiny girl from Sir John's arms, thanking him profusely.

Yet he said nothing.

Raymond rushed to his side, dropping to his knees. "Sir John, are you okay?" Yet he knew there was no hope. His master's body was crushed. Blood oozed from his mouth, his breaths shallow and rapid, what little life that remained quickly leaving him.

Sir John reached up and grabbed Raymond by the back of the neck, pulling him closer with his last remaining ounce of strength. "Save the scroll." His eyes fluttered and his body shook for a moment before giving up its final breath, leaving Raymond to weep without shame at the side of his master, of his friend, of his closest companion, that had reminded him every day of the young man's father who fulfilled those same roles so many years ago.

The scroll.

It was that brief period when he had thought he had lost Sir John after his father's death, that Sir John had met the young Muslim boy with the scroll. Protecting it after the boy's death outside Acre had become an obsession with Sir John, second only to the True Cross, and now that duty had been handed down to him. What he would do with it, at the moment, he had no clue.

And no care.

Feet pounded, and he looked up to find several Templars rushing to their aid, aid that had come too late, though Raymond found comfort in knowing that his brothers of the Order were present.

"Is he...?"

Raymond nodded at the man. "Yes."

"We'll take him inside so the Last Rites can be performed."

Raymond said nothing, instead standing back as four of his brothers lifted the crumpled body from the ground, solemnly carrying his friend toward the holy ground of the Vatican. The street was now silent, save the whimpers of the little girl who would continue her life, unscathed, hopefully with the example of the ultimate sacrifice paid, not lost with the passage of time.

The next few minutes were a blur, the other knights gently urging him forward, through the front gates of the Vatican, and finally once again to his friend's side, where several priests surrounded the body.

A hush fell over the room, the gathered crowd of onlookers parting. Raymond, his eyes blurred, peered up to see a white figure rushing toward them.

"What has happened here?"

"Your Holiness, this man died outside the gates, saving a little girl from a runaway cart."

"It's true, Your Holiness, I saw it with my own eyes. He sacrificed himself to save the little one."

Raymond's heart hammered as he wiped his eyes with the back of his hands, finally realizing who it was that stood before them. He struggled to his feet then bowed. "Your Holiness, forgive me."

"Rise, my son."

Raymond rose, but kept his eyes directed to the floor, and on his friend.

"You are a Templar?"

"Yes, Your Holiness, as was my master, Sir John of Ridefort."

"Ridefort?" The Pontiff's single utterance conveyed his shock. "Come with me."

Raymond's jaw dropped as the Pope spun on his heel and walked away. He stared at the retreating Pontiff then the body of his friend.

"Go!" hissed one of the priests, pushing him after the head of the Roman Catholic Church. Raymond willed his legs to move, a lurching gait finally turning into one of urgency as he struggled to keep up with the Pontiff. A few moments later, he found himself in a chapel, the sole occupant his holiness. He bowed once again, and a hand was placed on his shoulder.

"Look at me."

Raymond shook his head, his eyes glued to the man's sandals.

"Look at me, my son." The voice was firmer, though not angry. Raymond lifted his head, but kept his eyes down. A finger pushed his chin higher, forcing him to finally stare at either the Pontiff, or the ceiling. He chose the Pontiff. "That's better." The man smiled. "Your master, Sir John of Ridefort. He is the son of Sir Guy?"

Raymond's eyes widened, stunned his master's family should be known to the most powerful man in all of Christendom. "Y-yes, Your Holiness. The very same."

"Then you are one of *them*."

Raymond's eyes narrowed. "I'm sorry, but I don't understand."

The Pope stepped closer, raising Raymond's discomfort level considerably. "You are one of those who defend the True Cross."

Raymond's jaw dropped. "You-you know?"

The man smiled, patting Raymond's shoulder. "Of course I know. Your Grand Masters have informed every pope since you began. Remember, the Templars are *my* soldiers, and they serve at my pleasure. Your Grand Master was duty bound to inform *his* master."

Raymond's heart slammed.

We never should have come here.

Terror filled him as he imagined what was about to be said. What if the Pontiff demanded the cross be handed over? Their pledge had been three generations of peace, a time which had not yet passed, no semblance of a steady peace in these parts. Could he say no to the Pope? And if he did, would he be condemned to Hell?

He felt the finger on his chin again, his eyes having drifted to the floor.

"My words trouble you."

"Umm, n-no, Your Holiness."

Lord, forgive me for lying to him!

"Perhaps you fear I shall demand you hand over the True Cross?"

Raymond gasped, then snapped his jaw shut.

"Do not fear, my son. It may surprise you, but I agree with your pledge."

Raymond's eyes widened. "Wh-why?"

The Pope smiled. "Would it surprise you to know that much of my day is occupied by politics, and not religion?"

Raymond's eyes widened further, revealing his answer.

"The Fifth Crusade has begun, at great expense to the monarchs of Christendom. Can you imagine how they would react if they knew the

True Cross was here? To them, it belongs at the head of their armies. If word were to get out it was here, they might very well turn their armies around and march on me."

He smiled at the horrified look on Raymond's face at the very notion. "Not to worry, my son, I speak of hypotheticals. Yet my point still stands. At this moment, Christianity believes the True Cross is either in the hands of the Muslims, or has been destroyed by them. Either way, their anger is focused in the right direction. The True Cross is the holiest blood relic known to exist. It has healed the dying and made the dead rise again. It is proof that Our Lord Jesus Christ existed, and that he sacrificed himself for all our sins. Who are we, mere mortals, to say that it should be at the head of our armies, or mounted in our places of worship?"

He shook his head. "No, my son, for now, the best place for it is with you and your brothers, pure of heart, uninfluenced by the trappings of power or wealth. You must continue your mission and protect the True Cross from not only the heathens, but those who kill in His name, yet misunderstand His teachings."

Raymond nodded. "Yes, Your Holiness. You can count on my brothers to keep it safe."

The Pontiff squeezed his shoulder. "I know I can." He looked about the room, then back at Raymond. "You and your brothers have made a great sacrifice, and you should be rewarded. Your master, Sir John of Ridefort, shall be buried here, upon these sacred grounds, his entry into the Kingdom of Heaven assured for his honorable duty. I shall have a special tomb constructed for just this purpose, and all those who protect the True Cross shall be welcome here when they pass to the next life." He lowered his voice. "This must, of course, be kept quiet. For Templar Knights to be buried here will raise questions, questions that cannot be answered lest we trigger the very tribulations we discussed. But instruct your brothers, that when one of them falls, they are to be brought here, and buried with honor."

Raymond bowed deeply. "Thank you, Your Holiness. You honor my brothers and I with your words and your generous offer."

"Good, good. Now let us attend to your master."

"Yes, Your Holiness." He opened his mouth, then closed it, thinking better of what he was about to say.

"What is it, my son?"

Raymond shook his head. "It is nothing, Your Holiness."

"Speak the truth within these walls."

Raymond flushed. "It—" He stopped, looking about, searching for strength.

"Yes, my son?"

Raymond drew a deep breath. "I have one request, if I may."

"What is it?"

"My master's father, Sir Guy of Ridefort, is buried outside Acre. It was he who led the raid to retrieve the True Cross from the infidel Saladin. I would like permission to retrieve his body and bring it here, to be buried with his son."

The Pope smiled, placing a hand gently on Raymond's cheek. "You are the finest example of God's children I have yet to meet. Go and get your brother that I suspect means more to you than you reveal, and bring him here. He will be buried with honor with his son, and their souls will forever be protected from the evils of man."

Raymond collapsed to his knees, prostrating himself in front of his Pope, tears flowing onto the polished stone. "Bless you, Your Holiness. I pledge myself to you and to my Lord, for eternity."

Ridefort Residence

Saint-Pierre-la-Mer, France

Present Day

"You expect us to believe that?"

"Yes."

"And just take your word for it?"

Laura held up a hand, interrupting the back and forth between Jacques Ridefort and her husband. "You said you are the guardian of the True Cross. Does that mean you have it?"

Jacques smiled. "Finally, someone is paying attention." He gave Acton a look that left him feeling thoroughly admonished. Acton opened his mouth to protest then stopped himself. He smiled, realizing how one of his students must feel when he busted them for not listening.

He had been so distracted by what had happened on their way here, and the claim this man was a Templar Knight, that he had completely ignored the most important claim. "I apologize, Mr. Ridefort. May we see it?"

"It *is* why you are here." He beckoned his attendant to continue on, and their journey resumed.

Acton gestured toward an elevator. "I see you've installed some upgrades."

"We don't carry swords anymore, either."

Acton chuckled. "No, I suppose you don't." He nodded toward the chair. "May I ask what is, ahh…"

"Wrong with me?"

Acton blushed. "Sorry."

"I have pancreatic cancer, and will be dead within weeks, if not days. That is why I finally gave you the proof you were asking for. Your ignoring me could no longer be tolerated."

Acton was about to apologize again when he decided against it. He hadn't done anything wrong. He was contacted every day by some quack, and Jacques Ridefort had seemed no different. Until he finally provided the proof referred to. If he had done so three years ago, this meeting likely would have occurred that much sooner. He was not about to be made to feel guilty over something he was not responsible for, no matter how ill the man might now be.

"Well, I'm here now. Your home suggests your family has connections to what were once the Templars, and the fact you share the last name of several people buried under the Vatican and confirmed to be from the Order, suggests your ancestors very likely were Templars."

"Assuming it is your real name," said Laura, Acton happy to see he wasn't the only one not sure of what to make of the situation.

"I see why you two got married. You're both skeptics."

"We're both realists who've seen too many con artists in our day," replied Laura. "We'll need more proof than a driver's license and some old suits of armor with Templar crosses."

Jacques chuckled. "I'll give you more than that." He smiled as they entered a large room, a roaring fire off to the left with chairs and couches in a semicircle in front. "Ahh, here we are. Vincent, if you would."

The attendant, Vincent, bowed slightly, and headed for the opposite end of the room. He tipped a pedestal with a bust of what appeared to be the last Grand Master of the Templars, Jacques de Molay, and there was a clicking sound. He righted the pedestal, then stepped over to the wall and pushed, a portion of a wall-to-wall bookcase swinging inward, revealing a hidden doorway.

Laura looked at Acton excitedly, and they followed Jacques into the hidden room, Acton still skeptical, though if they were being led on, the hoax was one of the best he had encountered. Laura gasped first, and when Acton rounded the bend in the narrow passageway, he did as well.

Before them was what could best be described as a treasure room, overflowing with a large amount of gold and jewels, along with precious artifacts and art, but standing in the center of it all was an object so distinctive, so awe-inspiring, Acton barely took notice of the trove surrounding him. He instinctively made the sign of the cross as goosebumps rushed across his body, his heart slamming, his ears pounding, as his eyes devoured the holiest of artifacts he could imagine.

It *was* the True Cross.

He recognized it from period paintings and drawings, there little doubt this was it. It could be a replica, and whether the aged piece of wood embedded among the gold and jewels was the actual cross Jesus himself was crucified upon, there may be no way to tell. Yet his gut instinct told him this was, at a minimum, the cross carried at the head of the Crusader armies for almost two centuries, and if it were, no one had set eyes upon it for over 800 years.

"How?" was all he could manage, already circling it with Laura, taking it in from all sides, lights on the floor and ceiling all focused on it, giving it a radiant glow that made it appear even more holy than it might otherwise.

"My family, along with a small contingent, stole it back from Saladin's forces shortly after it was captured. It was a daring mission, and most of those who participated died, but nonetheless, my ancestors were successful. Under the blessings of the Grand Master, and of the Pope, my family was tasked with protecting it, and decided returning the True Cross to the leaders of the day would merely put it at risk once again. In time, it was decided that it couldn't be returned until three generations of peace had passed in either the Holy Land, or in Rome."

Laura glanced at Jacques. "I doubt you'll ever see that in the Holy Land. But Rome has been at peace for some time, arguably since the end of World War Two. That would be three generations, wouldn't it?"

Jacques smiled and Acton stopped his examination, turning to him. "That's what this is all about, isn't it?"

"It is now, though it wasn't when I first contacted you."

"What do you mean?"

"The four bodies you found were the first three protectors of the True Cross, and their trusted sergeant, Raymond, who was adopted into our family just before he died. When the Templars were betrayed, the promise given to us by the Vatican, to bury our honored dead on their hallowed grounds, was terminated, and the tomb sealed—the tomb they stumbled upon a few years ago, and that you were brought in to examine."

Acton nodded. "That matches with what we found, three generations of the same family, the last of which was entombed just before the Templars were arrested. So your intention was to make sure we knew who they really were?"

"Exactly. They deserved that honor, at least. And I had hoped to entreat the Vatican, through you, to have them returned to their final resting place, and left in peace and dignity."

Acton pursed his lips. "I can respect that. But there's one thing I don't understand."

"What is that?"

"Why the fake nameplates?"

Hyères, Kingdom of Arles

1240 AD

Raymond smiled as Sir Gervais entered, the new baby he had heard born only minutes before, cradled in his arms. And wrapped in blue.

"A son?"

Sir Gervais smiled, nodding. Raymond pushed up on his elbows, and his squire rushed forward, propping him up with pillows. "Let me see the boy."

Sir Gervais sat on the edge of the bed, a bed that had been Raymond's home for far too many months as of late. He was dying. He had held on these last few weeks in the hopes he would see his master's child born, the grandson of his late master Sir John, and the great-grandson of the man who had saved him from a life of destitution and probably crime, Sir Guy of Ridefort. He was past his due, but he had survived long enough to see the next generation born, the boy who would carry on their mission given to them by the Grand Master, and blessed by the popes themselves.

Peace had never won out in the Holy Land, and the kingdoms of Europe, including the Holy See, were ones gripped in intrigue and political machinations that ensured instability. The True Cross would remain hidden away, protected for generations to come, by this family, a family driven by duty and honor, and by inherent goodness.

Sir Guy had found him in a ditch, beaten and left for dead by ruffians offended by his audacity at asking for a bite of bread. Sir Guy had his squire nurse him back to health as they traveled on a pilgrimage to the Holy Land. During the course of this journey, where Sir Guy restored his health and taught him the ways of a knight, he learned of the Templars, and what it meant to devote oneself to one's God and His holy warriors.

By the time they reached Jerusalem, he had not only pledged his loyalty to his savior on the roadside, but to his Lord Savior, and His army on Earth, the Knights Templar. And during the two years of travel, he had made a friend, a friend he missed to this day.

Raymond leaned forward, staring at the bundle of pink skin, eyes squeezed shut, chubby cheeks a shiny, healthy red. "Tell me his name."

Sir Gervais smiled. "We named him after the greatest man we know, and the truest friend a family could ever have."

Raymond reached out and rubbed a bony finger against the little man's cheek. "The name, my boy, the name!" He smiled as the baby squirmed.

"Raymond."

Raymond froze, then stared at Sir Gervais. "Master?"

"We named him after you."

Raymond's chest ached, and his eyes glistened. There could be no greater honor than for nobility to name a child after a mere servant. Though they were brothers in arms, three generations of Ridefort fighting by his side, he never could have dreamed of such an honor bestowed upon a man found in a ditch and delivered into the hands of God all those years ago.

He had never asked for anything from this family, and they nothing from him. This young baby's progenitors, Sir Guy, Sir John, and now Sir Gervais, had been true friends, and had treated him like family. And now, so near death, he knew he had a legacy that would be handed down through the generations, the name Raymond of Ridefort to never be forgotten.

A tear escaped, rolling down his cheek as he beamed at his master, then at the boy. "You honor me, Sir. And you humble me."

Sir Gervais reached out and squeezed Raymond's shoulder. "You honor us with your service all these years. You have been my ever-faithful servant and companion these years, and I know from the stories of others, that you were there for my father and grandfather. I can think of no greater tribute to all you have given us, than to invite you officially into our family, with the birth of our son, and your godchild."

Raymond closed his eyes, the tears flowing freely now, as he pictured the men of this family he had been as close to as brothers, who despite their position always treated him as an equal, and who now, with the words of their descendant, were kin. "God put me in your grandfather's path that day, so many years ago. I dread to think what my life would be, had he not stopped to inquire of my wellbeing." He opened his eyes and reached out, taking the hand of Sir Gervais. "Your father and grandfather would have been very proud of you, as I know your son will be of you." Raymond leaned back in his bed, a smile on his face, tears staining his cheeks, his breath shallow and slow.

It is time.

He opened his eyes, smiled at the baby, then looked at Sir Gervais. "Goodbye, my friend."

Sir Gervais' chest heaved, and he forced a smile as tears filled his eyes. "Rest my friend. You will be with my father and grandfather, with your family, soon."

Saint-Pierre-la-Mer, France

Present Day

Pierre Ridefort stood at the rear of their vehicle, grabbing at his long hair, an impressive string of curses erupting from his mouth.

"What now?" asked his friend, Albert. "They're meeting right now about it, aren't they? Is it too late?"

Pierre looked at him then threw his hands in the air, more curses spat at the night. "Of course it's too late!"

Schmidt inspected the bandage he had just finished applying to his man's calf, someone from the car getting off a lucky shot. "It is *not* too late."

Pierre glared at him. "How the hell do you figure that?"

"This was not the original plan. This was an attempt to avoid having to execute the original. It failed because that damned car kept going after we shot the driver. If it hadn't, we would have succeeded."

"But we've lost the element of surprise. We'll never succeed."

Schmidt agreed. "Not with your original plan, but with my modified one, we will."

"What modified plan?"

"I bring in more men, and we take the chateau by force."

Pierre stared at him. "But that means killing everyone."

"Probably. At least a significant portion of them."

"But they're family!"

"Yes, they are. The question is what is more important to you? Them, or this thing you're trying to retrieve."

Pierre thought for a moment. The True Cross *was* the ultimate goal. And with his father dead, those who stood by him would automatically swear their loyalty to him.

If only the bastard would die!

But now, with his hand played, his father knew he was willing to kill to possess it, which meant he would likely take action tonight to see it returned to the Vatican. And once that happened, his family's duty would be finished, and his dreams of righteous glory and respect would be forever lost. His future son and grandson would never share in the honor his father and grandfather had enjoyed.

No, his father had to be stopped, and it had to be now. And the only way of accomplishing that feat would be by letting Schmidt's men loose on his own family, a family that had betrayed him by supporting his father.

"The Ridefort family's duty for eight centuries has been clear. My father is delusional, and so are those that follow him. If they die in our attempt, then so be it. There will be others to replace them in time, but if we delay any longer, our time will be up, and my family's legacy will be lost forever."

Schmidt stared at him. "So what are you saying?"

Pierre met his gaze. "I'm saying, do whatever it takes to get me inside."

Schmidt smiled. "I thought you might say that." He pulled out his cellphone and sent a text message, a helicopter in the distance quickly becoming louder. Within minutes, the sound was overwhelming, a spotlight shining down on them. Schmidt waved.

"Who is that?"

Schmidt turned to Pierre. "Reinforcements. We'll discuss the bill later."

Rome, The Papal States
August 5, 1307

Sir Raymond of Ridefort made the sign of the cross as the sarcophagus was sealed, his father, Sir Gervais, now consigned to the ages inside this tomb on the holiest of grounds, under the very walls of the Vatican. He slowly rounded the other three sarcophagi containing his great-grandfather, Sir Guy, his grandfather, Sir John, and humble sergeant and friend, kinsmen thanks to his father, and a godfather he had never known, Raymond of Ridefort.

Four souls, who had served their Order faithfully for three generations, who had sacrificed everything in the protection of the True Cross, buried with honor.

And one day he would be here beside them, his own days numbered.

He smiled at his son and grandson, standing at his side. "One day you will bury me here, and your sons will bury you. And perhaps someday, God willing, our family's burden will end, peace will reign, and our charge can be safely returned to the purview of man."

The next two generations bowed slightly, saying nothing. Sir Raymond turned and left the tomb, his son and grandson following, two priests sealing the door behind them. They mounted the stairs and wound their way through the corridors, arriving at the offices of Pope

121

Clement V, the priest who managed his affairs rising and opening the doors.

"Sir Raymond of Ridefort, Your Holiness."

Sir Raymond entered and bowed, Pope Clement rising from his desk, another man, previously unnoticed, turning in his chair in front of the Pontiff.

"Sir Raymond of Ridefort, may I present Sir Lambert, here on behalf of King Philip of France."

Sir Lambert rose, and the men exchanged greetings before Sir Raymond turned to the Pope. "Our business here is done, and my family thanks you once again for the continued honor bestowed upon us."

Sir Lambert squeezed his chin, tugging on his beard. "Yes, we have been speaking of this…honor."

Sir Raymond barely suppressed his shock, this a secret handed down for generations, and to his knowledge, known only to his family, the Grand Master of the Knights Templar, and the sitting pope. No others were to know. He stared at the Pope, seeking some indication as to what should be said. The Pope avoided his gaze, instead returning to his chair. Sir Lambert sat, but Sir Raymond remained standing, his son and grandson flanking him.

"Yes, we have been. I feel it is time that your burden be lifted, and the True Cross handed over to the Holy See. We are better equipped to protect it."

Sir Raymond's chest pounded and his fists clenched tightly. "But, Your Holiness, three generations of peace have not yet occurred. The oath has not been fulfilled."

The Pontiff dismissed his statement with a flick of the wrist. "Three generations was never something *I* agreed to, and from my understanding, was something the Templars came up with themselves. Who are you, *my* servants, to tell *me* what I as leader of the Holy See must adhere to?" He stared at Sir Raymond. "You will reveal to me, right now, where the True Cross is hidden."

Sir Raymond shook his head, jabbing a finger at Sir Lambert. "These are the words of the French King, not of the Holy See. They are the words of a debtor delivered by a snake to be spoken by you." He turned on Sir Lambert. "Do you think me the fool, sir? Your king owes the Templars a great sum of money for his foolishness against England and Flanders. His debts are due, and he has no means to repay them. He is merely trying to drive a wedge between the Templars and the Holy See to escape his obligations."

He stared at Pope Clement. "And you, sir, are playing into King Philip's hands. The Templars have protected the True Cross for over a century, and we will continue to do so until three generations of peace have been enjoyed by those who call the Holy Land or Rome their home. My oath is to God and His Son, our Lord Jesus Christ. It is not to any man, and it is certainly not to the King of France."

He spun on his heel and marched for the door, Sir Lambert leaping to his feet. A sword pulled from its scabbard and Sir Raymond spun, gripping his own yet not drawing, his son and grandson doing the same. "You would dare draw a sword in this sacred place? You would dare shed blood on this holy ground, the very ground where Saint Peter himself is buried? You call yourself a Christian, sir? I call you a coward and a heathen, and I would spit on the ground before you if it wouldn't be a desecration." He jabbed a finger at him. "Never shall the Templars yield the True Cross while men the likes of you and King Philip hold sway over the Holy See!"

The Pontiff rose. "Enough of this!"

Sir Lambert bowed slightly, sheathing his sword. "Of course, Your Holiness."

The Pope pointed at the door. "You will leave, now, while you can. But hear this. Until the True Cross is returned, never again shall a member of your family be welcome here, even in death."

Sir Raymond glared at the man, struggling to contain his seething rage. "And of the four that are already here?"

The Pontiff stole a quick glance at Sir Lambert, then returned to his seat. "I will not desecrate the dead, however their tomb will be sealed, never to be seen again by man."

Sir Raymond resisted jabbing a finger at the Pontiff. "You have made that promise on the holiest of ground, and my family will hold you to it." He bowed to the Pontiff, ignoring Sir Lambert, then left the room, his son and grandson in tow.

"What shall we do, father?" asked his son, Sebastien, when they were clear of the Vatican. Sir Raymond glanced over his shoulder at Saint Peter's Basilica and frowned. "We must protect the remains of our dead."

"But how?"

His jaw squared as he increased his pace. "I have a plan, but we must act quickly."

Ridefort Residence

Saint-Pierre-la-Mer, France

Present Day

Jacques Ridefort tore his eyes away from the True Cross, Acton's suspicions that it was a fake, waning. This man was clearly still enamored with what he had possessed his entire life, and he at least thought it genuine. He reached out, finally unable to resist touching that which He spent his final hours upon. A surge of energy rushed through him as his fingertips ran across the ancient piece of wood, a moment of true belief washing over him, unlike anything he had ever experienced before.

The scientist in him knew it was purely psychological, yet the spiritual side was equally convinced it was a truly rapturous moment, a true moment of belief, of faith. He inhaled deeply, closing his eyes as he finally pulled his hand away. He opened them to see Jacques smiling at him.

"You feel it, don't you?"

Acton couldn't resist nodding.

"It is something truly special, truly unique. I knew we were in trouble when my son touched it and felt nothing. I had hoped over the years he would mature and come to realize the burden placed upon our family, but alas, he did not. Instead, he became obsessed with the glory that its possession should bring him."

He sighed. "But I digress. You asked about the fake nameplates. The reason was quite simple. My ancestor, Sir Raymond, after meeting with Pope Clement on the day of the internment of his father, Sir Gervais, realized the church could no longer be trusted, the King of France, Philip, wielding too much influence. The meeting ended rather ignominiously, the Pope demanding the return of the True Cross, Sir Raymond refusing.

"In response, the Pope ordered the tomb sealed, and decreed that no future generations of the family would be buried there. While he promised to not desecrate the graves, Sir Raymond felt that with the Pope's blessing to their oath no longer in force, in the years to come, his father and grandfather's tombs might be desecrated for their connection to the True Cross.

He couldn't move the bodies, but he was able to have false nameplates created with the names of Templars he felt anyone in the future who discovered the tomb might decide were too pure of spirit to disturb.

"He and several others snuck into the tomb and added the fake nameplates, undetected, their deception going undiscovered. It turned out to be unnecessary, the tomb sealed and forgotten, what with the extended transfer of the papal court to Avignon. The bodies of my ancestors rested in peace for eight hundred years, until uncovered by you."

Acton sighed, the mystery finally explained, and explained to his satisfaction. Everything fit with the evidence already uncovered, and he had no reason to doubt this dying man's story, though he would certainly be looking deeper into it once he had the chance. He stared down at Jacques. "But that's no longer why we are here."

Jacques shook his head. "No. Now that I am nearly dead, it is time to return the True Cross to those who can now protect it best."

"The Vatican."

"Exactly."

Laura reached out and touched the bare wood, closing her eyes, and Acton noticed her shiver, a slight smile on her face. "If that's the case, why do you need us?"

"My son."

Acton reached for the cross again, then paused. "What about your son? Is he the one who tried to kill us?"

"Yes. He is determined to stop me from returning it, and I fear, will stop at nothing, including my death, to keep the True Cross in Ridefort hands."

Outside the Notre-Dame Cathedral
Paris, Kingdom of France
March 18, 1314

Sir Raymond stared through the mass of people in front of him, tears streaking his face, his son and grandson on either side, their own cheeks burning from the outpouring of grief. The downfall of the Order had been swift. Betrayed by Pope Clement V and King Philip IV of France, mass arrests of the Knights Templar had been carried out on Friday the 13th in October 1307. Those arrested had been tortured into false confessions of heresy, blasphemy, and sodomy, and despite Grand Master Jacques de Molay's retraction of his utterings made under duress, the bastard Preceptor of Normandy, Geoffroi de Charney, declared de Molay and the other leaders guilty of being relapsed heretics.

Yet their sentence was the most horrifying aspect of this entire farce orchestrated by King Philip to avoid paying what he owed the Templars. His eyes met de Molay's, the elderly man recognizing him, and smiling slightly, drawing in a deep breath of courage as the flames were set at his feet, his sentence about to be carried out.

De Molay raised his bound hands to his lips in prayer, continuing to stare at Sir Raymond, as if drawing strength from him, and Sir Raymond could see the difference in his demeanor, as if knowing he wasn't alone in this abomination of justice, would see him through it.

The fact his hands were bound in front of him, rather than behind him to the stake, was a testament to his powers of persuasion, and of how his executioners must feel about what they were doing.

De Molay lifted his gaze and stared at Notre Dame Cathedral, his lips moving. Sir Raymond lowered his head, reciting the Lord's Prayer, when the crowd gasped. He looked up to see the flames engulfing the Grand Master, who opened his eyes and stared back at him. Then in his dying breaths, he summoned the strength to issue one last gasp of truth.

"God knows who is wrong and has sinned! Soon a calamity will occur to those who have condemned us to death!"

And with those final words, he roared in agony, the crowd, once eager to see the execution of someone whose life was better than theirs, fell silent, the horror of it all too much even for them. Sir Raymond desperately wanted to look away, yet he didn't, maintaining his gaze at his master for as long as the man had breath within.

The courage displayed flowed through him, and he stepped forward, drawing a deep breath. "I swear to you Grand Master, and to God Almighty Himself, that within one year, His Holiness and the King shall join you to answer for their crimes here today!"

The crowd turned toward him for a moment, his son pulling him back, but Sir Raymond had no regrets in what he had said. For he meant it. This injustice would not go unpunished. De Molay raised his hands, stretching them out toward him, as if in acknowledgment, his agony-filled cries continuous, until finally, mercifully, the screams stopped, his head slumped, and he was no more.

The Poor Fellow-Soldiers of Christ and of the Temple of Solomon, the Knights Templar, were finished.

Saint-Pierre-la-Mer, France

Present Day

Pierre climbed into the black helicopter, his heart pounding as this was about to become very real. His friends were lined up to join him, Albert reaching out to be pulled inside.

Schmidt waved him off. "They should remain here."

"But I need them."

"Why?"

"To move the item."

"My men can do that."

Pierre shook his head adamantly. "Absolutely not. It could be damaged."

"What the hell is this thing? I think we're at the point now where we need to know."

Pierre debated the idea for a mere moment. "No, it's far too precious to risk."

Schmidt was clearly growing frustrated with him, his cheeks red, his nostrils flaring. "What do you mean? It's worth a lot of money?"

Pierre shook his head. "No, its value isn't monetary, it's spiritual. It is nothing men like you would be interested in."

Schmidt's eyes narrowed. "Men like us?"

"I'm sorry, I don't mean that as an insult, I just mean men who kill for a living."

Schmidt exchanged a look with his men. "You think soldiers can't believe in God?"

"I didn't say that. One of the Commandments is 'Thou shalt not kill,' and that is what you do for a living."

Schmidt shook his head. "No, the original Hebrew says 'Thou shalt not *murder*,' which is a completely different thing."

"And you don't think what you do is murder?"

Schmidt leaned back in his seat, the rotors hammering overhead. "Do you not see the double-standard here? We are killing people because *you* need them out of your way, and you think *we're* unworthy of whatever the hell this thing is? I'm sorry, kid, but *you're* the one who has tonight's blood on your hands, not us. If you hadn't hired us, nobody would be dead, and no one would be dying tonight. So what's it going to be? The whole truth, or do we bounce?"

Pierre looked at his friends, friends who weren't supposed to know the truth, yet did. And they hadn't betrayed him. These men, though, he didn't know, but if they did indeed leave, he had no hope of ever retrieving the True Cross, and that was unacceptable. He had to trust in God that these men, here to do his bidding for the greater good, were trustworthy enough to risk sharing the truth with. He sighed.

"It's the True Cross."

"What the hell is that?"

"It's the cross upon which Jesus Christ was crucified."

Schmidt laughed, the others joining in. "Bullshit."

Pierre shrugged, relieved. Doubters wouldn't covet what they felt was worthless. "It's what we believe."

133

Schmidt leaned out and closed the door, leaving Pierre's friends outside. "Let's go get your chunk of driftwood."

Roquemaure, France
April 20, 1314

Sir Raymond, his son and grandson at his side, waited patiently. For he had time. Pope Clement V was dying on the other side of the door they now waited before, eaten away from the inside. He was not long for this earth, but Sir Raymond needed to see for himself before his own life came to an end.

After the burning at the stake of Grand Master de Molay, his son and grandson had forced him into a hasty departure, afraid the crowd might turn on them for the curse he had yelled into the silence. They hadn't been captured, though word was spreading across the land of it, some now calling it the Templar's Curse, others, who claimed de Molay himself had uttered it, calling it the Molay Curse.

He didn't care what anyone called it. All he cared about was getting his revenge on those who had destroyed his order and dishonored all those that had done so much good for almost two centuries. There had been some debate as to what to do next, his son advocating a more cautious approach, wanting to leave things in the hands of God to exact revenge, advocating they focus on their sworn duty to protect the True Cross.

"They must never have it! These blasphemers, these sinners, cannot be trusted with it. It is our duty to protect it until the time is right, and we cannot risk our lives on this revenge you are so determined to exact."

Sir Raymond had been disappointed in his son at first, but he was right. Their duty was to the True Cross, though his duty to that original cause was almost over. He was near death himself, and it would be his son and grandson who would continue with that honor and burden.

Which left him free to fulfill his promise.

When word had arrived of Pope Clement on his deathbed, he had announced his intention to see him, and his son had insisted on coming. A faithful boy to the end. They made the journey to Avignon, to where Clement had moved the Papacy from Rome, something that should condemn him to the eternal depths of Hell as far as Sir Raymond was concerned.

When he had demanded an audience, he had fully expected to be turned away, perhaps even arrested, but instead, he had been redirected here, to Roquemaure, where the Pope was spending his final days away from his station.

A door opened and a priest appeared, beckoning them inside. "His Holiness will see you now."

Sir Raymond stepped through the door, his son and grandson following. He was taken aback at the frailty before him. The last time he had seen Pope Clement was when he had interred his father in the tomb reserved for those protecting the True Cross. That had been seven years ago, and time and illness had ravaged the man, yet there was no sympathy or empathy within Sir Raymond to offer this evil man who had destroyed so much, a puppet to the equally evil and cowardly King of France, Phillip IV.

Clement reached out a hand, and Sir Raymond, on instinct, took it. "I remembered your name at once, which is why I agreed to see you."

Sir Raymond said nothing.

"I—I owe you and your family an apology."

Sir Raymond's eyebrows rose slightly, yet he remained silent, still taking comfort in his hatred for this wretched soul.

"I let King Phillip wield too much power. I should have listened to God, and not to kings. I fear I shall go down in history a cursed man."

As you should.

"If you allowed me here to lift the curse I placed on you in Paris, you are wasting your breath."

Clement smiled. "My son, I am a man of God. I do not believe in curses."

A sneer curled up the side of Sir Raymond's face. "Yet here you lie, dying."

Clement chuckled then coughed. "My son, I have been dying for many years. There's nothing that can be done now, save a miracle from God."

Sir Raymond withdrew his hand. "No miracle shall come. Of that, I can assure you."

"Do you really hate me that much?"

"Yes."

"Should you die with a heart filled with hate, you may find yourself unworthy of Paradise."

137

"Then I will be joining you in Hell."

Clement sighed. "Perhaps, though I doubt it. You are a good man, merely engulfed in events beyond your control." He leaned his head slightly closer, lowering his voice. "You still guard the True Cross?"

"Of course."

The Pontiff nodded, lying back upon his pillow. "That knowledge will die with me. The Templars are no more. You cannot inform the next Pope of your oath and instructions, nor can I have the next Pope informed, as, again, the Templars are no more."

Sir Raymond paused, his hatred momentarily forgotten. "What does that mean?"

"It means, my son, that you must now decide what to do. Your oath was part of an Order that has now been disbanded and no longer has the blessings of this Church. And with my death, no one will know of your duty beyond yourselves. As far as anyone will be concerned, should you be found with the True Cross, you will be treated as thieves and heretics." He smiled. "Perhaps you and your family are the ones who have been cursed." His smile broadened. "I fear your torment will outlast mine." His eyes closed and a long, slow breath escaped, his chest failing to rise for another.

Sir Raymond didn't make the sign of the cross, and grabbed his grandson Henry's hand as he was about to make one of his own. "No remorse or respect will be shown for this man. He is responsible for the death of the Order, as much as King Phillip is."

Sir Raymond turned on his heel and left the room as Clement's staff surged in, the wails of mourners already filling the halls. They mounted their horses, leaving the property quickly, lest they be detained for some reason, and soon found themselves alone, outside of the town.

"*Now* can we return to our duty?" asked his son.

"We have seen one dead, yet one still remains. When I have seen him pass, only then will we return to our business, a business I'm afraid will be yours and *your* grandson's," he said, smiling at young Henry, yet to reach puberty.

Henry smiled. "How long will our family have to protect the True Cross, Grandfather?"

Sir Raymond sighed. "I fear it could be until the Second Coming."

"But how will we manage?" asked his son. "The Templars are no more."

Sir Raymond brought his horse to a halt, turning toward his son. "As long as there are men with honor in their heart, the Templars will exist. It is not our wealth or status that makes us who we are, but our devotion to God. What greater sacrifice in the name of our Lord could one possibly make, than to live in obscurity, guarding that which is His, from those who would commit atrocities in His name? We will continue our duty, for as long as is necessary, no matter how long that may be."

Ridefort Residence

Saint-Pierre-la-Mer, France

Present Day

Laura glanced nervously at her husband as he stepped closer to her. "Are we in danger?"

Jacques Ridefort shook his head. "Normally I would say no, but after the attempt on your lives, I'm afraid my answer is now 'yes.'"

"Then we need to get the hell out of here."

Jacques motioned toward the True Cross not three feet from Acton's mouth. "Language, Professor, please."

Acton's eyebrows shot up. "Oh shit, sorry!"

Laura placed a hand over his mouth. "He's truly sorry. Now, we obviously can't go out the front entrance, because that road is a deathtrap until you reach the town. Is there another way out?"

"Yes, we have several escape routes that have been built over the centuries for just such an occasion, but they are all known to my son."

"But he's after the cross, not us, correct?"

"Again, I would have said yes, but I'm at a loss as to why he would try to target you tonight if that were merely the case."

Laura chewed her cheek. "What happens to the cross when you die?"

Jacques paused. "Responsibility for it would be handed down to my first born son, Pierre."

"And then he can do with it as he pleases."

"Correct."

"So he can keep it in the family, rather than return it to the Vatican, despite your wishes."

"Correct."

"And"—Laura lowered her voice, bowing her head slightly—"you said you only have perhaps a few days left."

Jacques nodded. "Again correct."

"Then could this all be a delaying tactic? He must assume you plan to hand the cross over to us. By killing us, or at least preventing our meeting, he might have hoped to stop you from returning the cross long enough that you would die, solving his problem."

"Sounds pretty damned heartless to me," muttered Acton.

"My son, I fear, has no love left in his heart for me. He is consumed by a lust for glory and power. What you say, could very well be true. If I cannot hand off the cross to you tonight, then I will surely die before I can find someone else."

Acton's eyes narrowed. "Why not just have some of your people return it for you?"

Jacques sighed, his shoulders slumping. "I'm afraid I don't know who I can trust. Though my brothers and cousins who are here with me are loyal to me, they don't all agree with my decision. I fear should I give it to the wrong one, they may either not deliver it, or delay its delivery long enough for me to die, allowing my son to then rescind the order." He shook his head. "No, I need an outsider, such as yourselves, to fulfill my wishes. Only then can I be assured the cross is returned."

Acton frowned. "Well, as much as I'm honored you chose us, I think now that we are targets, we'll have to bow out."

Jacques sighed. "I was afraid you might say that. And now I fear all is lost."

Approaching the Ridefort Residence

Saint-Pierre-la-Mer, France

Schmidt held up his phone. "You lied to me."

Pierre's eyes narrowed. "Excuse me?"

"This cross. It isn't just some piece of wood, it's a fragment encased in gold and covered in jewels."

Pierre tensed. "I never said it was a piece of wood. You did."

"You said its value was spiritual, not monetary."

"It is! This is the most important Christian artifact known to exist! No price can be placed on it."

"Oh, I think I can come up with a price."

Pierre's heart hammered. "We had a deal."

"Yes we did, a deal based on a lie." He pointed to a second helicopter that had joined them. "And my expenses just went up."

"I know, and I will compensate you for it. Say, double what we agreed?"

Schmidt shook his head. "No, I want a piece of the action. Half of whatever you sell it for."

"But I'm not selling it! I'm trying to save it from my idiotic father returning it to the Vatican before he dies. I'm trying to keep it in the family, like it has been for eight hundred years."

Schmidt's eyes shot up. "The Vatican, huh? Now *they* have deep pockets."

"No! Don't even think about it! I'll triple what I was going to pay you."

"Now you're getting closer."

"Quadruple. But that's the best I can do."

Schmidt agreed, the others smiling at their increased payday. "Good. We have a deal. But if I find out you've deceived me in some other way, I may find it necessary to renegotiate." He slid open the door, peering outside as wind howled through the cabin. "We're here. This is your last chance to change your mind."

Pierre stared down at the chateau that had been his home for most of his life, filled with his friends, family, and memories. He closed his eyes, his heart hammering, then nodded. "Let's do it."

Ridefort Residence

Saint-Pierre-la-Mer, France

Acton placed himself between Laura and the door, as two men burst inside.

"Sir, two choppers are approaching. We believe it's an attack."

Jacques' lips thinned and his breathing became more rapid. "Pierre, how could you?" He looked at the men. "Execute the escape plan."

"Yes, sir." They disappeared, and Jacques turned to Acton and Laura. "Will you please take it with you?"

Acton shook his head. "No, I'm sorry, but this isn't our fight, and frankly, it's not fair of you to ask us to risk our lives for this. You have people, have them take it. If you didn't trust them, you could have called the Vatican yourself and had them come to collect it." He sighed. "I'm truly sorry, but you have to let us go." Acton looked about. "Now, where can we find one of those escape routes you talked about?"

Jacques pointed at the far wall, and his attendant walked over, pushing against it, another dark passageway revealed. "Follow it to the end. It will take you outside, on the coast. From there, just head south and you'll reach the town within half an hour." Jacques leaned forward. "Please, I'm begging you to change your minds."

Laura shook her head. "No, James is right. This is simply too dangerous. I'm sorry."

Acton took her hand and headed for the tunnel. He turned back as the two men returned with others, pieces of a large flat crate carried between them. "Good luck, Mr. Ridefort."

But the dying man ignored them, instead staring at the True Cross as it was lifted from its reliquary and placed into the crate, leaving Acton to wonder if he would ever see it again.

Schmidt leaned out the side of the chopper and aimed his Heckler & Koch MG4 at the chateau's defenders. He squeezed the trigger, a burst of lead spraying across the courtyard, sending the enemy below scattering, one dropping from what was likely a leg wound. The other chopper circled, laying down fire as well, another defender collapsing.

The entire complex lit up as emergency lighting flooded the area, inside and out, providing the defenders with a clear view of anyone approaching the walls, but also of themselves to any aerial attack. They apparently had never planned on this, their entire way of thinking geared toward a ground assault.

As he continued to fire, he watched as these so-called Templar Knights scurried like cockroaches, and he glanced over at Pierre, tears running down the boy's face. He felt for the kid. These men were, apparently, his family, his friends, people he had grown up with.

Yet none of that mattered anymore.

This was war.

Father against son, and his father would lose. They would retrieve this holy artifact, over the man's dead body if necessary, then get their payday. Four times their original agreement, though with double the number of men now involved, it was closer to only double. Still a good haul, but this True Cross had him intrigued. From the few minutes of Googling he did, it suggested it was a fairly large artifact, at least eight feet tall, if not a dozen, and was, at a minimum, plated in gold, if not solid gold, with jewels embedded throughout. It was worth a fortune to those who believed in what it was, but melted down, it would still be worth millions, and be easy to fence.

He continued to fire, short, controlled bursts, most of the courtyard cleared, the defenders that had survived now having found cover. He understood how the conquistadors must have felt centuries before as they confiscated priceless treasures from the Incans, Mayans, and Aztecs. Then melted them down for transport. These trinkets had meant nothing to the Spaniards, yet everything to those they had been stolen from. He could understand how believers would feel this cross in its current form would be priceless, the very idea of melting it down, unthinkable. And he wasn't even sure how he felt about it.

He was raised Christian, yet hadn't set foot inside a church in over a decade, if not longer, and wasn't a praying man. Did he believe in God? He supposed, though he wasn't certain. He didn't buy into the Bible, though the idea that Jesus was real didn't bother him. He didn't deny it, he simply didn't care.

And this cross, even if it were real, meant nothing to him, again, something he didn't care about. Yet for some reason, his inner voice kept telling him to just take the payday and forget the cross. Leave it to the believers.

We'll see.

He leaned back, adjusting his headset. "Let's get down there. Chopper Two, provide cover, over."

The pilot banked hard to the left, dropping their altitude rapidly before righting them. His team rappelled out the sides, and he followed suit, leaving Pierre in the chopper with his wounded man, staring down after him. His feet hit the ground and he unclipped his rope, surging toward the outer wall as his men spread out. He reached it, not having fired his weapon, and in fact, hadn't heard a single shot since they had landed. All-clears sounded through his comm.

They must all be inside.

He glanced at a few bodies in the courtyard.

Or dead.

"Chopper Two, begin your insertion, over."

"Roger that."

The second chopper hovered over the courtyard, the rest of his team jumping out and scattering to the edges. "Chopper One, bring our VIP, over."

The pilot acknowledged, and Schmidt stepped into the courtyard as the chopper landed. He urged Pierre out, and his wounded man waved at him. "Kill that sonofabitch that shot me, okay?"

Schmidt grinned. "Consider it done."

Acton led the way, a flashlight found on the wall when they first entered the tunnel, lighting the way. They could hear the dull thuds of gunfire through the stone walls, but there was no way of knowing who was winning. He hoped, of course, that Jacques and his forces would prevail, yet he had his doubts they would. Whoever had ambushed them in the car was well-equipped and well-trained, the only thing ruining their plans the fact the chauffeur had activated the cruise control, allowing the built-in safety features to take over when he was shot.

And if Jacques' people managed to secret the cross away, then in his rage, the man's son just might kill everyone left, in an attempt to find out where it had been taken.

They came to a fork in the tunnel, with no indication as to which way to go, both routes still descending. "Umm, what now?"

Laura took the flashlight and aimed it at the floor of one tunnel, then the other. "Neither looks like they've been used in years, if not centuries."

Acton pointed to the left. "That one seems a little steeper. We're on the coast so they can't go below the water table. Let's just hope they both come out somewhere, and it doesn't matter where."

Laura led the way in silence, their footsteps echoing in the confined space, the gunfire either stopped, or whatever medium had been carrying the sounds through the ground, was no longer near them. Laura cursed as they rounded a bend, their path blocked by a cave-in that didn't appear recent. "Well, we're not getting through that," she muttered. "Let's try tunnel number two."

They backtracked, then made their way down the second tunnel, walking for several minutes, Acton about to express his doubts as to the sanity of Jacques Ridefort, when Laura held up her fist. He stopped, and she turned around.

"Do you hear that?" she whispered.

He cocked an ear and at first heard nothing. He opened his mouth to say so, when he finally heard it.

Water!

He nodded, and they proceeded onward, slower this time, tiptoeing, not sure if they were about to walk into someone working for Jacques' son, or a drop-off into some water-filled pit with no hope of escape.

Laura held up a fist again, and Acton stopped, straining to hear what had her concerned. Voices. Two men, speaking in French. Laura inched forward, light reflecting off the shiny slick stonework surrounding them. As they continued, it became brighter, though not much more, the light artificial and dim.

Acton pointed at a channel of water ahead, their path coming to an end at its edge, a wall on the other side. This was some sort of hidden dock underneath the chateau, carved out by Mother Nature and the hand of man.

Laura peered around the corner and her shoulders relaxed as she sighed. She stepped out, her hands up slightly. "Gentlemen."

Acton quickly followed, not pleased at her foolhardiness, yet breathed his own sigh of relief as he recognized Jacques' attendant Vincent, and two of the men who had helped package the cross. Acton's eyes bulged slightly as he saw the crate in the back of a boat, bobbing gently in the cavern they now found themselves, along with several others, the hidden cavern large.

"I see you found your way."

Laura nodded. "Yes, but how did you get here quicker? The other route was blocked."

"We took a shortcut." Vincent jerked a thumb over his shoulder, and Acton cursed at the sight of a freight elevator. "And you couldn't have let us use it?"

"No, it's reserved for the cross."

A PA system crackled, an excited voice in French echoing off the stone walls. "Reinforcements to the treasure room! Reinforcements to the treasure room!"

The three men checked the lines to make sure the boat was secure, then headed for the elevator.

"Wait a minute, you're just going to leave it here?"

Vincent shook his head. "No, you're with it."

"We're leaving."

Vincent frowned, then pointed at the water and the opening to the outside. "That's your choice. You'll have to swim for it. You'll find the beach just a little ways to the right."

The elevator door opened and the three men climbed aboard. "Good luck, Professors."

The doors closed and Acton cursed, staring at the crate holding the cross. He looked at Laura. "We can't just leave it here."

She frowned. "Normally I would agree, but what can we do? If we stay, we have no idea who's coming through those doors next. If we go, then aren't we in effect stealing it?"

Acton folded his arms and grabbed at his chin, squeezing it tightly as he paced, the timbers of the dock creaking with each step, leaving him to wonder just how old it was. "If we take it, and return it to the Vatican as he said he wanted, then we aren't stealing it. We're merely doing what he wanted."

"Yes, but then we're going to have whoever is upstairs after us. We have no weapons, no backup, and no transportation beyond this boat. How the devil are we going to get it to Rome all by ourselves?"

Acton sighed, scratching behind his ear. "You're right, of course." He stared at the water and the opening leading to the Mediterranean Sea. "To hell with it, let's get our asses out of here and let them deal with it. If they win, the cross is safe, and if they lose, then they would have come after us and probably killed us anyway if they've got helicopters at their disposal."

Laura's eyes widened slightly. "I forgot about those." She jumped into the water, disappearing momentarily from sight. She resurfaced and looked at him. "Coming, dear?"

Acton grinned then dove in after her. He bobbed up beside her, treading water. "Do you think we can book an earlier flight to Spain? I think we're probably going to want to be out of France sooner rather than later."

"I'll buy the damned plane if I have to."

Acton laughed then stopped when more gunfire echoed from overhead, the sounds carried through the elevator shaft or the opening to the outside—which, he didn't know, nor care. "Let's get a wiggle on. I have a feeling it's about to get crowded in here."

Pierre directed Schmidt and his team toward the treasure room, the resistance nonexistent. He had counted perhaps half a dozen of his family lying in the courtyard, yet had only seen two inside, both running away. He had ordered Schmidt not to shoot, and, remarkably, his command had been followed, though if one were to return and injure or kill one of his men, Pierre had little doubt Schmidt would take it out on him.

He didn't trust him. Hiring Schmidt had been a mistake, though how he might accomplish his goals without him, he had no idea. These mercenaries were supposed to be a scalpel, not a broadsword, and unfortunately, that was what they had become. He should have stuck to the original plan, of secretly infiltrating the chateau and stealing the True Cross. Instead, they had gone with Schmidt's plan of killing the professors and preventing the meeting they assumed was the handover.

And because that plan had failed, they had lost their element of surprise, the scalpel approach no longer possible. All because of Schmidt. Pierre's plan might have resulted in no casualties, yet now half a dozen of his family and friends were dead or dying, and they were about to enter the one room where if a last stand were to be made, it would be there.

Which would mean even more deaths.

"Just up on the left."

Schmidt slowed their advance, approaching the closed door. His men took up position on either side, two covering either end of the hallway. He reached out and tried the knob unsuccessfully, sending Pierre's stomach into flips.

They're inside.

Schmidt pointed at the lock, and one of his men quickly placed a small explosive on it. They all stepped back and turned away, the blast making quick work of the lock. Schmidt and one of his men both tossed flash-bangs inside, the roar overwhelming, Pierre gripping at his ears, but too late. Stunned, he stumbled around in circles as the team rushed inside, gunfire erupting as he slowly regained his senses.

And by the time he did, the weapons fell silent, and that could mean only one thing. He stepped inside, and his eyes traveled the room. And he dropped to his knees, his shoulders slumping as sobs racked his body.

What have I done?

Schmidt hauled him to his feet. "Cut that shit out. There'll be plenty of time for you to mourn later. Now, where is this cross?"

Pierre pulled in a deep breath and wiped his eyes on the back of his sleeve. He headed for the pedestal with the bust of Grand Master Jacques de Molay, and tilted it toward the wall, the bookcase to his right clicking. He returned the pedestal to its former position, then pushed on the bookcase, revealing the hidden treasure room. Schmidt motioned for two of his men to proceed. A flash-bang was tossed inside, Pierre opening his mouth to protest, but it was too late. He covered his ears in time, squeezing his eyes shut, then when the ruckus was over, followed the team in, thankful this time there was no gunfire.

As he rounded the corner, he waved his hand in front of him in a futile attempt to clear away the smoke. He stepped over to the wall and cranked up the ventilation system, the room quickly clearing before he returned it to its normal setting. He turned back and cursed, the True Cross gone, the rest of the family's treasures accumulated over eight centuries, left untouched.

With Schmidt and his team eyeing them.

He spotted his father's wheelchair sitting near the stand where the cross had been mounted, an envelope on the cushion. He stepped forward and picked it up, his name written on the front. He opened it, removing a single folded sheet of paper. He unfolded it, and his chest ached.

I forgive you.

Love, Dad

He dropped into the chair, battling the tears as Schmidt's men split their attentions between the blubbering boy and his family's loot.

Schmidt turned to him. "I think we've found our payment."

Pierre's eyes widened. "Are you kidding me! This is a hundred times more than we agreed to! A thousand!"

Schmidt shrugged then slapped the machine gun hanging from his neck. "He with the gun negotiates the price."

Pierre jumped from the chair, advancing on Schmidt. "You double-crossing sonofabitch!"

Schmidt turned slightly, the barrel of the gun now pointing at Pierre. He stopped. "I suggest you calm down."

Pierre glared at him, then walked over to the wall, slamming his hand against a large red button by the door. An alarm sounded, and a red light in the ceiling flashed. He stepped through the door. "You've got ten seconds. I suggest you follow me."

Schmidt eyeballed him. "What did you just do?"

"I activated a safety measure. Five seconds."

Schmidt marched for the door, waving at his men. "Let's go, now!" His men scrambled after him, looking confused, one still filling his pockets with gold. "Hans! Now!" Hans glanced at him for a moment, the greed evident in his wide eyes, then returned to stuffing his pockets.

Pierre pulled Schmidt through the door, the mercenary's foot clearing the threshold just as dozens of sharp metal spikes shot up from the floor, spaced less than a foot apart. Hans cried out as he was impaled, a heavy door dropping from the ceiling and cutting them off from the room.

"Hans!" Schmidt slammed a fist against the stone now blocking their path, two of his men rushing forward, grunting as they futilely pushed against it. Schmidt turned on Pierre, charging toward him. "Open that door, now!"

Pierre stumbled backward, shaking his head. "I can't. It won't open for hours."

Schmidt grabbed him by the shirt, lifting him from the floor. "But my man is in there! Open it now!"

"It's impossible! And-and don't bother with explosives, the entire room will collapse. He-he's already dead. You saw him."

"You killed him."

Pierre shook his head. "No, *you* did."

Schmidt's eyes flared, Pierre's choice of words clearly unwise.

"I mean, it was his fault. He disobeyed your orders and got greedy. If he had of listened to you, he'd be alive now. It's nobody's fault but his own."

Schmidt tossed him into a chair, eying the massive stone where the opening to the treasure room had been. "What *is* this place?"

Pierre stood. "It's the home of the last of the Templars, with booby-traps and secret passageways built over eight hundred years. You were never getting that gold."

Schmidt glared at him. "The price just doubled again."

Pierre decided it wouldn't be worth the shortened life expectancy to argue the point, instead walking over to another shelf and revealing yet another hidden gem. An elevator. "Let's go. If they took the cross anywhere, they took it to the docks under the chateau."

Schmidt signaled for two of his men to follow, and they all boarded the freight elevator, Pierre reaching through the bodies to press the button to take them to the bottom. The elevator shuddered then began the descent, this secret exit installed in the seventies by his grandfather. It was slow and loud, but would deliver them to the hidden dock within minutes.

He just prayed his father and the True Cross would still be there when they arrived.

"Did you hear that?"

Laura nodded at Acton as they cleared the opening, several explosions heard overhead followed by a burst of gunfire, then silence. "I think someone just lost."

"Yeah, but who?"

Acton was about to continue swimming when the PA system in the cave behind them crackled to life with the voice of Jacques Ridefort.

"Professors, if you are still there, we have lost. Please take the cross, I beg of you. If you don't, it could be lost forever. Please, professors, if you can hear me—"

There was a loud sound that overwhelmed the system, then what sounded like gunshots.

"Pierre! How could—"

The PA cut off, and Acton closed his eyes, saying a silent prayer for the man and his compatriots. He opened them, then looked at Laura.

"What do you think?"

Her eyes were wide with fright, but he knew her too well to not know her answer. "We have no choice. If they can't save it, then we have to."

Acton grinned. "I had a feeling you were going to say that." He turned, and they both swam rapidly back toward the entrance to the hidden dock. Laura climbed over the edge of the boat as Acton hauled himself up onto the dock, freeing the lines. The engine roared to life as the elevator chimed. Acton spun toward it, the doors opening, a young man and three others, heavily armed, visible.

"Go! Go! Go!"

Acton dove into the boat as Laura gunned the engine, landing painfully overtop the crate.

"Stop!" shouted someone from behind them, gunfire echoing, bullets tearing at the rock as they shot out of the cave and into the open sea. Laura banked hard to the right, killing the enemy's line of sight, and raced them down the coast, toward the town.

Acton picked himself up and sat beside her, glancing back to make sure their precious cargo was still intact. It was, no damage from the bullets evident. "What the hell are we going to do with this thing?" he asked as the lights of the town became visible.

Laura shot him a quick look. "I have no bloody idea. We need to find someplace to hide while we figure it out."

Acton frowned. "Then maybe heading toward the town isn't such a good idea."

Laura shook her head. "I'm not dying for this thing, and there's safety in numbers. I doubt they'd do anything in public."

The town rapidly approached, the boat equipped with a pair of impressive engines that were quickly reducing the amount of time they had to make a decision. But Laura was right. They needed to surround themselves with people. Even if they were discovered, it was more likely they'd survive any encounter if there were witnesses.

Something behind them caused him to turn and search the night sky for the source. A beam of light sliced through the dark, illuminating them, and Acton cursed as a chopper rapidly overtook them.

"We've gotta get off this boat, now!" He searched for anything they could use, his eyes coming to rest on a scuba tank. He grabbed it and shrugged it over his shoulders, testing the regulator, a burst of air filling his mouth. They were almost at the port now, dozens of pleasure craft visible, the public they needed for protection only a couple of miles away. Gunfire sprayed the water in front of them, then tore into the prow of the boat.

"Let's go!" Acton pushed Laura over the side then dove in after her as the boat was torn apart by a heavy machine gun. He broke the surface, searching for Laura, finally spotting her to his left. He swam toward her, grabbed her hand and pulled her under. He handed her the buddy regulator, and she took several breaths as he flipped over on his back to see bullets streaking through the water.

Suddenly a massive explosion rumbled overhead, their boat ripped apart, flames throwing a bright glow over the waves above as the fuel ignited.

Laura pointed, a large rectangle to the right puzzling him for a moment, before he realized what it was. It was the crate holding the True Cross. On instinct, he kicked toward it, Laura following, and soon reached the crate as it slowly sank. He pointed toward the shore and Laura nodded. They both grabbed the crate, kicking hard as they tried to move it away from the wreckage now descending around them, flames still lighting the water overhead. They managed to float it about half a mile, if not a little farther, from where Acton hoped anyone might search for it, before it finally hit bottom.

He pointed to shore, and they quickly reached a deserted beach about a mile north of the port, both flopping on the sand, gasping for breath. Acton shrugged the tank off his back then rolled over, reaching out for Laura's hand. "Are you okay?"

"Yes, I think so." She sat up on her elbows and watched as the chopper circled the area then banked away, the searchlight cutting out as it headed back toward the chateau. "Now what?" asked Laura, sitting cross-legged beside him.

"Let's call Giasson. Maybe he can help."

Laura reached into her pocket and pulled out her phone. "Fried."

Acton frowned, retrieving his own. He cursed. "Mine's shot too."

"Okay, we're going to have to find a phone, and keep our heads down. Since we were targeted, I think we can be sure they know what we look like, and they're going to have eyes in the town soon, if they don't already."

Acton climbed to his feet and gasped, grabbing for his side.

Laura jumped up beside him, concerned. "What?"

He felt for the pain, his fingers coming to rest on something sticking out his back, just below his right kidney.

"Oh my God, you've been wounded." Laura knelt down. "It looks like a piece of shrapnel from the boat. We need to get you to a hospital."

Acton grimaced as Laura carefully felt around the piece of metal. "That's the first place they'll be looking for us."

Laura stared up at him. "I don't think we have a choice."

Schmidt guided the boat as Pierre and the others sat in the back. The sputtering flames from the wreckage that had carried the True Cross were visible just ahead, and other pleasure craft were already converging on the area. Schmidt cut the engine, leaving them in the dark, half a mile from the explosion site. He turned around.

"This is close enough." He pointed to his two men, already geared up. "Go."

They both flipped over backward into the water, then disappeared into the inky blackness. And they waited, Pierre's knee hopping with nervous energy.

"What if they don't find it?"

Schmidt glanced at him. "They will. There's no way two professors, one a woman, were able to drag that thing to shore."

"What if it floated?"

Schmidt shook his head. "My men in the chopper reported seeing it sink with the wreckage. It's down there. When they find it, they'll tag it with a locator, and we'll come in with the right equipment to retrieve it."

"But what if the authorities find it first?"

"My men are already acquiring what we need. The authorities will be searching for bodies first, then worrying about what's on the bottom. We've got time."

Pierre stared at the wreckage as the first emergency craft arrived, its blue lights flashing, a loudspeaker ordering the civilians out of the area. Pierre closed his eyes, not as convinced as Schmidt was that this would end well. His eyes shot open.

"They were the only two on the boat!"

Schmidt eyed him. "Yeah. So?"

"Well, where's my father?"

Jacques Ridefort sat on the deck of his yacht, watching through binoculars as the authorities began their search. Things hadn't gone according to plan, and unfortunately, there was little he could do about it. And while he had no emotional connection to these two professors, he did feel they were good people, and he hated to see good people die. It was unfortunate, but what was more unfortunate, was that the crate now lay on the bottom of the sea, soon to be discovered either by the authorities, or, more likely, the forces hired by his son to steal the True Cross from him.

He did feel bad about tricking the professors into taking the boat. His attendant had already safely moved him through another tunnel, where he had given his emotional plea to the two, cameras showing them still within earshot. He had then faked an explosion and gunfire simply by batting his fingertips against the microphone, then delivered a panicked line, before cutting off the mike.

They had bought it.

And paid the ultimate price.

He sighed as he lowered the binoculars, making the sign of the cross. He turned to Vincent. "Ready?"

"Yes, sir."

"Then let's proceed. There's little time to waste."

Laura flagged down an ambulance, its lights flashing and sirens blaring as it raced toward the port. The driver slowed, rolling down his window.

"What's wrong?"

Laura responded in flawless French. "My husband was injured when a boat exploded. We were swimming, and he was hit with something." She pointed at the bloody wound, and the man's eyes bulged, bringing the ambulance to a complete stop.

He climbed out, his partner rushing around from the other side. Within moments, James was in the back of the ambulance receiving treatment. "We need to take him to a hospital, Madame."

Laura glanced at her husband who shook his head slightly. "Can't you just patch him up here? We're leaving on an early flight, and we can't afford to miss it."

The paramedic shook his head. "No, I don't dare risk removing this."

James reached over and yanked it out, gasping in pain as blood oozed from the wound.

"James!" cried Laura, her eyes wide as she stared at him. He gave her a look, the paramedics delivering a string of curses as they quickly dealt with the new situation. Within minutes, they had calmed, and James had a smile from some good drugs. Laura's heart hammered, and she wished she could have an injection too. "So? Is he going to be okay?"

"Yes, Madame. The wound is clean, and no arteries were hit. That was a very stupid thing your husband did, but the bleeding has stopped. We still need to take him to the hospital, however, just to be safe."

James sat up, wincing slightly. "No. I don't have travel insurance. I'll get it looked at when I get back stateside."

The paramedics protested, but he climbed out regardless, gingerly holding his side. "Thank you, gentlemen," he said, his words slightly slurred. "I'll be okay."

Laura held her hands against his shoulders. "I don't think this is a good idea. Let's go to the hospital like they say."

He shook his head, leaning in. "If they're looking for us, that's where they'll start, then I'm dead anyway."

"What did he say?"

Laura waved off the curious men, James' voice not as quiet as he thought it was. "It's just the drugs."

The driver shook his head. "Crazy Americans."

Laura smiled. "I'm British."

The man frowned, jabbing a finger at James. "He isn't. He's going to kill himself." He threw his hands up, another string of curses erupting. "I don't care. Let him kill himself. What do I know, a highly trained professional? Apparently, he knows better."

They shut the doors and climbed into the ambulance, moments later its siren back on as it continued to the port, leaving them on the side of the road.

"You're beautiful when you're worried."

Laura glanced at him. "You're stoned."

"Yes, yes I am. Call me Cheech."

She slung his arm over her shoulder, and they continued into town, a hotel visible just ahead. "If you die on me, I'll kill you."

Approaching the Ridefort Residence

Saint-Pierre-la-Mer, France

Captain Durand rode in silence up the winding road toward the chateau he had stared at for years as a boy, imagining what great battles had taken place at its gates—then as an adult, learned to ignore, the massive structure simply one of thousands dotting the landscapes of Europe. Fascinating to the tourists, just another trivial thing to the locals.

When word had come of gunfire and explosions at the chateau, he had volunteered to take the call. He had always wanted to get through the gates of the private structure, to see what was inside, and to likely have his boyhood fantasies crushed.

And this might be his only chance.

He couldn't recall hearing of anyone being let inside, the four walls with surrounding fencing a mystery to all that lived here for time immemorial.

They pulled up to the gates, the entire structure bathed in moonlight and little else. He stepped out and could see no evidence of anything untoward, an eerie silence surrounding him. He walked up to the gates, searching for a buzzer, when a door built into the side opened, and a man stepped out, one he recognized from around town, though never realized resided here.

"Monsieur Ridefort, I didn't know this was where you lived."

"Captain Durand. How can I help you?"

Bernard Ridefort appeared slightly disheveled, his hair a mess, matted from heavy sweat, his eyes darting about, as if searching the grounds.

He's not happy I'm here.

"We had reports of gunshots and explosions coming from here."

Bernard stared at him for a moment then laughed. He batted a hand. "Sorry about that. Just some fireworks we were having some fun with. With these walls, I guess it might sound like gunshots."

Durand watched the man's eyes, not convinced. "If that's the case, then I'm sure that's all it was. I'd be remiss, however, if I didn't at least take a look around. May I?"

He stepped closer, and Bernard retreated inside, closing the door slightly, bracing it with his shoulder. "I'm sorry, but I cannot permit that."

"Why?"

"This is private property, and I have strict instructions that no one is allowed on the premises without permission."

"That is rather inhospitable. I'm sure an exception can be made for the police."

Bernard shook his head. "I'm afraid not. I'm afraid I must ask you to leave."

Durand bowed slightly. "As you wish. I will return with a warrant."

Bernard's eyes widened slightly. "That's your choice. When you do, we will cooperate fully."

The door slammed shut and Durand returned to his car, his driver turning them around.

"What do you make of it?"

Durand pursed his lips. "He's definitely hiding something."

Off the coast of Saint-Pierre-la-Mer, France

Pierre flinched as Schmidt's men returned, their heads breaking the water just to his left. The first removed his mask and shook his head. "We couldn't find it."

Schmidt hauled him into the boat. "You've been gone almost an hour. Did you search the entire area?"

The man shrugged off his scuba tanks, placing them against the bulwark. "As best we could. There's no way we'd miss a crate as large as you described. It either wasn't on the boat when we hit it, or someone already got to it."

Schmidt shook his head. "No, our guys in the chopper saw it. It was definitely on the boat."

The man shrugged. "Then someone got to it, because it's not there."

Schmidt cursed, Pierre's stomach flipping with the news. If the crate with the cross was already gone, then these professors must have had help. It made no sense, though. How would they have known they'd need help before they even arrived tonight? It hadn't even been an hour since their boat had been sunk. Who could have possibly helped them so soon?

None of it made sense.

Unless Schmidt's guy is wrong.

"That's impossible."

Schmidt glanced over his shoulder at him as he hauled his second man into the boat. "What's impossible?"

"That someone could have retrieved it already. Nobody knew it was going to be there. It would take special equipment, definitely a boat, and there were no boats except the authorities. There's no way somebody already got it."

Schmidt's man glared at him. "Are you saying I'm lying?"

Pierre's eyes shot wide. The thought hadn't occurred to him, but now that it had, it made perfect sense. Schmidt wanted the cross for himself so he could sell it. How could he possibly trust Schmidt's men to tell the truth? They were probably just shining him on, allowing him to think the cross was already gone, then they'd come back later and retrieve it.

He opened his mouth to accuse them of just that, when he snapped it shut, rethinking things. If he revealed to them that he knew, they might kill him right here, then the cross would be lost to his family forever, though he was sure those who had survived would stop at nothing to retrieve it.

But he didn't want to die. Not like this, not so young, not before he had enjoyed the fruits of a lifetime of labor. He met the man's glare, deciding to work with his original hypothesis. "I didn't accuse *you* of anything. What I meant was that it must be there, just not where you looked. The professors had no idea why they were coming here tonight, so they had no reason to prepare anything with respect to taking the cross with them. They would have had no need for backup, and even if they had some, that backup could not have known the cross would

170

have ended up on the bottom of the sea. It is simply inconceivable that someone has already retrieved it."

Schmidt regarded him for a moment, his head slowly bobbing. "I agree." He looked at his men. "Either you missed it—"

"We didn't."

"—or it wasn't where you were looking."

Pierre stared at the water. "Maybe the crate got caught in the currents and was carried away from the wreckage."

Schmidt sat at the controls, the engine roaring to life. "If that's the case, then hopefully it's been pulled far enough away that they won't find it while searching for the bodies."

Pierre stared back at the scene as the engines carried them away, Schmidt keeping their speed reasonable so as not to draw any unwanted attention. His theory made sense to the others, though there was one problem with it.

After spending over twenty years in these waters, he had never known there to be much of a current where the boat had exploded, and certainly none strong enough to carry a large, heavy crate, any significant distance. He stared at the back of Schmidt's head.

They're lying to me. They have to be.

Ridefort Residence

Saint-Pierre-la-Mer, France

Bernard Ridefort watched as the body of Simone Chartrand was carefully removed from the Maybach and placed on a tarp, two of the survivors of the assault carrying it to the crypt under the chateau. He quickly wiped down the seat of blood, then threw a large sheet over it and climbed in, driving the car to the garage, a garage that a century before had been stables, now only half a dozen horses on site.

He positioned the car carefully, his nephew directing him, an open palm signaling he was lined up properly. He climbed out and stepped aside, his nephew operating the controls, the car lowering out of sight to an underground chamber the police would never find unless they knew where to look.

He jogged over to make sure his youngest cousin was doing his job properly, a large hose washing the blood from the cobblestones, his free hand spraying bleach from a pump bottle. "How's it going?"

His cousin glanced back at him. "Almost done."

"Excellent work. When you're finished, take the metal detector and sweep the area for bullets and shell casings again."

"Yes, sir."

Bernard glanced back at the garage to see the car gone and the horses now repositioned over the secret entrance, hay and droppings shoveled over the area.

No police officer will be getting their nose into that.

As he supervised the cleanup, he glanced at his watch, unsure of how much time they had left before Durand returned with his warrant. When he did, there could be no evidence of the tragedy that had occurred here. Their leader, Grand Master Jacques Ridefort, was gone and now safe, and young Pierre had failed to steal the True Cross.

And despite his actions today, their duty hadn't changed.

The cross was still under their protection, and they couldn't do that if the police arrested them all. Until it was delivered into the hands of the Vatican, this chateau must remain in Templar hands.

He sighed, the mantle of responsibility heavy on his shoulders. It was a travesty what had happened here tonight. So many friends and family dead or wounded, and a family's honor destroyed.

If I ever see Pierre, I'll kill him myself.

He paused, watching his young cousin roll up the hose, as he contemplated his nephew's death.

If I were Pierre, where would I be hiding?

Hôtel Neptune

Saint-Pierre-la-Mer, France

"Were you able to reach Hugh?"

Laura shook her head, helping prop up her husband in one of the two beds in their cramped room. It wasn't what they were used to staying in when it came to paid accommodations, but it was far more hospitable than a tent in the desert. And the three-star nature of their room wasn't her concern.

It was James' wound.

The bandage was soaked through, so she had removed it, laying down several towels in an attempt to save the mattress. Blood continued to ooze, though it was much slower than when they had checked in last night. Yet that was little comfort.

"We need to go to a hospital."

He shook his head. "No, I'll be fine. But we're going to need supplies."

Laura pulled out her phone to make a list when she remembered it was dead. She found a pen and hotel stationary in the corner of the room on a small table. She grabbed it, then sat beside him. "Okay, we obviously need gauze and tape, and some sort of disinfectant."

"Hydrogen Peroxide. Polysporin?"

"I think you'd need quite a few tubes of that to do any good."

He chuckled. "True. I'm going to need lots of water and easy calories. Juice, milk, soup."

Laura glanced around. "We don't have a refrigerator here, or any way to heat stuff."

"I can eat it cold. I just need to keep my strength up and keep my fluid intake high. I need to give my body a chance to replenish the blood I've lost."

"What about infection?"

"He gave me a shot of antibiotics, that much I remember. That should keep me good for a few days. If we're not safe by then, this wound will be the least of our worries."

Laura nodded, jotting everything down, then stood. "Are you going to be okay alone?"

"I was for over forty years before I met you."

"Oh, you didn't live with your parents for any part of that?"

He grinned. "I was a very independent child."

Laura gave him a look. "Remember, I've seen you with your mother. You were a little mamma's boy, I think you Yanks call it."

"Hey, don't culturally appropriate my sayings just to insult me with them."

Laura's eyebrows rose. "Now I know you're not well." She tore the page off the pad and stuffed it into her pocket, opening the door. "I'll be back as quickly as I can."

He nodded, giving what appeared to her to be a weak thumbs up. She didn't like it, and if he didn't show signs of improvement soon, she'd be forcing him into a hospital for his own good.

She closed the door and left the small hotel as quickly and inconspicuously as possible, the desk clerk busy with other guests, leaving her unable to ask for directions. As she walked deeper into the town, she kept her eyes open for a drugstore or some grocery that might carry what she needed, then spotted a kiosk selling phones. She pulled the small travel wallet she always carried on her from her pocket, her purse and luggage back in the Maybach. She opened it, the Euros slightly damp, but her ID and bank cards still there.

She eyed a nearby ATM. The people searching for them were criminals, so they shouldn't be able to tell that she had accessed her accounts, and she needed more money than the couple of thousand Euros she had. She needed an untraceable phone so she could reach out to their network for help, and she'd need transportation out of here, perhaps quickly, should something go wrong. Not to mention the True Cross sitting offshore, under twenty feet of water.

Though that would have to wait. Her priority was getting James to safety.

She decided to damn the torpedoes.

She strode over to the ATM and withdrew the limit the machine allowed, stuffing the bills inside her jacket pocket then ducking into a store to more discretely distribute them on her person. She headed for the kiosk and purchased a new phone, immediately activating it after getting directions to the nearest pharmacy, then racked her brain for a number to call.

She wanted to reach Hugh Reading to let him know what had happened. As an Interpol Agent, he was in the best position to advise

176

them, and even help them, but she didn't know his number—it was stored in her dead phone. One of the problems with modern devices was the lack of a need to memorize numbers anymore, something she hadn't fully appreciated until this moment.

The hotel!

She knew the name of the hotel he was staying at, so perhaps she could reach him that way. She spotted the drugstore and rushed toward it, her eyes drawn to the port to her left, a heavy police presence still evident as their investigation and search for bodies continued.

She entered, quickly purchased her list including the liquid based calories James wanted, a fully stocked fridge located at the back of the store. Canned soup she would grab on her way back at a corner store she had spotted. She paid and left, hurrying back toward the hotel, her eyes on the activity across the street.

Her heart slammed when she saw a man standing among the crowd, staring at the street instead of the port. But it wasn't his conspicuous behavior that had her panicked—it was the fact she recognized him as one of the men that had come off the elevator before they made their escape in the boat. He turned away.

Or was he?

She tried to calm herself as she continued forward, her bags heavy with the water and juice. She had only seen the men for a brief instance when they stepped off the elevator and opened fire. She had been concentrating on getting them out of the hidden dock without running into the walls.

She glanced back and saw him staring directly at her. His eyes widened, and she forced herself to look directly ahead and keep her pace steady. But he had seen her, of that she had little doubt. And his reaction suggested he had recognized her, so she was correct in her belief he was one of the men who had tried to kill them last night.

She didn't want to turn her head again in case he hadn't recognized her, but she had to know if she was being pursued. She risked a quick glance, and her heart slammed as she saw him on her side of the street, closing the distance rapidly, apparently unconcerned if he were noticed. She focused on the sidewalk ahead of her, tunnel vision setting in as her panic grew.

Breathe!

She inhaled deeply and held it for several seconds before slowly exhaling, repeating the tactical breathing exercise her SAS security chief had taught her.

And it worked.

Quickly.

She looked about for a police officer, but found none—all evidently behind her, at the port. She had no weapon and no means beyond her hands to defend herself.

And he probably had a gun.

They were likely after the True Cross, so might not want to kill her, though once she divulged its location, she was a witness with no reason to be left alive.

She had to either lose him or stop him.

Her eye caught an umbrella stand sitting in front of a tourist shop, a dozen walking canes giving her an idea. She made a beeline for the store, grabbed two of the heavier canes, then entered the store, quickly making her way to the back. She placed her bags from the drugstore on the floor then waited, peering at the door from behind a shelf lined with gaudy souvenirs.

It took only moments for the man to appear in the doorway, his head on a swivel as he searched for her. He headed down the aisle toward her position, peering over the shelves, still trying to spot her.

He was only feet away now.

She emerged silently, swinging the cane in her left hand, the solid piece of wood braced at her elbow, and nailed his knee, hard. He winced, dropping slightly, as the other cane swung up and caught him under the chin. He fell backward and she continued her assault, hammering him repeatedly as he tried to block the blows, instead only inflicting more pain upon himself.

She stepped back and let him struggle to his knees before she lashed out with the cane in her left hand. Both his hands dropped to push the blow aside, leaving him completely exposed for the swing of the second cane. It connected with the side of his head, leaving him in an unconscious, crumpled heap on the floor.

She reached down and pulled his gun from his holster and stuffed it in her belt, then grabbed her bags and headed out of the store, the shoppers and staff staring at her, mouths agape, unsure of what to do. She held up the canes.

"Thanks, but they're a little too heavy for my liking." She dropped them in the umbrella stand and lost herself in the crowd.

We have to disappear. Now.

Ridefort Residence

Saint-Pierre-la-Mer, France

Durand sighed, shaking his head. They had found nothing. Well, that wasn't entirely correct. They had found nothing incriminating. It was a fascinating search, the treasures and heirlooms impressive, those who lived here clearly enamored with the Templars of old. None answered any questions beyond the basic "yes," "no," or "I don't know" responses typical of uncooperative witnesses.

About all he had gleaned was that no one lived here, they just worked here, humoring the owner by pretending to be knights. The owner was very ill, was out of town receiving treatment in Switzerland, and couldn't be reached. They had heard the same helicopters as some locals had reported, had been playing with fireworks while the owner was away, and that was it.

When questioned about what appeared to be recent damage to the stonework, they had an answer for that too. Crossbow practice, again while the boss was away. Nothing illegal, no evidence of a shootout, and as far as he was concerned, not a truthful man among them.

Yet there was nothing they could do. The warrant covered searching for evidence of foul play, and they could find none. It was over.

A horse whinnied nearby and he paused, turning toward the stables. He strode over, scratching one of the beasts behind the ear, wishing he had a treat to feed the magnificent creature. The waft of horse dropping filled his nostrils, something that reminded him of when he was a child on the farm, and he smiled.

Then he looked at the floor and frowned. There were an awful lot of droppings. He turned toward Bernard. "Who cleans these stables?"

Bernard nodded toward a young man standing near the wall. "He does. Why?"

Durand pointed at the floor. "It doesn't look like it's been cleaned in at least a day. And that's not nearly enough hay for them. And where's their water?" He paused, his eyes narrowing. He opened the gate and stepped inside, Bernard following.

"Please don't disturb the horses, Captain. They're already upset enough with all these strange people poking around."

"I'll just be a moment." He carefully navigated his way around shit and hooves, coming out behind the horses to find half a dozen stalls, cleaned with fresh hay and water, all empty. "Why aren't they in these?"

Bernard flushed slightly, staring at the ground.

Now I have you.

The young man responsible stepped forward. "I just finished cleaning them. I was about to put the horses back when you arrived."

Durand's eyes narrowed, again a perfectly good explanation given. "You don't do them one at a time?"

The young man shrugged. "I think they like to be together while I do it. You know, have some social time with their own kind."

Durand frowned, again a perfect answer. Too perfect. He stared at the floor, covered in straw and excrement. Something wasn't right. He sniffed the air, the stench overwhelming, but there was something else there. It smelt like…

Gasoline!

He searched about for a source, a jerry can or something, and found none, yet the smell was distinct now that he knew it was there. "Do you service cars in here?"

"Yes, when the horses are in their stalls." Bernard motioned toward the floor. "Not now, of course."

Durand felt himself getting frustrated, another perfectly reasonable answer.

Perhaps there's nothing here to find. Perhaps it is all innocent.

He kicked at some straw, revealing a seam in the stone floor underneath. His eyes narrowed, and he looked about, finding a broom standing in the corner. He grabbed it, then swept along the seam, soon revealing a large rectangle in the floor, and two very nervous men. "What's this?"

Bernard shrugged. "It's always been like that."

"Bullshit."

Bernard shrugged again. "Believe what you want."

Durand tossed the broom into the corner then grabbed a pail, filling it with water from one of the horses' troughs. He gently poured it over the seam then stopped, holding up a finger for everyone gathered to be quiet. The water slowly seeped away, and he could hear dripping sounds. He smiled and stood. "Either you open this, or I will. And you won't like my way."

Port of Saint-Pierre-la-Mer, France

Schmidt stood near a group of police officers and paramedics, all chattering about the events of last night. While the exploding boat was of interest to the crowds gathered, especially the unconfirmed rumors of hearing gunfire and a helicopter, the police were preoccupied by the activity at the chateau.

The assault hadn't gone unnoticed, though apparently when the police finally arrived, the survivors had buttoned up the place and refused entry without a warrant, denying anything had happened. By the time the place had been searched today, all evidence of anything untoward having transpired was cleaned up.

No bodies, no blood, no bullets, though apparently there was some evidence of scarring to the stonework, that the residents explained away as the result of damage from crossbow practice.

"We went through that place with a fine-toothed comb but found nothing. The Captain sent most of us to go help down here."

"I heard on the radio a request for a jackhammer and crew to be sent up. Any idea what that's about?"

The cop shook his head. "No idea. I know something happened there. They claimed fireworks, but I know something happened."

"What's the Captain have to say about it?"

The officer shrugged. "Before I left, he said without any evidence, there's nothing we can do. And he's right. We'll probably never know what happened, though maybe this jackhammer thing changes things."

"Maybe it *was* nothing. Those people have always been a little special. Doesn't the guy's son think he's a Templar or something insane like that?"

"Bah, that's just a phase. That Pierre's always been a bit of a troublemaker, but he's generally harmless. Just drinks too much and thinks he's God's gift to the ladies."

"Now I know he's crazy. Everyone knows *I'm* God's gift to the ladies."

They erupted with laughter and Schmidt continued walking along the pier, a pair of exhausted paramedics sitting on the bumper of their rig. He approached them. "Any luck finding them?"

They both shook their heads. "Nothing. The currents must have carried them away. If they haven't been found by now, they're dead."

His partner flicked his cigarette. "I still say it was that guy from last night."

Schmidt's eyebrows rose slightly, but he kept his silence, sometimes the best way to get information out of people was simply to let them talk.

"I doubt it. Why wouldn't they have said something?"

"Think about it. It was definitely a piece of shrapnel in the guy's side. How the hell did that happen? We found them near the location of the explosion, then they refused to be taken to the hospital. That sounds to me like they had something to hide."

"You watch too many spy movies."

"Yeah, and guess what, the world has spies! Just because you see something in a movie or read it in a book, doesn't mean it can't happen in real life."

His partner dismissed his argument with a wave of the hand. "I don't buy it. But if you want to report it, go ahead. I'll back the *facts* but not the conjecture."

Schmidt was already almost out of earshot, zero doubt in his mind that the paramedics were talking about his missing professors. They were alive, he was wounded, and they probably knew where the crate was.

His comm squawked.

"Joachim has been beaten up, over."

He came to a stop, pressing his finger against his earpiece. "Repeat that?"

"Joachim. Some woman apparently beat the living shit out of him with a stick. They're taking him to the hospital now."

Schmidt cursed as he resumed walking, his pace much quicker than a moment before. "Get there and make sure he doesn't say anything stupid. I don't need him blowing this operation while he's on painkillers."

"Yes, sir."

"And transmit the location where he was found to the team. We'll start searching for this woman from there."

"Do you think it's the female professor?"

He grunted. "Probably. I just overheard a conversation. They're both alive, and he's injured. They're holed up somewhere. Let's start searching the hotels. We'll find them."

Off the coast of Saint-Pierre-la-Mer, France

Pierre sat offshore, the boat bobbing gently on the water, an idyllic setting if his life weren't falling apart. He stared up at the chateau, visible through the morning haze on top of the hill overlooking the town, and it appeared as peaceful as it ever had, no outward evidence of the horrors he had committed there the night before.

Much of his family was dead, by hands paid for with his own money, and for what? He didn't have the cross, and his father was still alive, otherwise the banner flown at the front gate, even visible from here, would have been removed. Schmidt's report was that the police had searched the chateau and found nothing, his brethren having cleaned his home of the sins he had committed, the bodies probably already moved to the crypt below for honorable burial later.

And he felt sick about it.

Yet he was more determined than ever to retrieve the cross. For if he didn't, then all those brave men that had defended it against him, would have died in vain.

Schmidt's man on the boat put a finger to his ear, listening, then smiled.

"What?"

"She's been spotted, and he's wounded."

Pierre sat up. "They're alive?"

The man nodded. "Both of them. We'll have them shortly."

Pierre beckoned for the comm gear and the man frowned, but unhooked it from his ear, handing it to the man paying the bills. Pierre clipped it around his ear and pressed the earpiece. "Schmidt, this is Ridefort."

"Go ahead."

"I understand you have a lead on the professors."

"Yes. She's been spotted."

"Good. Make sure you don't kill them, they're the only ones who know where the item is."

"Understood. And once we've recovered it?"

Pierre stared up at the chateau, picturing the dead, then closed his eyes. "Kill them."

Hôtel Neptune

Saint-Pierre-la-Mer, France

Laura smiled at the desk clerk and held up her bags. "Shopping!" He returned the smile, her tone that of the crazy tourist with too much money, though he might have been curious as to why a tourist would be excited with a bunch of bags from a drugstore.

She took the stairs, the elevator out of order, noticing some blood splatter on her blouse. She had washed her clothes in the hotel bathroom last night, certain she had removed all of the blood from their chauffeur, so this must be new.

Must be from today's beating.

She frowned, quickening her pace, hoping to reach her room without encountering anyone, and within minutes had managed just that.

"Hey, babe."

She smiled at James, placing the bags at the end of the bed, quickly pulling out her loot. "How are you feeling?"

"Thirsty."

She held up a bottle of orange juice and he nodded. She twisted the cap off, breaking the seal, then handed it to him. He slowly sipped it down, then his sips became gulps as she sorted through the medical supplies. He looked pale, sweaty, and his bandage was too red for her liking, but when he finished off the bottle, she had some renewed hope for him.

"I'm thirsty and starving. Any food?"

She cracked the seal on some coffee creamer.

"Ooh, the breakfast of champions!"

She handed it to him. "Sorry, I couldn't get to a grocery store." She gently pulled off his bandage, the seeping to a minimum now. She grabbed the bottle of hydrogen peroxide and a few pieces of gauze. "This might hurt."

"Hurt me, baby."

She resisted the urge to smile, then poured some of the fluid over the wound, bubbles appearing for a moment as it did its job. He winced, then kept drinking his breakfast. She repeated the process several more times, patting it dry each time, before applying some Polysporin around the wound, which in the light, and properly cleaned, appeared much smaller than it had earlier. It was still a good couple of inches long, but seemed clean and uninfected.

"I need to sew it up."

This had James' eyes shooting open, his container of cream removed from his mouth. "Umm, I'm not a pin cushion."

"No, you're walking wounded with an invincibility complex."

"You know me so well. But I'm not walking."

"You will be. They found me."

James became concerned. "Who?"

"One of the men that attacked the chateau. I took him out, but now they know at least *I'm* alive, and they'll be looking for me."

James frowned. "This isn't good."

"No." She grabbed the phone out of her pocket. "I picked up this."

"Ooh, good thinking."

She grinned and handed it to him, then produced a curved needle and some thread from the pile of supplies.

His eyes widened. "Sadist."

"Do you know Hugh's number?"

He shook his head. "No, it's in my phone."

"Okay, call the international operator and get the number for his hotel. We need to reach him and let him know what's going on, then we need to get out of here."

James dialed the phone then pressed it against his ear. "Hey Greg, it's me."

Laura's eyebrows shot up as she realized he had called his best friend instead of the operator.

Okay, not a bad idea, actually.

"Just a second while I put you on speaker. Laura's here." He eyed the phone for a moment, trying to figure out how to accomplish his task, then pressed a button. "Can you hear me?"

"Loud and clear. What number's this?"

"Our phones were ruined, so Laura grabbed this one when she was out. Ouch!"

"Sorry." Laura pulled the needle through, then the thread.

"What's wrong?"

"Oh, well, we've gone and done it again."

Laura paused her needlework. "Don't include me in this one. I told you I had a bad feeling."

"Oh no, what have you two gotten yourselves into this time?"

"Hey, we're—*I'm*—totally innocent in this. We went to the meeting, but on the way, we were ambushed. They tried to kill us, but we managed to make it to the chateau. While we were there, the same people assaulted the place, and we escaped through a hidden tunnel then used a boat to get away. But they followed us in a helicopter, shot it up, and the boat exploded. We managed to get off just before, and make it to shore, but I got a huge piece of metal—"

"Small piece of wood."

"—stuck inside me. I got patched up, but we figured it was best to avoid the hospitals in case they were still looking for us."

"My God, what is it with you two? Where are you now?"

"In a hotel, but we won't be here much longer. Laura's sewing me up—"

"She's what!"

"She's putting in stitches so I can travel. But we need your help."

"Anything."

"You've got Hugh's contact info?"

"Yes."

"Good, call him, tell him what's going on, and give him this number."

"Will do."

"And call Giasson at the Vatican. Tell him as well."

"Why would he be involved?"

"Tell him we have the True Cross."

"What the hell is that?"

"No time to explain. He'll know. True Cross. Got it?"

"Yes."

"Good." James winced once more as Laura pulled the thread through again. She smiled an apology at him.

"Our phones are toast, so we have no way to reach Dylan. Do you think you still have that direct line to the CIA?"

"No idea, but it's worth a try."

She could almost hear their friend smile and panic at the same time. CIA Special Agent Dylan Kane was a former student of James', and had helped them out on occasion. Milton had been caught up in events recently requiring contact with Kane, and had discovered his phones had been redirected to one of Kane's CIA teams. It had rattled him, to say the least.

"Okay, tell everyone that Pierre Ridefort is behind this, our host's son. He's trying to take the True Cross, thinks we either have it or know where it is, and he's already killed a bunch of people at the chateau to get it. We're getting out of town in the next few minutes. I'll try to contact you once we're safe."

"Okay, Jim. I'll start making those calls right away."

"Thanks, Corky."

"I'm booking a flight over there now so I can punch you in the throat."

James grinned, as did Laura. Milton hated that nickname.

"Don't bother, you'll be doing it in person soon enough." James ended the call.

"Turn it off, will you? I don't want it ringing and giving away my position if I'm followed again."

Acton turned it off as Laura completed her final stitch, snipping off the excess thread. "Is that sterile?"

She shrugged. "No idea, but we'll hopefully get to safety before it becomes a problem."

He nodded. "Right. In a survival situation, don't worry about getting sick from the water in a few days, just drink the damned stuff and save your life today."

Laura finished patching him up then stood.

"What's the plan?"

She gathered the scraps from her handiwork as she thought. "I think our best bet is to rent a car and put as much distance between them and us as possible. We can call my travel agent and have her send a jet to the nearest airport, then get stateside. We'll be safe there."

James' eyes widened. "You're seriously going to just leave the True Cross on the bottom of the Mediterranean?"

She stared at him. "You're not?"

"Hell no! We need to retrieve it. God only knows what's happening to it down there. This is a piece of history that is irreplaceable. It's confirmation of an entire faith!"

Laura sighed, the archaeologist in her sympathizing with his position, yet the wife in her wanting to protect her wounded husband from certain death if they were discovered. "Just what would you have us do?"

"Rent a truck, a boat with a winch, and a couple of locals who won't ask any questions."

She stared at him. "You're delusional."

He laughed, his head dropping back on the pillow. "You're right. If I didn't have this damned wound, the two of us could handle it, but if I try any heavy lifting, this thing's tearing open, expert sewing job or not."

"So we're going with my plan?"

He frowned. "Yeah."

"Good." She moved all his drinks closer. "Fuel up. I'm getting us a car."

Hotel Barcelona

L'Estartit, Spain

Interpol Agent Hugh Reading lay in his bed, his CPAP mask in place as he tried to ignore the sun pouring in around the edges of the thick curtains. It was long past the time to get up, though he had barely slept last night, the drunken tourists partying until at least 3 a.m. if not 4, not a wink of sleep achieved until they had passed out.

L'Estartit was always a tourist town, but when he had come here as a kid with his parents to scuba dive, it had been off-season and quiet. He had never been here in the height of tourist season, and he swore he'd never do it again. It had lost the charm his mother spoke of, true of most tourist towns whose populations would swell over the summer.

It might as well have been Spring Break in Florida, something his younger self might have enjoyed, but not a fifty-something old bastard with sleep apnea and joints that protested every morning when he woke.

Yet the noise of L'Estartit couldn't spoil the trip.

Nothing could.

His son Spencer was with him. One week in the sun, on the beach, scuba diving, father and son bonding. It was more than he could have hoped for just a year ago, yet here they were, together, just the two of them, and he was confident the boy—young man—was enjoying himself.

No awkward silences, no mood swings. Just smiles and laughter.

They had been estranged since his divorce, well over a decade of almost no communication, the boy shutting him out of his life despite his mother's best attempts. The divorce had been as amicable as it could have been, and he didn't blame his wife for the situation that developed. Eventually, he had given up pressuring the boy, instead, hoping that over time, he would come around. He'd send the obligatory cards and gifts at the appropriate times, and never received a thank you.

But a couple of years ago, in a renewed attempt at reconciliation, his son had taken his call. Conversations had begun, then some lunches, then some pints, and eventually, this vacation, which was working out brilliantly.

He couldn't be happier.

Good food, good company, and a good view.

Yes, the beaches of Spain had their good views even an old bastard like him could appreciate through sunglasses. His mid-twenties son's head was on a swivel, and the good-looking lad had many smiles returned. Reading had no doubt if he were caught staring, arms would be crossed and disgusted looks delivered as his victims hurried away.

But he was an old pro.

He never got caught.

It was enough to put the spring back in his step, and on occasion, remind him that he was still a man with a libido, a libido that needed stroking, the last woman he had been with dying in his arms, expressing her love for him. His chest ached and his eyes watered as he tried to push the memory of Kinti away.

He tore off his mask and turned off the life-saving machine. He had been diagnosed with sleep apnea a couple of years ago after he caught himself falling asleep at the office. When he was diagnosed, he hadn't been concerned. "Who cares if I snore? I live alone." Yet as his doctor had explained, snoring wasn't the issue, it was the fact he would stop breathing, and that could cause heart damage. When he stopped breathing, his blood pressure shot up, and it could cause Left Ventricle Hypertrophy, a thickening of the heart wall, that could eventually cause heart failure. He had been tested and was fine, his sleep apnea caught in time, but the entire experience had pissed him off.

He had heard of sleep apnea most of his adult life, yet thought it simply meant you snored and stopped breathing sometimes. If someone had told him it could kill him and how, he might have paid more attention. Why that wasn't advertised, he had no idea. But now he had his CPAP machine, and loved it. He felt at least ten years younger. He had been waking up dozens of times an hour. Not enough to be aware of it, though enough to ruin his sleep patterns, leaving him exhausted the next day.

Now that he was properly sleeping through the night, he was a new man, or at least a renewed one. Though not so much today. He needed at least six hours on the machine, preferably seven, yet had only managed five. He'd need a nap this afternoon.

He stretched out a yawn, then growled when his phone vibrated on the nightstand. He could smell bacon and eggs through his door, his son apparently giving up waiting for him to make an appearance.

Good to know the lad can cook.

199

He picked up the phone and his eyebrows rose as he saw the call display.

Greg? Isn't it three or four in the morning there?

He swiped his thumb. "Greg, what are you doing up at this hour?"

"Hey, Hugh, what do you think? Jim and Laura are in trouble."

Reading tensed, reaching for the pad and pen he kept with him wherever he went, now sitting on his nightstand. "What's happened?"

"The details are sketchy, but Jim just called. Apparently, someone tried to kill them on the way to their meeting in France, then the chateau they were at was assaulted. I guess there are people dead, and Jim was wounded in an explosion. People are still after them, and they're going to try and get out of town before they're found. They apparently found the True Cross. That's what this is all about."

"The True Cross?"

"Yes, it's supposed to be the cross Jesus was crucified on."

Reading whistled. "Well, if that's not worth killing over, I don't know what is."

Milton chuckled at his sarcastic tone. "Yeah, there's nothing like religious icons to bring out the best in people. Anyway, they asked me to contact you, because their phones are dead. I'm going to text you their new number so you can reach out to them, okay?"

"Got it. Send me it now, and I'll call them right away."

"Good. Let me know if you hear anything."

Reading nodded. "Will do."

He ended the call and waited for the phone to vibrate. It did, and he jotted down the number just in case, then transferred it to his contacts.

He dialed, and an automated message indicated it was out of range or turned off.

Why the bloody hell would they turn off the phone?

Saint-Pierre-la-Mer, France

Schmidt stepped out of yet another hotel, the search for the professors so far fruitless. This might be a small town, but during tourist season, like now, it was jam-packed, the usually sleepy hotels bustling with activity. Showing desk clerks the photos of the professors on his phone, without being able to claim he was with the police, was proving to be pointless, suspicions heightened since last night's events limiting his options. He had more success bribing doormen and bellhops, than going inside and questioning clerks who were more likely to be under the watchful eye of management. Yet even that had proven a waste of time so far.

He checked his phone for the location of the next hotel, then continued down the street, his eyes constantly scanning for the professors, or any other suspicious activity, such as someone ducking down an alley or rapidly changing direction to face away from him.

But he saw nothing. His man Joachim, severely beaten by Laura Palmer, was in the hospital now, under the careful watch of one of his men. He was conscious, and would apparently make a full recovery, the unprovoked attack not meant to kill, just to disable.

He wouldn't underestimate her like Joachim had.

He knew nothing about these two beyond what he had found on the Internet, and they had proven more resourceful than he would have expected of two academics. They had evaded the assassination attempt, evaded capture, survived the explosion on the boat, got the drop on one of his highly trained men, and continued to elude him. They had skills, acquired somehow, which was making his job far more challenging than he had expected.

And far more interesting.

He loved the chase, and this was a chase. As long as he succeeded in the end, he didn't particularly care how long it took.

But he had to win.

Losing wasn't an option with him. He would find them, recover the cross, then kill them. The contract would be fulfilled, he'd receive his payday, then he'd decide whether to take the True Cross for himself, and kill Pierre Ridefort, should he object. Pierre was a punk-ass spoiled kid, who had thrown a years-long temper tantrum, and deserved a good beating.

No man who wanted his own father dead was a man.

From what he could tell, Jacques Ridefort had done nothing wrong, merely threatened a brat's inheritance.

Grow up, you self-entitled self-absorbed millennial twit, and be a man. Make your own way in the world, instead of relying on Daddy to take care of you.

Schmidt had little time for Pierre's kind, and no respect for many of his generation. In the Army, he had seen them, little snowflakes who couldn't take the reality of reality, washing out in the first week or two, which was fine. He didn't want a sniveling weasel with him in the foxhole when the shit hit the fan. His Army days were behind him, but when evaluating men for assignments like this, he'd hack their social media accounts and see the types of posts they had.

If they were Social Justice Warriors, he'd immediately exclude them. He didn't need delusional people who had to retreat to their safe spaces if they heard an opinion that contradicted their own. He didn't need people who hugged their teddy bears and cried when they lost an election.

There were always winners and losers in life. If you lost, then you sucked it up and moved on, and tried to win the next time out. You didn't sit around for four years crying and whining and throwing a fit. You got on with your life, made the best of the situation you could, then next time, tried that much harder.

And that was the problem with the kids today. They had been raised in environments where score wasn't kept, where no one was to blame, where bullying wasn't tolerated, and where no one failed.

That wasn't life.

Kids left the bubble of school for the real world, and had absolutely no concept of how to react when things didn't go their way. For their first twenty years, nothing that had ever gone wrong was their fault, it was always the system's. They never lost a game, they never failed a course, they were always given an extension on a deadline.

Then when they had their first real choice to make, the choice clear in their minds, it had to be some conspiracy when they lost, someone had to have cheated, someone had to have lied, because they were raised to believe they were always right. It was inconceivable that they could have lost. And after a youth spent being encouraged to fight for what they thought was right, even if they were factually wrong, that's what they did. On social media, in protests, on campuses.

Schmidt had no time for it.

Finish school, get a real job, take your lumps, and improve yourself. If you don't like the results of a vote, don't demand another vote. The systems in democracies had worked for decades in most cases, for centuries in some. Why should they change just because one generation thought it was rigged because they didn't win?

He growled at a group of teenagers, walking four abreast down the sidewalk, forcing others to go around. He shoved his way through, a string of French curses thrown at his back, his hand slowly reaching for his weapon.

Now, now. Calm down.

He looked ahead at the next hotel, just as someone turned quickly down a side street. He picked up his pace and reached the road, staring down to see what appeared to be a woman, dressed in white, running.

It had to be Laura Palmer, the clothes definitely not workout wear.

He pushed through the crowd and broke out into a sprint, his footfalls echoing through the tight street. The woman glanced over her shoulder and he smiled.

It was her.

And she wasn't getting away this time.

Laura didn't recognize the man, but there was no doubt he recognized her. It was his haircut and demeanor that had aroused her suspicions, evidently accurately. She ducked down the next street, running past the tourists as quickly as she could, dodging around a group of seniors and into another laneway, doubling back the way she had come.

She had to shake him and get a rental car. James was in no condition to defend himself, and the only way out of here was by vehicle. If she knew Milton, he would have already contacted Reading, and he would already be taking action, but he would also be walking right into the thick of things, without knowing what was going on.

It could get him killed.

She was sure Milton would have told him about the violent altercations last night, but Reading was a "storm into danger type" when it came to his friends.

Oh God, I hope he doesn't bring his son!

She checked over her shoulder and saw her pursuer closing the gap as she turned back onto the main street, stepping onto the roadway and running with the traffic rather than battling the more unpredictable pedestrians. She spotted the car rental place the desk clerk had told her about, but instead ran past it—there was no way she could rent a vehicle from here.

Then a thought dawned on her, and she nearly smacked her forehead for being so stupid to have not thought of it before. She pulled out her phone as she hurried across the street, toward the port, and dialed her travel agent's number, a number she knew well, that predated her smartphone. She had planned on calling her to charter a flight for them once they were mobile, but why put her to use now?

The precious woman answered on the first ring. "Laura, so good to hear from you!"

She decided to play it cool, not wanting to frighten the woman. "Hi there, no time to talk. I need you to rent us a car in Saint-Pierre-la-Mer, at the Eurocar agency on Boulevard des Embruns. Got that?"

"Eurocar agency in Saint-Pierre-la-Mer on Boulevard des Embruns. Got it. For when?"

"Right away. Tell them I'll be picking it up in a few minutes, and to have it ready to go. We're in a hurry. No pre-check BS either. I just want to walk in, show ID, and walk out with keys."

"Is something wrong?"

"No, just in a hurry, that's all."

"Ok, consider it done. Do you want me to call you at this number to confirm when it's ready?"

"No, just call me if there's a problem." Laura ended the call, stuffing the phone back into her pocket, then fished out a few 100 Euro notes, clasping them tightly in the palm of her hand. She ran down the pier, searching for a boat with a local, spotting several. She stopped at one who had some scuba gear, and held up the notes.

"Three hundred Euros if you take me out right now, no questions."

The man stared at her for a moment, when someone in the next boat stepped onto the dock. "You don't want his boat, Mademoiselle. It's completely unreliable."

She glanced at the new arrival, then at the man in the boat. "Is this true?"

He shrugged, a silly grin emerging. "Imagine if Jag made boats."

Laura chuckled, then pointed at the other man's boat. "And yours?"

"Guaranteed to give you a smooth ride."

"Can you take me now?"

"Sure, Mademoiselle. The pretty lady wants a boat ride, the pretty lady gets a boat ride."

Laura freed the lines to the surprise of the man, then jumped in. "Quickly, please."

He climbed in after her and fired up the engine. As they pulled away, she spotted her pursuer as he reached the pier. He sprinted toward her then gave up, shouting at some of the other boat owners, apparently not having as much success as she had. She lay down flat so he couldn't see her, the captain glancing back at her, curious.

"Are you okay?"

She nodded, then noticed he had scuba gear as well. She pulled out another couple of bills. "Two hundred more if you let me borrow your scuba gear. I'll return it to the dock before the end of the day."

He eyed her, slowly shaking his head. "I don't know. That stuff is expensive, and, well…"

She pulled out five more. "Another five-hundred. That's one thousand Euros total."

He grinned. "The lady wants scuba gear, the lady gets scuba gear."

She rose slightly and stared at the pier, not spotting any sign of pursuit yet. She quickly donned the gear, testing the regulator, then pointed to a large yacht nearby. "Go behind him and stop. When I go over, head south for ten minutes, then circle back. Take your time. If anyone asks where I went, just tell them the truth."

The man's eyes narrowed as he steered them around the yacht, cutting the engine. "Are you in trouble? Do you need help?"

She shook her head. "Don't worry about me. Just a bad date I'm trying to dump."

The man's eyes widened, his jaw dropping. "Ahhh, I see. Some men just can't take no for an answer."

She smiled as she sat on the edge of the boat. "Thanks, my friend. You'll get your gear back soon." She tipped over the edge before he could say anything, then cursed as she remembered her phone was in her pocket, unprotected from the water.

Too late now.

Giasson Residence

Via Nicolò III, Rome, Italy

Mario Giasson smiled at his two young daughters, giggling as he Charlie Chaplin'd their breakfast to the table.

"You're so funny, Daddy!" laughed Zoé.

He grinned as he put two plates of rösti potato pancakes in front of them, then two glasses of ice-cold milk. "Today, we eat like I did when I was a kid."

Zoé raised her hands in the air. "Yay!"

"Now, don't tell Mommy when she gets back. She'll say I'm trying to make you fat." He poked Zoé's stomach, eliciting squirms and giggles. He had decided a treat was in order while his wife was away visiting his mother-in-law, and he loved to spoil his children.

It was always good fortune when his wife visited the in-laws. Without him. His mother-in-law seemed to have a perpetual hate on for him, about the only good thing he had ever done was father two grandkids for her. Other than that, it didn't matter that he was a good husband, father, and provider, with a prestigious job as Inspector General and head of the Corps of Gendarmerie of Vatican City State. He would never win with her, no matter how much Marie-Claude loved him and defended him.

So whenever he was asked if he wanted to come, he made sure he had a good excuse. This time it was legitimate, a head of state arriving in a couple of days that would preoccupy his time. The kids had begged to stay, a friend's birthday party this weekend, and his wife had reluctantly agreed. He had sold her on the idea of some father-daughter time, at which she had smiled.

"Any excuse to avoid my mother."

He had grinned. "Who, me?"

His wife understood. He would never please her mother. He was Swiss, his mother-in-law Italian. Anything less than an Italian man wasn't good enough for her daughter. It had bothered him the first few years, but not anymore. There was no changing her. They would lead their lives, and as long as his mother-in-law never said anything bad about him to the children, he couldn't care less what she said behind their backs, or his.

He just knew it hurt his wife, and had noticed that her trips to the home where she had grown up, were becoming fewer with time. If his mother-in-law wasn't careful, she'd lose her daughter altogether.

"You okay, Daddy?"

He looked up from the pan he had been staring at, then at Zoé. "Yes, dear, just thinking."

"About what?"

He slid the rösti onto his plate. "Mommy."

"Aww, do you miss her?"

He smiled. "Of course." He sat and took a sip of his coffee before attacking his Swiss treat, the potato and onion concoction something he had eaten almost every day in the mountains of Switzerland.

And it hadn't made him fat.

His phone vibrated on the table and he glanced at it, the call display indicating it was the office. He tensed slightly, a call rare unless something was wrong. He took the call as he swallowed. "Yes?"

"Sir, it's Ianuzzi. I have an urgent call for you from a Dean Gregory Milton from St. Paul's University in Maryland."

Giasson's eyes narrowed. "The name sounds familiar. Isn't that Professor Acton's university?"

"I believe so. He says it's most urgent."

"Okay, put him through." Giasson wiped his mouth with his napkin then rose from the table, heading for his home office.

"Monsieur Giasson?"

"Yes, Dean Milton, is it?"

"Yes, I'm a friend of Jim Acton, whom I understand you're quite familiar with."

Giasson smiled, his encounters with the archaeology professor always memorable, and almost always life threatening. "Yes, I consider him and his lovely wife friends."

"Good, good. Listen, I just got a call from them. They're in the south of France, in Saint-Pierre-la-Mer. There's been an attempt on their lives—"

"Oh no! Are they okay?"

"Yes, but Jim has been wounded. I got the impression he was going to be okay, but they think those responsible are still after them."

"I'm not sure what I can do, but I'll do whatever I can to help. Have you called the police?"

"I've already called Hugh Reading, and he's on it. But Jim asked me to call you."

Giasson's eyes narrowed. "Why?"

"Because he says he has the True Cross."

Giasson collapsed into his chair, his jaw dropping. "Did you say the True Cross?"

"Yes."

"And you're sure he has it?"

"Apparently so. That's why they're trying to kill him."

"Who?"

"They were supposed to meet a Jacques Ridefort. Apparently, his son Pierre is behind the attack."

"Ridefort? As in the knights found under the Vatican a couple of years ago?"

"The very same."

Giasson wiped his hand over his shaved head. "Is he bringing it here?"

"I have no idea. I quickly Googled it, and I think it's fairly large, so I don't know how they can try to evade these guys and save it."

Giasson leaned forward. "He *has* to save it. This could be the most significant find since…well, ever!"

"I think his life is more important than some relic."

"Not just some relic, sir, but *the* relic. If he indeed has found it, it could have profound consequences. Where did you say he was?"

"Saint-Pierre-la-Mer."

"Okay, do you have a pen?"

"Yes."

He quickly gave Milton his cell number. "If you talk to him, give him that number. I'm going to speak to my people and see what we can do from this end."

"Okay, if I can reach him, I'll let you know."

Giasson ended the call and leaned back in his chair.

The True Cross! It can't be!

Milton Residence

St. Paul, Maryland

Gregory Milton checked his watch again for the umpteenth time. It was barely four in the morning. Sandra was already sitting beside him, listening to the calls he was making, getting updated through the conversations and the brief moments between. He turned to her.

"One more call."

"Who?"

"CIA."

Her eyebrows shot up. "Dylan?"

"They can't reach him because their phones are fried. I think I remember them saying he had installed an app on their phones so they could contact him securely. Without it, there's no way to reach him directly."

"So you're just going to call up the CIA and ask for him?"

He shook his head. "Nooo, I'm hoping that I still have that direct line."

Sandra shivered. "Oh, God, I hope not. That was kind of creepy."

A few months ago, he had called the CIA on an urgent matter, and found himself immediately talking to someone on the inside who knew everything about him, his phones tapped so any calls he made to a CIA number would be automatically directed to Kane's contact. He didn't know who the man was, though he sounded young.

And he had delivered.

He just wondered if this was something left enabled, or was he about to waste his time. With the number of times his friend got in trouble around the world, he wouldn't be surprised if the CIA had left the "direct" line open.

He looked at his wife. "Do you want to do the honors?"

Her eyes widened. "I'm not talking to them."

He laughed. "No, I mean look up the number like you did last time."

"Oh." She grabbed her tablet and within moments had the number for him. He dialed, and a woman answered. A young woman.

"Dean Milton, my name is Sonya. Is there a problem?"

He sucked in a quick breath, his heart hammering, the very idea this had worked, terrifying.

What else are they listening to?

"Umm, hello. I, ah, need to speak to Dylan Kane."

"I'm afraid that's not possible. Is there something I can help you with?"

"Well, ah, Jim—James—Acton and his wife, Laura Palmer, seem to be in, well, in trouble again."

"Details."

"Umm, I received a phone call from them a few minutes ago. They said someone had tried to kill them on their way to a meeting. They managed to escape, but they're still being pursued."

"Where?"

"Saint-Pierre-la-Mer, France."

"Do you have the exact address?"

"Ah, just a sec." He grabbed his notepad and read off the address for Ridefort's chateau, along with the new phone number. "That's one of those pre-paid phones. Their regular phones aren't working."

"Understood."

"Will you be able to help them?"

"I can't make any promises, sir."

"And Dylan is unavailable?"

"Yes."

"What about those guys in Delta he knows?"

"They're unavailable as well."

"How can you be—"

"Sir, they're unavailable. I'll do what I can, but I'm afraid your friends might be on their own this time. Goodbye."

The call abruptly ended, and Milton returned the phone to its cradle. He looked at his wife. "I don't think I'll ever get used to that."

"Me neither. Are they going to help?"

He stared at her for a moment, replaying the conversation. "I'm not sure. Dylan and Delta aren't available. She said she would see what she could do, but then said that Jim and Laura might be on their own this time."

Sandra bit her finger, worry on her face. "God, I hope they'll be okay."

Leroux/White Residence

Fairfax Towers

Falls Church, Virginia

CIA Analyst Supervisor Chris Leroux moaned in delight as his girlfriend, CIA Agent Sherrie White, straddled his back, delivering a *very* early morning surprise hot oil massage almost as good as sex.

Almost.

If life were to give him a choice between the two for some reason, there was no doubt which one he would choose. There was nothing like making love to the incredible woman now providing him with so much exquisite pleasure, and though he would love for this to last forever, it would soon be his turn to return the favor.

And that always led to his most favorite thing.

Sometimes life gave you a choice, and you were able to choose both.

Life is good.

She finished with an incredible hard though not painful pulling of his hair, the grip firm yet loose enough to let the hair slowly slip through. She repeated this several times, and the stress in his scalp faded away with her ministrations. And it was awesome. She was the first to have ever done that for him, in fact, she was the first to ever give him a massage.

He had never thought he would like it, a stranger's hands rubbing all over his body, but he trusted her implicitly, and when she had first offered, despite his hesitations, he had acquiesced, and now it was a regular part of their lives.

She slapped his ass. "My turn."

He rolled over, Chris Jr. waving at her.

"Someone's happy."

He grinned. "I have nothing to say on the matter. He's his own man."

She handed him the bottle of lotion then lay down, her spectacular body laid out before him, causing him to shake his head in appreciation. He poured a generous portion of the viscous fluid on her back, then worked his magic. The first time he had tried this, he wasn't very good, but with practice, he now thought of himself as quite proficient, her moans and groans suggesting he was right.

As he got more into it, his entire body joined in, and after only a few minutes, the massage was forgotten, and she reached behind her, grabbing him. "Now!"

He groaned, there no doubt what she meant, and there was no doubt they both needed it. He backed off slightly, ready for the reward they had both been working toward, when the phone rang.

"Are you freakin' kidding me!" She stared back at him. "If that's Dylan, tell him I'm putting a hit out on him."

Leroux growled in frustration, wiping his hands on a nearby towel then grabbing the phone. "Hello?"

"Sir, it's Sonya. I hope I'm not waking you, but we just received a call from Dean Gregory Milton, Professor James Acton's boss."

Leroux dropped onto the bed, frustrated. "What is it now?"

"Apparently someone tried to kill Acton and his wife in the south of France. They were hoping to reach Special Agent Kane, but he's on assignment in Istanbul. Should we ignore this or take action?"

Leroux sighed then his eyes widened as Sherrie rolled over and straddled him, deciding to take care of business herself, the tool of choice him. He moaned.

"Sir?"

"Ahh, nothing. Just stretching. Umm, what do you have that's actionable?"

"An address and a new phone number."

"Okay, run with it, I'll be in shortly."

"Okay, good—"

He ended the call, tossing the phone aside and reaching up for Sherrie's shoulders, pulling her down on top of him. "I've gotta go."

"Not until I'm done with him."

"We kind of come as a package deal."

She grinned at him mischievously. "That's exactly what I had in mind."

Hotel Barcelona

L'Estartit, Spain

Hugh Reading stared at the screen on his son's laptop, searching for the quickest flight to get him to Saint-Pierre-la-Mer, a town in France he had never heard of, but where two of his best friends were in trouble.

"Dad, forget the plane."

"Huh?"

"It's too slow." His son stuck his phone in front of Reading's nose. "Look, it's only a two-hour drive from here."

Reading's eyebrows shot up as he grabbed the phone, the route laid out, Google assuring him it was only two hours and three minutes from where they sat. He smiled. "Now that's bloody brilliant." He began to rise when his son pushed him back in his seat with a hand to the shoulder.

"Eat your breakfast. You're going to need it."

Reading eyed him. "Just what are you implying?"

"That you're old." Spencer grinned. "Now, I'm going to go pack."

"Woah, wait a minute. You're not coming with me."

"Why not?"

"Because it could be dangerous."

"Well then, good thing I'll be with a copper."

Reading stared at him. "I'm being serious. Men with guns tried to kill my friends."

"Well, Europe is filled with men with guns now. And if I'm going to be a cop, I'll need to learn to run toward the danger and not away."

Reading's eyes shot wide, his jaw dropping slightly. "Excuse me?"

"I'm going to be a cop. I put my application in last week."

"Bloody hell!" Reading leaned back in his chair. "Does your mother know?"

Spencer shook his head. "I was kinda hoping you'd tell her."

"Bollocks to that! I've managed to go over fifteen years without her screaming at me. I'm not going to start now. You want to learn how to defuse incendiary situations, start with your mother."

Spencer frowned. "Maybe I just won't tell her until I've completed that part of my training."

Reading chuckled. "You wait that long, and your friends might be investigating the new lump under the rose bushes."

"Then what should I do?"

"Be honest. And don't tell her in the bloody kitchen."

"Why?"

"Too many sharp objects. And don't do it in the car, she'll crash the thing."

"Now you've got me really worried."

Reading laughed, then became serious. "Is this what you really want?"

Spencer nodded. "Yes."

"Then tell her that. She'll come around eventually. But if this is what you want, then you have my support."

Spencer grinned. "Thanks, Dad." He turned on his heel, leaving for his room. "Now I'm going to pack. Eat your breakfast."

Reading didn't bother arguing, but his breakfast remained untouched.

My son, a copper?

He sighed. Twenty years ago, he wouldn't have been concerned at all. But with all the problems the UK had today with terrorism and immigrant communities that refused to integrate or respect the law, he wasn't sure he wanted his boy on the frontlines without a gun.

And he definitely didn't want him in the south of France facing some unknown criminal element.

He stared at his plate, bacon and eggs in the shape of a happy face. He chuckled then picked up his fork. Spencer was an adult, old enough to make his own decisions. And if he refused him now, he might just set back the progress of the past couple of years, perhaps irreparably.

He just prayed he wasn't about to regret this selfish indulgence.

Off the coast of Saint-Pierre-la-Mer, France

Pierre was going nuts with all the waiting. So far, the search had proven a failure, and he was powerless to do anything about it. He couldn't go to the chateau as it was now enemy territory, he had no idea where his father was, the cross was on the bottom of the sea, and he couldn't even go home in case the authorities were searching for him, or his father's loyal subjects were waiting to kill him.

And what made it worse, was he was stuck on this boat with a man whose idea of conversation consisted of grunts and huffs. He half expected the man to point them toward the nearest caves and start painting.

He reached into his pocket and pulled out his cellphone.

"No cellphones."

"Why?"

"They might track it."

"Who?"

"The police."

"Why would they? They don't know I'm involved in anything."

"The police are searching the chateau right now. They know your family is involved in something."

Pierre shoved the phone back in his pocket. "Do you think they'll find anything?"

The man shrugged. "That's up to your father."

Pierre frowned. His father wasn't there, that much he was pretty sure of.

What would you do if you were in charge?

He thought for a moment. He wasn't sure. His father always made the decisions. He could—he would—ask his uncles. They were older with more experience, so would know what to do. He chewed on his cheek then stopped.

Is that why he doesn't want me to carry on? He doesn't think I have enough experience?

He resumed chewing. It made sense. His father was dying far before his time. It should be at least another twenty years before he should expect his son to take over the responsibilities of the family. But surely this had happened before. Five, six, seven hundred years ago, the average life expectancy was nowhere near what it was today. Men his age had to have been taking over from their dying fathers. What was so different now?

He picked at a hangnail.

The difference is you don't know what to do.

A hundred years ago, would his great-great grandfather have known what to do if he were thrust into this duty at his age? He had a feeling he would. He had to admit he hadn't embraced the training, physical or mental, preferring to play his video games and hang out with friends, his nose on his phone rather than his books.

He hadn't cared.

There was time.

And now there wasn't.

If he had devoted himself to the family tradition, would his father be so quick to return the True Cross to the Vatican? Perhaps not. Yet it didn't matter. What was done was done. He was who he was, his father would be dead shortly, and the cross would be his once they recovered it.

Then the family would be his to control.

And for that, he needed their ancestral home. He had no idea who had survived the attack last night, but he was sure they were taking action to protect the family's legacy.

What would you do?

He drew a deep breath.

I'd hide all the evidence that anything had happened.

It was the only thing that could be done. To do otherwise, would invite too many questions, questions the family couldn't afford. He stared up at the chateau, the sun climbing in the sky, and wondered what might possibly be going on up there.

Ridefort Residence

Saint-Pierre-la-Mer, France

Durand stood back as the jackhammer did its job, breaking away the stone that he felt confident was hiding something these men didn't want found. He watched as they were huddled together, under guard, at the far side of the courtyard.

Suddenly the sound changed, metal on metal, and the two-man crew stopped, turning off the machine. One kicked away the stone with his steel-toed boot then cursed.

"What is it?"

"There's a metal plate under this. I'm betting this whole thing is just stone on top of metal."

"Well, that would make sense, wouldn't it? If it's some sort of panel hiding some secret hideaway underneath it, it would need some sort of support."

The foreman yanked his hard hat off his head and scratched. "Nobody told me about any secret whatevers. I was told to bring a crew to chop up some concrete."

"So you can't do the job?"

"Not *this* job. We can clear off the stone for you, but you're going to need a cutting crew to get through the next layer."

"Then get a cutting crew!"

The foreman growled then pulled out his phone, calling his company. Durand marched over to the suspects, Bernard Ridefort stepping forward. "Why don't you just open the damned thing so we can all save ourselves a lot of time?"

Bernard shook his head. "I have no idea what you're talking about. Like I said, it's always been like that. This castle has been here for hundreds of years. Who knows what's underneath it."

Durand frowned, and was about to leave when he noticed something. "Where's the kid?"

Bernard's eyes narrowed. "What kid?"

"The young guy who takes care of the horses."

Bernard glanced around. "No idea. Bathroom?"

Durand turned toward the officer watching them. "Where'd the kid go?"

He shrugged. "I don't know. Nobody's left."

Durand cursed. "Okay, search the place. He has to be somewhere."

Port of Saint-Pierre-la-Mer, France

Laura came up under the pier where she had hired her boat. She removed her diving mask and surveyed the area, not spotting her pursuer. With any luck, he was still chasing her boat, which she noted hadn't returned yet, the man apparently following through with her request.

She pulled herself up onto the dock, two locals spotting her, eager to help a woman with soaking wet, clinging clothes. "Thank you, gentlemen, I appreciate all the attention." She smiled at them, the two graying men grinning back. She pointed where her boat had been, then at the scuba gear. "Can you see that he gets this back?"

"Absolutely, Mademoiselle, we'll take care of that for you."

His friend pointed at his boat. "Join us for a drink?"

Laura smiled and held up her ring finger. "Sorry, boys, but I'm taken." She almost giggled at the disappointment. A woman came rushing toward them, a towel in her hand, admonishing the "dirty old men."

"You poor dear, did you have an accident?"

Laura smiled as she took the towel, quickly drying her hair and exposed extremities. "No, just lost a bet." She handed the towel back. "Thank you so much for your help." She rushed off, not wanting to risk the premature return of her boat, or that which she presumed carried her pursuer. She glanced at her watch, thankful it, unlike her phone, was waterproof.

The car must be ready by now.

Off the coast of Saint-Pierre-la-Mer, France

Schmidt pointed at the boat he had spotted earlier with Laura Palmer, and his generously paid captain steered them toward the craft, now coasting leisurely along, a broad smile on the owner's face. They pulled up beside him, the two men apparently friends.

"Where's the woman?" asked Schmidt, as pleasantly as he could.

The man eyed him suspiciously. "And what business is it of yours?"

Schmidt reached for his weapon but decided against it, too many police in the area to risk a radio call going out for help. "She's a friend."

"Unlikely."

The man gunned his engine, though not before Schmidt got a good look in the back.

Empty.

He cursed. "Take me back to shore. Fast."

His captain complied, and Schmidt moved to the rear of the boat. It was time to face the fact that he was dealing with no ordinary woman. She had obviously gone overboard and swam back to shore, which meant she had bigger balls than most men he was used to dealing with. They had no idea where she and her husband were holed up, and he had no doubt they were making plans to get out of town. They might only have minutes before they were gone.

And once they were, there was no way they would find them. They needed more eyes than they had, eyes that were everywhere. He pulled out his phone and called Pierre Ridefort.

"This is Schmidt. I've lost her. I think we need to assume they're going to get away."

"What should we do?"

"I think it's time we enlisted some help, but it's going to be expensive."

"I've got the money. Tell me what you need."

Corpo della Gendarmeria Office

Palazzo del Governatorato, Vatican City State

Mario Giasson sat in his office with half a dozen of the Vatican's most learned scholars seated in a semi-circle in front of his desk. He had been forced to wait for the babysitter to arrive, but had taken the time to get the ball rolling through phone calls, this meeting arranged to find out if Gregory Milton's claims were even possible.

And from what he was hearing, they were.

Remotely.

"The True Cross was presumed destroyed by Saladin in Damascus, shortly after he captured it. King Richard and others offered massive sums for its return, amounts so obscene, that it was quite remarkable Saladin refused the offers. It could have funded his armies for some time."

Giasson nodded at Father Jonathan Brandis, the foremost expert on the True Cross the Vatican had to offer. "But that would make sense, wouldn't it? If he didn't actually have it, then he had nothing to bargain with."

Brandis bowed his head slightly. "This is true. History assumed he destroyed it so that the Christian armies could never possess it again. If he never had it, or somehow lost it, then yes, it could be the reason he never ransomed it."

Giasson leaned back in his chair. "So then we agree it's possible that Professor Acton has found the True Cross?"

"You said he's in the south of France?" asked Father Francis.

"Yes."

"Then I doubt it. I can see no reason it would be there of all places."

Brandis waved a hand. "Don't be so quick to dismiss the possibility. When the Crusades were over, the knights returned home, and many were from France. Perhaps one of them had the cross and took it with him."

Murmurs of dissent filled the room.

"Now wait. We have historical accounts that say Saladin absolutely had the cross. We can all agree on that, at least?"

Heads bobbed.

"And we can agree that none of Saladin's people would have dared take it from him, agreed?"

Again, heads bobbed.

"Yet we have no account of him actually destroying it, which is something you think he would do in a quite public manner, and which history would have recorded."

Grunts of assent.

"Then I think it's logical to at least consider the possibility that he lost it somehow, and that can only mean it was stolen. And if it was, it had to be by Christians, and it would have had to have been done shortly after its capture, otherwise Saladin would have had time to destroy it."

Francis leaned forward in his chair, excited. "Right, and Jerusalem fell very shortly thereafter, and the defenders were forced to leave the Holy Land. Those who had found the cross might not have had any choice but to take it with them, back to Christendom."

Giasson held out his hands. "Soooo?"

Francis smiled, his eyes wide. "It's definitely possible."

A commotion outside the glass walls of his office had Giasson looking then gasping. His Holiness was walking toward his office, smiling and exchanging pleasantries with the staff. Giasson leaped from his chair and opened the door for him. "Your Holiness, I wasn't expecting you."

"There is something I would speak to you about."

"Of course, sir, but I could have come to you."

The elderly Pontiff smiled, motioning for the others to return to their seats. "Sometimes it is good to stretch one's legs, or so my doctor would have me believe."

Giasson pulled up a chair for the man. He waved it off. "Standing is apparently good as well." He smiled at the room. "I understand you have had some interesting news."

Giasson bowed slightly, surprised, yet not, that the Pontiff had been informed. "Yes, Your Holiness, I received word today that Professor James Acton, whom you've met, may have found the True Cross."

The Pope regarded those gathered. "And what do you gentlemen think?"

The response was noncommittal, Father Brandis finally speaking. "I believe it's definitely possible. Even if it's not true, do we dare risk not investigating?"

The Pope nodded. "I tend to agree with you, Father." He turned to Giasson. "Is Professor Acton bringing it here?"

Giasson shook his head. "I'm afraid there was an attempt on his life, and that of his wife. I'm not exactly sure of the status right now, only their location."

"And that is?"

"Saint-Pierre-la-Mer, in the south of France."

"Then I think you should be there, investigating this, rather than here, don't you?"

Giasson bowed. "Absolutely, Your Holiness."

Operations Center 3, CIA Headquarters

Langley, Virginia

Sonya Tong bit her tongue at Randy Child's annoying habit, instead focusing on tracing the professors' movements after they arrived in France. The youngest analyst on the team spun again in his chair, staring up at the ceiling, just enough of him in the periphery to be annoying. The nightshift was bad enough. Working it with Child made it worse.

His console beeped.

He dropped a toe, bringing his spin to a halt. "I got something!"

Tong rose from her station and approached his. "What have you got?"

"I've been monitoring the Dark Web like Leroux suggested, and got this." He pointed at the screen. "Someone just took out a contract on our two professors. Half-a-mil each, alive."

Tong smiled then frowned. "Well, at least that means they're still alive, and whoever wants them must need something from them. That gives them a better chance of not dying in a hit."

The doors to the Operations Center opened and Chris Leroux entered, appearing in far too good a mood for this hour. Tong's stomach flipped, remembering his girlfriend had returned from assignment only hours ago. Tong had a crush on him, a hard crush, an inappropriate crush, yet knew he was madly in love with a woman way out of her league. And with the glow he had, she had no doubt Sherrie White had worked her magic on his wand.

She giggled at the thought.

"Something funny?" asked Leroux, all smiles.

"No, umm, sorry, sir." She motioned toward Child's station. "Randy just found out that a contract has been put out on the two professors. Half a million each."

"Dead or alive?"

"Alive."

"Well, that's good news. What have you discovered?"

She picked up a tablet from her desk, directing his attention to the wall of displays that curved across the entire front of the room. "Here's footage of them landing at Béziers Airport, France, last night. They're picked up by a chauffeured Maybach"—Child whistled in appreciation—"without incident, then we have nothing on them from a video perspective."

"No traffic cameras or anything?"

"It's a small town, so they don't have much. We're going through ATM footage and other security cameras to see if we can catch a glimpse, but I don't think it's really necessary. We were able to track their phones." She tapped at the tablet, and a map appeared with a route traced from the airport, several glowing red dots indicating cellphone towers that had picked up their devices. "This is the route we think they took. From what Dean Milton told us, their destination was some castle just outside of town along the coast." She tapped, some Google images appearing. "This is their destination, and as far as we can tell, they reached there. At least their phones did. But there's something interesting."

Leroux glanced at her. "What's that?"

"Well, I ran an analysis, and it appears that for the last half of their trip, the driver was speeding, significantly by the end of it, then they came to an abrupt stop near the castle, then nothing."

"Nothing?"

"Their signals cut out until about half an hour later." She tapped again. "We got a brief signal from two coastal towers from both phones before they cut out after about five minutes. Then nothing since."

Leroux's eyes narrowed as he approached the screen. "This is a fairly significant distance from the last signal. At least a mile or two by the looks of it. It's odd that no towers picked them up in between."

"Not necessarily," said Child in mid-spin. He tapped at his keyboard, an aerial view of the castle appearing. "It's a dead zone."

Leroux turned to him. "What?"

"Check it out. There's no cellphone activity at all around that castle. I'm guessing they have some sort of jammer installed."

Leroux's eyes narrowed. "That's odd. What the hell are they hiding?"

Tong shrugged. "Apparently they were paranoid for good reason, if Dean Milton's description of his conversation with Professor Acton is accurate. Someone tried to kill them on the way there, which matches with the speeding vehicle, and then someone apparently assaulted the castle." She brought up another display. "We have reports of an emergency call placed to the local police about weapons fire at the castle, then a warrant being issued this morning for a search. Something must have happened there."

Leroux's head bobbed slowly. "Okay, so it sounds like there's something to this." He motioned to the tablet. "My understanding is their phones are no longer working. What about this new number we were given?"

"That's a weird one as well. We traced it for about an hour, then it went offline. It came back on a for a few minutes, then that's it."

"Could they have just turned it off?"

"Perhaps, but why? It's their only lifeline. And the last signal is again from a coastal tower."

Leroux crossed his arms and tapped his chin. "Could they be going in the water?"

Tong's eyes widened as she stared at the screen. "That makes sense! They reach the castle, where there's some sort of jamming device. If they left, we should have picked them up on one of the surrounding towers, but we didn't. We picked them up over here"—she pointed at the coastline—"which could make sense if the castle had some sort of other…" She hesitated to say it.

"What?"

She looked at Leroux, then away. "No, it's too far-fetched."

Leroux grunted. "What? That a thousand-year-old castle might have some sort of escape tunnel to the sea?"

She flushed, his brilliance never ceasing to amaze her. "Exactly."

"I think it's more than possible. Escape tunnels were par for the course back then. So if they did have an escape route, then it's very possible they were on a boat. They leave this tunnel, the cellphone towers pick them up again, then go dead a few minutes later."

"Because they had to jump in the water."

Leroux turned to Child. "Why do you say that?"

Child motioned toward the screen, tapping at his keyboard, several French news sites appearing. "Looks like a boat exploded last night in Saint-Pierre-de-Sol, and some witnesses claim they heard a helicopter and gunfire."

Leroux nodded. "Well, I think we've explained their phones. They got wet and stopped working. And if there were helicopters and weapons fire, then whoever is after them is well-funded and determined. What has me wondering though, is what's changed?"

Tong's eyes narrowed as she used the opportunity to stare at him, his mind fascinating in how it worked. "What do you mean?"

"Last night they try to kill them, and now a contract is put out on them that stipulates they should be delivered alive. What changed?"

Tong pursed her lips, drawing in a slow breath. "I can only think of two things. One, whoever tried to kill them last night wasn't supposed to, or two, between then and now, they've discovered that the professors have something they want."

Leroux grinned at her. "*Exactly* what I was thinking. I'm guessing that it's the latter. What do we have on this new number of theirs?"

Tong tapped at her tablet, a map appearing on the display. "We show it activated a couple of hours ago. It kept in a very narrow area, then a call was made to Dean Milton's home. It went offline, then came back on. A short call was made to a travel agent, then it went offline again near the port. We're running that call down, but the agent apparently is in an important meeting."

"Probably arranged some sort of transportation. We need to know what that's about." Leroux exhaled loudly. "Could their new phone have ended up in the water too?"

Tong shrugged. "Possible. More likely they just turned it off."

"But that's their lifeline. Turning it off seems rather shortsighted."

"Maybe they were being followed and couldn't risk it ringing?" suggested Child.

Leroux nodded. "Possible, but it doesn't matter. Keep monitoring for that phone to come back on. I'll go talk to the Director and get official clearance to work on this, but in the meantime, keep running with it. We need to figure out who's trying to kill them and why, before someone takes that contract and finds them first."

Spanish-French Border

Hugh Reading accelerated as they cleared the border between France and Spain, recalling a different time when he was younger and the border was guarded. He had severe allergies as a child, and had been prescribed some sort of medicine—what, he couldn't remember—that was a powder you sniffed up your nose. He was having a particularly bad attack, so hauled out his medicine and began to take it—much to the horror of his father who looked in the rearview mirror as he slowed at the border, finding his son with powder covering his nose as if he had just snorted a few lines of cocaine.

Funny today, apparently not so much back then.

He glanced at his son, doing the navigating. "How much longer?"

"About an hour."

"Try the number again."

His son hit redial on the new cellphone number Milton had given them, then shook his head. "Still off."

Reading slammed his fist into the steering wheel. "Bloody hell! Why would they turn it off?"

Spencer grunted. "From what you've told me about them, maybe they're dead."

Reading glared at him. "Don't ever make jokes like that. Ever!"

Spencer flushed, shrinking away toward the door. "Sorry," he mumbled.

A wave of regret washed over Reading, and he reached out, squeezing his son's shoulder. "Sorry, son, I'm just afraid for my friends, because you're right, they could be dead, and that thought terrifies me. These are good people, and they don't deserve to die. Especially when *this* time, I don't think they've actually stuck their nose where it doesn't belong."

His son sat up a little straighter. "*This* time?"

"They have a knack for getting themselves into situations they shouldn't. Too many times it's by not minding their own business."

Spencer looked at him. "You mean they're do-gooders?"

Reading chuckled. "You could call them that. They do like to help people."

"What, they're Social Justice Warriors?"

Reading outright laughed. "I don't think I've ever heard Jim described like that. That's like calling Hitler a Jew-lover. Social Justice Warriors listen to only one side of an argument, theirs, and refuse to even let the other side speak. They are the worst kind of protestor. They don't believe in debate or free speech, and too often feel that if you don't agree with their quite often incorrect or naïve position, you should be thrown in jail, or worse, killed.

"Jim has a wide range of views, most I agree with, but some I don't, but he will *always* listen to someone else's opinion and debate them rationally. In his classes, I'm taken to understand that he has zero tolerance for disrespectful discourse on either side. It's quite the shock to the SJWs that take his class, expecting to be able to just shout down their opponents. More often than not they find themselves tossed from the class, or the course altogether."

Spencer stared at the road ahead. "Must make it hard to fill a class, what with the way most of my generation is."

"Jim told me that since he's become a bit notorious in the archaeology community, he's had a long waiting list."

"So he's a *rock* star of archaeology?" Spencer grinned at him. "Get it?"

Reading gave him a look. "I do. Millions wouldn't, but *I* do." He frowned. "We're going to have to work on that sense of humor."

Spencer laughed. "Mom says I'm the funniest guy she knows."

Reading shook his head. "Now I *know* she's lying. *I'm* the funniest guy she ever knew."

Spencer stared at him. "Now *that* I can't imagine."

Reading shook a fist at him. "Don't make me show you how funny I can be."

Spencer laughed, holding up his hands in mock defense. "Okay, okay, you're a funny guy!" He held up his phone then pointed. "Get to the right. We're turning off soon."

Reading checked his mirror and changed lanes, his mind returning to the task at hand, and praying his friends had simply turned off their phone.

But he knew them.

And he expected the worst.

Port of Saint-Pierre-la-Mer, France

Laura walked down the pier, attaching herself to a group of tourists as she tied her hair back in a ponytail and rolled up her ruffled sleeves, making herself look as presentable as possible.

It wasn't easy.

She hadn't seen a shower since yesterday morning, too exhausted to take one at the hotel last night, and too worried about James to take one this morning. That wouldn't normally be an issue if it weren't for the fact she had been swimming twice in salt water, had a physical altercation with one assailant, evaded another at a sprint, and had been otherwise running on adrenaline for twelve hours. She was sure she didn't smell the greatest, though her husband always said she smelled like roses.

God, I love that man.

She said a silent prayer for his quick recovery as she broke off from the group, making a beeline for the car rental agency. She saw a Renault out front, a man with a clipboard standing beside it, searching the crowds.

"Hello, I'm Laura Palmer," she said as she approached, extending her hand. "Someone was supposed to call ahead to arrange a vehicle?"

"Yes, Mademoiselle." She held up her left hand. "Apologies, Madame. Here are your keys, your paperwork, and you're set to go. The bill has already been taken care of. You have unlimited mileage, and I was told to include the insurance option."

Good thinking!

"Thank you."

"Just sign here, and initial here." He indicated two places on his clipboard, and she filled them in, handing it back and taking the keys.

"Thank you!" She climbed in and fired up the engine as she adjusted her seat and mirrors. She waved at the agent then pulled into traffic, heading for the hotel only minutes from where she now was. She breathed a little easier as she came to a stop, glancing over at the port.

And her heart raced.

A boat was docking, her pursuer standing tall in the bow, scanning the area. She could have sworn his eyes came to rest on her for a moment, but that was impossible.

If I can see him…

Traffic moved again, and she pressed the gas.

Let's go people!

Ridefort Residence

Saint-Pierre-la-Mer, France

Captain Durand stood in the courtyard, staring at the cutting crew as they did their work. The young man who tended the horses still hadn't been found, and in the confusion, the count had dropped by one more.

It made no sense.

They had started with eight, now they had six, two having disappeared before their very eyes. He turned back to do another count when there was a shout then a crashing sound, followed by breaking glass. He rushed toward the crew as they stepped back, a large hole now visible. Durand held out his hand to one of the uniformed officers.

"Flashlight."

One was slapped in his hand as he knelt by the hole, directing the beam into the darkness below. And he gasped. A car was underneath where he was kneeling, with what appeared to be a bullet hole through one side of the windshield, and a chunk of metal in the other.

I knew it!

He stood and pointed at the wall. "Get me that ladder."

Two of his men grabbed it and lowered it into the hole. He climbed down and played the beam around the large room, the light coming to rest on a nearby panel with light switches and two buttons with arrows.

He tilted his head up to look at the hole. "Everybody clear away from that seam. I'm going to try and open it from down here."

"Yes, Captain!"

He heard the sounds of movement overhead as the cutting equipment was hauled away.

"All clear!"

He headed for the wall and flicked the first switch. A line of lights at the far end came on. He flicked the next switch, and another batch lit up. He repeated this until the entire area was bathed in bright light. He turned off the flashlight, shoving it in his jacket pocket as he surveyed the area.

He was alone, and it seemed to be a garage of sorts, nothing truly unusual here except for the state of an impressive Maybach with a damaged windshield, the driver side torn apart by bullet holes, and evidence it had been in a rear-end collision.

With a sheet covering the driver seat.

He eyed the two remaining buttons, one with an up arrow, the other with a down. He wasn't sure what to do. The car was already down. Pressing the up button would logically send it up. He eyed the ceiling, the placement of several rails suggesting the floor above would drop then slide away. He pressed the up button and motors kicked in, the floor overhead lowering about a foot before sliding open, the ladder clattering to the floor, and a dozen curious faces revealed, staring down at him.

The car jerked and rose. He took his thumb off the button and it stopped. He pressed the down arrow, and the car lowered. He let go once it returned to its former position. He picked up the ladder and repositioned it. "Get me that Bernard fellow that's in charge. He's got some explaining to do."

Bernard Ridefort watched as their secret was revealed. From this underground chamber under the stables, the police would soon have access to most of the chateau's secrets.

Though not its most important.

The treasure room.

It had already been locked down, a key now needed to access the secret chamber, that key located in a safety deposit box in Paris with no links to anyone here. Unless the police broke down the wall, they'd never find it.

But none of that was relevant.

They had plenty of "real" money in banks and deposit boxes around the continent, the treasures in the secret chamber priceless and irreplaceable, and not used to fund their operations. Those arrangements had been made centuries before and continued to this day, updated from time to time to take advantage of modern financial methods.

The Order would continue, though not here. After almost 800 years, they would be forced to move. But who would lead them? Sir Jacques would be dead soon, and his son was a traitor, though their new leader by right.

And Bernard would never follow him.

None of them would.

Pierre must die.

And should he, there was no male heir. It had never happened in the eight centuries they had been guarding the True Cross. He was the next in line if proper succession was followed. He was the oldest brother after Jacques, and if the lone male heir were dead, it would fall to him and his bloodline to continue, including his own son, close to Pierre's age, but different from that traitorous bastard in every way important. He would be a worthy Grand Master some day.

The two guards turned as the excitement surrounding the garage grew, and Bernard slowly backed toward the wall, motioning with his hand for the others to do the same. He kept his eyes flicking between each officer, watching for any sign they were about to turn, it essential their escape go unnoticed for at least a few seconds.

He took a quick glance over his shoulder and saw the remaining men all gathered together at the wall. He held his hand out to his side, checking the officers once again, then dropped it. He backed up slowly, careful to not make a sound, and passed through a hidden opening in the wall, a trompe-l'œil, an optical illusion that would fool anyone not expecting it. He ducked out of sight then quickly followed the others down the hidden corridor buried within the outer wall.

Someone shouted.

"Sir! They're gone!"

Durand tensed at the shout from overhead. "What?"

"They're gone!"

He hurried up the ladder and was hauled up the last few feet. He rushed into the courtyard, staring at the far wall where the men had been held, the two officers assigned to guard them standing there, looking about uselessly, avoiding eye contact.

"Where the hell did they go?"

"I don't know, sir. One minute they were there, the next they weren't."

Rage built inside Durand as he glared at the two idiots. "How the hell do half a dozen men disappear while you're watching them?"

No response.

"Well?"

"I, well, we were watching that secret door open, sir, then when I looked back, they were gone. It couldn't have been more than a few seconds."

"Idiots!" Durand looked about, no possible means of escape within sight, just a long, unremarkable stone wall, stretching from one end of the courtyard to the other. He stared at the wall, searching for something, anything, when his eyes narrowed.

What is that?

He leaned to the left, then to the right, something not right about the wall directly ahead of him. He wasn't sure what it was, but something didn't appear natural. He stepped toward it, the two idiots following, and stopped several feet from the wall. He leaned to the left then right again, this time the effect more pronounced.

Something was definitely wrong.

It appeared as if part of the wall was shifting its perspective out of sync with the rest. He reached out to touch it, and found empty space. He cursed, the optical illusion instantly broken as his mind resolved what it was seeing. He stepped forward, several feet beyond the wall, a passageway behind it revealed.

And no sign of their suspects.

Port of Saint-Pierre-la-Mer, France

Schmidt was pissed. This woman was good. Too good. Which was why he had put out the contract on the two of them. It was now clear they would likely evade him and his men. With the right incentive, surveillance cameras would be hacked, transport records accessed, and the ugly underbelly of society would go to work, greed overcoming most scruples with the right motivation.

And a million American dollars for the capture of both would be enough, especially for the hackers. They would sit back in the safety of their own homes, or their Russian or Chinese government-sponsored offices, and work the data, sending him a location. He had used them before, and it worked.

Sometimes very quickly.

Gone were the days when hitmen roamed the continent, waiting for a contract. They still existed, but the days of hunting down someone through physical clues and guile had been shoved aside by computer algorithms and CCTV cameras.

His phone vibrated and he pulled it out, swiping to see the message.

Laura Palmer just rented a car at Eurocar on Boulevard des Embruns

He tapped the button, cursing when he saw the map, the agency not half a mile from where he now stood. He broke out into a sprint, dodging the tourists and locals on the pier, then reached the road, the rental agency just ahead. He jogged to the lot then gathered himself, catching his breath as he straightened his clothes and hair. He entered the small office, smiling at the young man behind the counter.

"Hello, I'm Professor James Acton. Was my wife Laura Palmer just in here?"

The clerk's eyes widened slightly. "Yes, she was. Not ten minutes ago. Were you supposed to meet here?"

Schmidt laughed, shaking his head. "Sorry, just a miscommunication I guess. You know how it is. Can you help me out though? Did she say where she was going?"

The clerk shook his head. "Sorry, sir, she didn't."

Schmidt frowned, putting on a show as he tapped at his chin. "I wonder if she went back to the hotel. Do you know which way she went?"

The clerk seemed happy to answer at least one question helpfully. "Yes, sir. When she pulled out, she went to the right."

"Ahh, the hotel. Thank you very much." He smiled and pushed open the door before turning back. "So, what kind did she manage to get?"

"Sir?"

"The car? What kind?"

"Oh, a very nice one, sir. A Renault Latitude. Blue."

"Sounds great!" Schmidt left, striding toward the sidewalk as he activated his comm. "All units. Palmer now has a rental vehicle. A blue Renault Latitude. She was last seen heading north on Boulevard des Embruns. She's almost definitely going to pick up her husband. Let's focus on the hotels north of my position."

The traffic was heavy and slow, and he needed wheels. He spotted a bicycle rental shop and smiled.

Laura breathed a sigh of relief as she spotted someone pull out of a parking spot across from their hotel. A car ahead of her braked and she cursed. It drove past the spot, slowing to parallel park, when she cranked the wheel and jammed her front end in, hopping the curb before spinning the wheel to the left and dropping back onto the road, the spot hers in an asshole move if there ever was one.

She jumped out of the car, ignoring the fist-shaking driver, and weaved through the traffic to the hotel. She waved at the desk clerk then rushed up the stairs, unlocking their door. She found James asleep on the bed, empty juice bottles littering the linens as he gently snored. She didn't want to disturb him, but there was no time to waste.

She stepped over to the bed, checking the bandage, finding it dry on the outside, a good sign. She grabbed the shopping bags and stuffed their medical and foodstuffs inside, then looked about the room for anything she might have missed.

Nothing.

She sat on the edge of the bed and gently shook his shoulder. "James, darling, time to wake up."

He moaned and turned toward her, his eyes fluttering open. He smiled. "Hey, babe, did you save us yet?"

She gently slapped his shoulder then stood. "Let's go. I've got a car outside and we're all packed." She helped him to a seated position, swinging his legs off the bed. She slipped his shoes on, then helped him into his jacket, zipping it up to hide his bloodstained shirt. "You ready?"

"As I'll ever be."

She draped his arm over her shoulder then helped him from the bed. He took a few timid steps toward the mirror, gripping his side, then straightened his hair as best he could, then his jacket.

"You okay?"

He nodded. "Let's just get to the car, quick."

She opened the door and they headed down the hall, toward the stairs.

"What took you so long?"

"I was spotted. I had to rent a boat to get away."

"A boat? Is that why you smell like you've been swimmin' with da fishes?"

She chuckled. "I'll explain in the car."

They reached the stairs and took the first step, James wincing. "Okay, this is going to be difficult. We had to pick the one hotel without a functioning elevator."

"Even if it had one, would you take it under these circumstances?"

James frowned as he took the next step. "You're right. No escape if you're caught in it. Next time though, remind me not to get wounded in an explosion caused by madmen in a helicopter with automatic weapons."

"Deal."

Laura helped him down the next few steps until they reached the landing. James leaned on the railing, gasping for breath. "This sucks. And those pain killers are wearing off."

"They're in the bag. I'll give you some when we get in the car."

"Is that supposed to be incentive for me to go faster?"

She grinned. "At least you haven't lost your sense of humor."

"Why don't you dangle a stick in front of me with a few Tylenol on the end. You'll have me sprinting in no time."

"Okay, that's enough, Seinfeld. Are you ready?"

He nodded and took the next step on his own, Laura stepping ahead of him, allowing him to put a hand on her shoulder and lean on her, the process quicker than carrying some of his weight over her shoulder. "When we get in the car I want to call Greg, see if he's heard anything."

Laura glanced back at him. "We'll have to get a new phone."

"Again?"

"Yeah, it got ruined when I had to swim for shore."

"You really did have an adventure while I was asleep."

"You have no idea." She rounded the corner and smiled at the desk clerk, then froze, ducking back and pushing James against the wall with her arm. He yelped in pain, and she slapped her hand over his mouth.

Schmidt showed the desk clerk the photos of the two professors, the man's eyes widening slightly as he glanced behind Schmidt. He spun but saw no one. A faint cry stopped him from turning back.

Was that inside?

He couldn't be sure. The small lobby was empty. There was a set of stairs directly ahead, and to the right, an out of order elevator occupied most of the far wall. But something had drawn the clerk's attention, and someone had made that sound.

A sound of pain.

Acton is wounded.

If he were to assume Acton was the man the paramedics had been talking about, then he had a serious wound to his side. And if the elevator were out of order, he'd have to take the stairs.

He strode quickly toward them, reaching for his weapon.

Laura looked about desperately for some means of escape. She spotted a utility closet to their right and rushed toward it, pushing it open. James limped toward her as footfalls echoed in the marble lobby. He reached her and stepped inside. She followed, squeezing into the cramped space, and pushed the door shut.

A clicking sound from behind startled her, the room bathed in light, James having found the chain controlling the lone overhead bulb. She checked the doorknob and found no way to lock it from the inside. The footsteps grew closer.

"Take this." James handed her a doorstop from one of the shelves and she smiled, dropping down and shoving it under the door, gently kicking it as hard as she dared, wedging the door shut. The footsteps were close now, just outside the door. Her pursuer walked past, and she breathed a sigh of relief. Suddenly he stopped and rushed back.

The entire door rattled as he tried the handle. She pushed against the door with her shoulder and the wedge with her foot, as hard as she could. The man put his shoulder into it, and the top half of the door bent inward slightly, then bounced back. He tried again, then growled in frustration, the footfalls receding back toward the front desk.

An exchange occurred between the clerk and the man, then more receding footfalls, then nothing. She kicked the wedge clear and James turned out the light. She opened the door tentatively, and heard a gasp. She poked her head out and found the desk clerk standing there, his mouth agape.

"What was that all about?"

Laura shook her head. "I'm not sure. He's been following me all morning. He's some creep we met at a bar last night." She glanced out at the lobby. "Where did he go?"

"He left, but I think he's across the street. Is that blue car Madame's?"

"Yes."

"I think he's watching it." He started for his desk. "I'm calling the police."

Laura reached out, grabbing his arm. "No, no police. That will just cause delays. We're leaving now, anyway." She frowned as she stared at the car through the glass doors, so close yet so far. "We'll need to find another way to the airport." She looked at the clerk. "Is there a back way out of here?"

He nodded. "I'll show you." He eyed James with concern. "Are you okay, Monsieur?"

"Yeah, just some food poisoning last night. Should be a fun plane ride."

The clerk shook his head, frowning. "You poor people. I really hope you don't hold this experience against our lovely country."

Laura smiled as he led them toward the rear entrance. "Not at all. I don't think that man was French."

"Definitely not! His French was excellent, but he was definitely German. Perhaps Swiss or Austrian, but definitely not French."

"Neither were the oysters," added James. "I'm sure they were Spanish."

The clerk smiled. "Of course they were, of course they were. There is no such thing as bad French oysters." He pushed open the door then pointed to the right. "Go that way. You should be able to find a taxi to take you to the airport."

"Thank you so much for your help." Laura led James into the back alley and the door was hastily closed behind them, leaving her with the distinct impression the clerk was happy to be rid of them. It was only then that she realized she hadn't checked out. "We forgot to pay."

James glanced at her. "You're not thinking of going back, are you?"

She put an end to the internal debate. "No, you're right, that would be daft."

"Damned bloody daft."

She gave him a look. "Don't try to curse British, dear, you just sound even more American." They started toward the street, the going slow. "When this is all settled, I'll call and pay the bill."

James winced. "You do that."

They were approaching a street, cars and pedestrians visible. She directed them to a set of steps and helped James sit so he could catch his breath.

"What now?" he asked.

She frowned. "I'm not sure. We need to get out of here, but need a car to do it. I don't have a phone anymore, and I'm not sure how many rental agencies are in this town. It's not like I can go back and get a second car."

"We need a phone."

"Right." She paused. "Do you think Hugh is coming?"

James grunted. "If I know him, he's already here."

"Then we need to let him find us."

"How?"

She sighed. "Maybe we need to stop running."

James' eyes narrowed. "What do you mean?"

"I mean, if we're on the streets, we can be spotted. And the longer they don't see us, the more likely they're going to think we escaped."

"Riiight."

"So, maybe we should just stay put and see what happens."

James' eyes widened. "That's bold or stupid."

"I prefer bold." She glanced up at the door he was sitting in front of. "Care for a bite?"

Operations Center 3, CIA Headquarters
Langley, Virginia

Sonya Tong turned toward Leroux as he entered the room. He had been gone a long time, well over an hour, though in that time they had discovered little until just a few minutes ago.

"Problem?" she asked him, his expression troubled.

"Yeah, something big's brewing. We're probably going to be pulled off this any minute now. What's the latest?"

"Nothing much until just now. One Laura Palmer rented a car in Saint-Pierre-la-Mer about half an hour ago."

Leroux's eyebrows shot up. "Well, that's good news. That should mean they'll be able to get out of immediate danger."

"Right, but there's still the matter of the contract out on them."

Leroux nodded. "Any eyes?"

Child raised a hand as if still in class. "I managed to access a few cameras. When Sonya found the rental, I was able to pull this up." He pointed at the screen and security footage was shown, clearly from an ATM, the occasional customer blocking the view.

"What am I looking at?"

"An ATM camera. Look across the street. You can see the rental agency. Now wait for it…" He raised his hand for dramatic effect, then dropped it, tapping his keyboard, freezing the image. "There. Isn't that Professor Palmer?"

Everyone leaned toward the screen as Child isolated the image and enhanced it.

"Yeah, that definitely looks like her. Play it forward, let's see what she does." The image jerked forward, a second at a time, and several dozen frames later Palmer, and the car disappeared from the shot. Leroux nodded. "Okay, so it looks like she rented a blue car. Do we have any other cameras showing it?"

Child shook his head. "We're working on it, but…" He tapped a few keys and a satellite image appeared. "We've got a sat going over the area now." A few more keypresses and a crystal clear image of the town of Saint-Pierre-la-Mer appeared. Child zoomed in. "This is the rental agency where she picked up the car. We didn't see it again, so I think it's safe to assume it went north, since it didn't pass back in front of the camera." He manipulated the image to follow the street north, when Tong jumped from her seat and pointed.

"There. Is that it?"

Child zoomed in on a blue car, parked along the street he had been following. "Let me see if I can get a plate." A few keypresses and they had an angle shot, the first few letters visible.

"That matches the rental agreement we pulled," said Tong, "but there could be thousands of vehicles with those first few letters."

Leroux agreed. "Yes, but look at the bumper. That's a rental agency sticker." He glanced at Child. "Where is that?"

Child zoomed out slightly, showing the immediate area, then popped open another screen, Google Street View appearing. He swung the image around.

"Wait!" Leroux stepped toward the screen. "Back it up a bit. Thirty degrees to the right."

Child complied, and Leroux smiled.

"How much are you willing to bet that they're staying at that hotel?"

Child grinned. "I'll bet my day's wages against yours."

Leroux gave him a look. "I think you're grossly overestimating how much I make." He glanced at Tong. "Give them a shout, see what happens if you ask for them."

Tong nodded, pulling up the number online. She dialed, the conversation on speaker for everyone to hear.

"Allô, Hôtel Neptune, comment puis-je vous aider?"

"Umm, bonjour, parlez-vous Anglais?"

"Yes, of course, Madame, how may I help you?"

"I'm trying to reach some friends of mine, James Acton and his wife, Laura Palmer. Can I have their room please?"

"Umm, I'm sorry, Madame, but I need a room number."

Child snapped his finger, pointing at the screen, a voice stress analysis display indicating serious anxiousness on the part of their hotel clerk.

"I'm sorry, but I don't have that. The message from them was garbled. You can't just put me through? It would mean so much to me."

Leroux smiled at the sweetness dripping from Tong's voice.

Didn't know she had that in her.

"I'm sorry, Madame, but there is nothing I can do."

"But they are there, right? I do have the right hotel?"

The stress indicator shot through the roof. "I'm sorry, Madame, there is nothing I can do. Au revoir." The call ended and Tong removed her headset, smiling at Leroux.

"I think it's pretty safe to say they're there, or at least were."

Leroux nodded. "Agreed. Get that intel to Agent Reading. He might be able to do something with it."

Tong's comm panel beeped and she grabbed her headset. "Sir, it's for you." She handed it to Leroux who fit it over his head.

"This is Leroux." He paused for a moment. "Understood." He handed the headset back, then turned to the room. "Shut it down. We're now on a Priority One tasking from the Director. The professors are on their own." Leroux paused, turning to Tong. "But make sure Agent Reading gets that last bit of intel."

Tong nodded. "Consider it done."

Approaching Saint-Pierre-la-Mer, France

Reading glanced at Spencer. "Did you get that?"

Spencer held up his phone. "Already found it. Hôtel Neptune. We're fifteen minutes from there."

"Good. Let's hope they're still there."

Spencer nodded then turned to his father. "What are we going to do if they are?"

"Get them out."

"How?"

Reading's eyes narrowed. "Huh?"

"I mean, if it were that easy, wouldn't they have already done it? I mean, just get in a car and leave, right? Something must be keeping them there."

Reading stared ahead at the coastal traffic, his lips pursed. Spencer was right. Something must be wrong, something must be preventing them from leaving.

And that something had to be dangerous.

"Jim's wounded, so that might be keeping them in place. Laura might not be able to get him to the rental."

"That's a possibility, but if he's in that bad a shape, wouldn't she have called for an ambulance?"

Reading nodded. "Possibly, but if someone's looking for them, especially if they know he's wounded, then they'll be watching the hospitals."

Spencer fell silent for a moment, then pointed ahead. "Keep right up here."

Reading followed his son's directions, impressed the boy—young man—was giving him directions with plenty of warning, suggesting he had some experience behind the wheel himself. He knew he had his driving license, but had never been the passenger with him.

And I won't be today.

"You didn't answer my question. What are we going to do if they're still there and someone is watching the place?"

"Sneak them out somehow."

Spencer's eyes shot wide. "Sneak them out? How the bloody hell are we going to do that?"

Reading grunted. "Let's just hold that thought. We don't even know if they're still there."

Spencer stared at him. "So, you're making this up as you go."

"Yup."

"Is that how you normally do things?"

"Yup."

"Is that wise?"

"Probably not."

"Umm, I guess we shouldn't mention this to Mom, huh?"

Reading glanced at his son. "We'll take it to our graves."

Spencer grinned. "Sounds good to me. If she finds out, she'll never let us go on vacation again."

Reading tensed, the boy right. He sighed. "We're *definitely* taking it to our graves."

Off the coast of Saint-Pierre-la-Mer, France

Pierre sat up straight, his chest pounding with the news he had just received over the comm. "You're sure they're still in town?"

"Absolutely," replied Schmidt. "I'm outside their hotel right now with the rental car about fifty meters from my position. I think they're within walking distance. My men are converging on the area now."

"Do you have enough?"

"What do you mean? Men?"

"Yes."

"I have another half-dozen on standby that can be here within the hour. But it will cost you."

Pierre stared at the chateau. Once things settled down, he'd retrieve the riches trapped within, and settle any bill with ease. Money wasn't the problem. Time was. He needed to capture the professors before they escaped, otherwise the True Cross would be lost to him forever. He stared at his chaperone, picking at his fingernails with a hunting knife.

More of these cavemen could be dangerous.

His biggest fear was someone shooting the professors before they could get the location of where they hid the cross. But Schmidt's people knew the job. They were professionals. And if the professors escaped the confines of the town, they had the entire continent in which to hide.

His jaw squared. "Call them in."

Approaching French Airspace

Mario Giasson wasn't happy. He never liked kneejerk reactions to situations, but who was he to tell the Pontiff he was wrong to send them to France without a plan. It was a 90-minute trip, expedited by the fact their chartered jet was designated a Vatican diplomatic flight, leaving him little time to figure out what they would do when they landed, though the time had been well spent.

The academics were huddled together, excitedly discussing the possibilities, mostly focused on how to positively identify the cross when it was recovered.

If it was recovered.

His concern was the security aspect. An attempt had been made on his friends' lives. That meant there were hostile forces at play, and he was heading into the thick of things with four academics and two security personnel besides himself, licensed for small arms only.

He didn't care what the four men arguing behind him thought, they were remaining with the plane until he could be certain it was safe. He just wished he knew what was happening. News reports indicated a boat had blown up last night in Saint-Pierre-la-Mer, with those aboard still missing. His personnel back at the Vatican had managed to find reports on social media claiming a helicopter and automatic weapons fire were heard before the explosion, and also reports of another incident at the chateau the professors were apparently heading to, involving more gunfire.

Whatever was going on was serious, and dangerous. The *only* official reason he was here now was because the Pope had *suggested* it, otherwise he would have been content to remain at the Holy See and wait for word from Acton and Laura. He couldn't be involved in any official capacity. If the Vatican were caught interfering in private affairs in France, it could cause a diplomatic row. Even this flight was classified as an academic undertaking to investigate the discovery of a religious artifact, something that occurred at least several times a year, therefore nothing out of the ordinary that needed to be minded by the French authorities.

But if they went in and ended up in a gun battle...

He sighed.

This isn't smart.

Yet if his friends were in trouble, part of him did feel obligated to help. Though as Mario Giasson, not the Inspector General of the Holy See.

The stewardess approached. "We'll be landing in a few minutes. Please fasten your seatbelts."

Giasson nodded, tightening the lap belt, his time over for planning their next move.

Ridefort Residence

Saint-Pierre-la-Mer, France

Durand still couldn't believe what had happened. *All* of them had escaped. The tunnel he had discovered eventually split off into several others, fresh footprints found on the far side of the outer wall, the men long gone, transport probably arranged by the first to have escaped.

It was clever, the method they had used, and as he thought back upon it, the residents, not his men, had chosen to congregate near their secret exit. They had planned for this contingency all along.

Very clever.

He had put out a bulletin on them, but he had no doubt they would get away. This was a free country, and they weren't about to lock down the south of France to find eight men who had probably done nothing wrong beyond defending themselves. They hadn't yet found the body of whoever had been shot in the car—there was too much blood and brain matter for the victim to have survived. The car was registered to this address, so the residents likely hadn't shot their own man, and he had just received a report that bullet casings had been found several miles away along the road, a sustained gun battle apparently having occurred.

And a gun battle needed two participants.

The backend damage to the car suggested they had eventually been rammed, and residue from a busted taillight had been found just outside the gates to the chateau. His mind was quickly filling in what had happened, especially when luggage and travel documents belonging to two professors were found in the trunk.

It was his theory that the driver, their victim, had been sent to pick up the two professors. On the way back, they were ambushed, the driver shot. Blood patterns suggested the occupants had pulled the driver out of his seat and taken control. A gun battle ensued with the car eventually rammed from behind. The fuel would have been cut off, ending the pursuit, but it happened just before the gates.

And judging by the weapons cache his men had found a few minutes ago, those who lived here were armed to the teeth, and probably able to fight off whoever had pursued their chauffeured Maybach. All of which meant the men who resided here were likely innocent of any crime beyond lying to the police, hiding the body, and possessing illegal weapons. Still crimes, though nothing he was genuinely concerned about.

What did have him puzzled was why they wouldn't have called the police? A crime had occurred. A horrific crime. Yet they were covering it up. It was safe to assume that if anything else untoward had happened here, if the reports of gunfire and explosions within the walls were correct, that there was a second attack.

And if that were the case, it suggested to him that whoever the perpetrators were, they were after the passengers of the Maybach. Professors James Acton and Laura Palmer.

Who are you? Why do they want you dead?

He frowned. And was the explosion in the harbor last night related to all this? If the reports of the helicopter and automatic weapons fire before the explosion were accurate, then it had to be. This was a peaceful town. There was no way there would be two separate incidents involving heavy weapons fire and aerial assaults. They were definitely connected. But why? What was so important about these professors?

One of his officers jogged up to him, holding out a phone. "Sir, I have that call for you."

Durand took the phone. "Hello, Dean Milton?"

"Yes, how can I help you?"

"Monsieur, I'm Captain Durand of the National Police. I'm investigating an incident that occurred last night in Saint-Pierre-la-Mer. I'm not sure if you've heard of it—"

"I have."

Durand's eyebrows shot up slightly. "I take it you know of our town due to the fact one of your professors arrived here last night?"

"Yes. Please tell me you've found him. Is he all right? Are they all right?"

Durand's eyes narrowed as his heart rate picked up a few beats. "Tell me, Dean Milton. Why should they not be all right?"

Les Mouettes Restaurant

Saint-Pierre-la-Mer, France

Acton smiled as their lunches were brought to their table, a booth tucked in the back of the restaurant giving him a good view of the door, and quick access to the rear exit. He was feeling a little better, his appetite back with a vengeance, and he was eager to get some solid food into him, hopeful the calories might give him some of the stamina he feared he might need at any minute.

"Looks wonderful," smiled Laura at the waitress, Acton agreeing with an extended sniff.

"Smells good too."

He tackled it with gusto, Laura pacing herself slightly better. He was determined to not miss out on a bite, the delicious tastes and textures unfortunately mostly lost on him as he hoovered in the food while keeping a watchful eye on the door. He paused, fork in midair.

"What?"

Acton watched a man pass the windows lining the front of the restaurant, peering through the glass. Acton leaned out of sight, fairly confident he couldn't be seen by anyone outside in the bright sunlight, yet he wasn't willing to bet his life on it. "Someone's looking through the front window." He leaned back over slightly, his right eye just able to see part of the window, then a little more as he continued to chance it. He breathed a sigh of relief. "He's gone. Probably just looking for a place to eat."

"Probably."

They resumed their meal, Acton noting Laura had picked up her pace slightly, though still wasn't matching his prison-quality display. He was on edge, more so now than a moment before. It had been over half an hour, if not approaching an hour, since they had decided to hide in place. In the excitement, he had lost track of time, too much of it a blur of pain and panic.

Pierre Ridefort's people had found their hotel and their rental car, and were probably swarming the area. He had no idea how many they were up against, but it had to be a fairly significant number, perhaps a dozen or more—you didn't assault a well-defended castle with just half a dozen men.

And it had been more than twelve hours now. More people could have been brought in.

He growled slightly. "I wish we had a phone. I'm going crazy not knowing what's going on."

Laura agreed as she took a sip of her Pepsi Light. "I'll ask the waitress when she comes back if she knows where we can buy one. I'll go grab it while you stay here."

He shook his head. "I don't think we should split up."

She disagreed. "No, you'll slow me down. I can get there and back in a third of the time if I don't have to help you. Besides, I think we're—" She froze, her jaw dropping, her fork slowly lowering to the table as her right hand inched to her side.

"What—" He stopped as a man entered his peripheral vision on his right. A man with a hand in his pocket, there little doubt his jacket was happy to see them.

"Professors, you've given us quite the chase, but it's over."

Schmidt flicked his weapon slightly at Laura Palmer. "Uh-uh, Professor. Hands where I can see them."

Laura's hand returned to the table and Schmidt leaned forward slightly, smiling at the gun sitting on the bench beside her.

"I don't believe that belongs to you, Professor."

She said nothing, instead glaring at him. She continued to impress. Most would be terrified right now, and perhaps she was, simply hiding it remarkably well. He found himself strangely attracted to his adversary. She was beautiful—not Hollywood beautiful in an artificial way; more Jackie Kennedy beautiful. Naturally attractive without flaunting it. He had no doubt if she were dressed up for a Friday night on the town, she could stop traffic, but he had a feeling she wasn't the type. This woman liked to get her hands dirty, would never back down from a fight, and probably preferred jeans with a slice of pizza and a bottle of beer, rather than an evening gown with canapes and champagne.

He motioned toward Acton, feeling a little jealous. "Now, why don't you pay your bill and come with me."

Acton stared up at him. "Sorry, but I don't have any cash. Would you mind?"

Schmidt smiled slightly, why these two were a couple, clear. "Don't tempt fate, Professor."

Laura reached into a pocket, pulled out a 100 Euro note, and placed it on the table. "Let's go," she murmured, sounding defeated.

It raised alarm bells.

He stepped back then paused. "When you get up, I better see that gun sitting on the bench."

Laura frowned, a hand movement behind her suggesting she was returning the weapon to where he had last seen it.

I knew you weren't that easily defeated.

His admiration ticked up another notch. "To the back." They shuffled forward, Acton clearly in some discomfort, which would make his job a little easier. Exploiting a wound for pain was an effective torture technique, and it also prevented him from running too far or too fast.

He reached over and grabbed Joachim's gun, stuffing it in his other pocket, then followed them out the rear entrance and into the alleyway. "That's far enough."

They both stopped then turned to face him.

"Now, tell me what I want to know, and you'll live."

Acton stared at him, the picture of ignorant innocence. "What do you want to know?"

Schmidt smiled. "You know exactly what I want to know, Professor. Where is the True Cross?"

"The what? True Cross?"

"Yes."

Acton shrugged. "No idea what you're talking about."

Schmidt drew his weapon and aimed it directly at Laura's chest. Acton stepped in front of her. "Kill her, and you'll get nothing."

Schmidt chuckled. "Professor, I don't really care if I find the True Cross. It means nothing to me, but a lot to my employer. I get paid whether I find it for him or not. So don't think for a moment I won't hesitate to kill your wife."

"You'll have to kill us both."

Schmidt shook his head, enjoying an adversary with unexpected balls. "Professor, again you're mistaken. I'm going to kill *her*, not you. You'll have to live with the knowledge that you could have saved your wife by simply telling me where you hid some old piece of wood." He stepped slightly closer, though maintained enough distance that he could get a shot off should the injured man, favoring his side, make a move. "Now, Professor, ask yourself, is your wife's life worth less than some relic of the past?" He held up the gun slightly. "And if the answer is yes, I think you two should consider investing in marriage counseling. Or good divorce attorneys." He leaned over slightly to get a better view of Laura's face. "Then give me a call." He winked.

She gave him a look. "Don't flatter yourself."

He tossed his head back and laughed. "Oh, God, I like you." He flicked his gun at Acton. "You really are a very lucky man. Are we really still standing here having this conversation? How can there be any debate in your mind on what's the right thing to do here? Prove you love your wife"—his face became all business as he stretched his arm out, pointing his Glock 17 directly at Laura's head poking out from behind Acton's shoulder—"or she dies, right now."

Interpol Agent Hugh Reading entered the rather nondescript hotel, he was sure chosen by his missing friends for that very reason. He flashed his ID to the desk clerk, who appeared slightly rattled, his movements rapid and uncertain, his cheeks flushed and fingers struggling to hold a pen that incessantly tapped on a pad of paper in front of him.

"I'm Agent Reading, Interpol. I'm looking for two people, a Professor James Acton and his wife, Professor Laura Palmer." He brought up a photo of the two of them in his apartment last year, showing the man the picture. "Have you seen them?"

The clerk's eyes darted to the left and Reading looked. Elevators.

"Well?"

"N-no, I haven't."

Reading's eyes narrowed and he leaned in, his imposing frame dwarfing the little man behind the counter. "You don't sound too certain." He backed away slightly, swiping his thumb over his phone's screen, bringing up a photo from the same night with the three of them together, arms around each other, laughing. He showed it to the clerk. "They're friends of mine. *Good* friends. And they're in trouble. I'm here to help."

The clerk's eyes shot wide as he stared at the photo, then his shoulders slumped, visibly relieved. "They were here. Someone was after them, but they hid in the utility closet over there." He pointed to a stairwell to the left of the elevators. "The man following them left. I think he might still be out front."

Reading headed for the doors, peering through the glass as he searched the throngs of tourists. "What did he look like?"

"Umm, your height, slightly thinner, thirties, short blonde hair, dark tan. Dangerous."

Reading glanced at Spencer, also searching.

"What was he wearing?" asked his son, Reading smiling at the excellent question.

"Umm, I-I don't remember. Something dark, I think. I-I really don't remember, sorry."

Reading grunted, not seeing anyone who matched the description that appeared to be anything but what they were. He returned to the desk, Spencer remaining at the door. "Are my friends still here?"

The clerk shook his head. "No, they left. Maybe half an hour to an hour ago."

"Where did they go?"

"No idea, but I can show you which way they were heading."

Reading nodded. "Show me."

The clerk headed for the stairwell, then past the steps to a door at the back of the hotel. "They went out this way then to the right. From there, I have no idea." He paused. "Wait! I think they said they were going to the airport."

Reading pulled out his card and handed it to him. "If you see them or the man who was following them, call me."

"Yes, yes I will." The clerk beat a hasty retreat back to his desk as Reading pushed open the rear door and stepped into an alleyway. He looked to the right and his heart skipped a beat. He shoved a hand out, pushing Spencer back inside. He held a finger up to his lips and the boy nodded. Reading pointed down the alleyway and the boy's eyes bulged at the sight.

Acton and Laura were standing not one hundred paces away, hands slightly raised, with a man pointing a gun at them both.

A man with his back to Reading.

Acton stepped slightly closer to the man, moving to the side to block his shot. Somebody entered the alleyway behind their gunman, the door that swung open appearing to belong to the hotel they had been staying at. His heart pounded a little harder, wondering if he should call out for help, there little chance of their captor getting a shot off at the new arrival in time.

But he stopped.

Is that—?

It was, yet it couldn't be.

Reading.

He focused his eyes on the man holding the gun as Reading approached from behind.

You need to give him cover. Talk!

"You don't have to do this. I'll tell you what you want to know."

"I thought you might."

Reading picked up a glass bottle from a case put out for recycling.

284

"Where is it?"

Acton frowned. "Well, I don't know exactly where it is. I'd have to show you."

Reading was less than fifty paces away now. Laura sucked in a quick breath.

She sees him. Don't give him away!

"Bullshit. No games, Professor, or she dies."

"I mean it. I don't know this area. We pushed the crate through the water as it sank. I know where we came out on shore, and it's only a couple of hundred feet from there. I can show you, and you'll find it easily, but I have to see the beach."

Twenty paces.

"You expect me to believe you were able to relocate the crate, while it sank, underwater?"

Ten paces.

"We had scuba gear."

Reading stepped on something and it snapped, something insignificant, a stray plastic bottle cap perhaps. It didn't matter. The man spun toward the sound as Reading swung. The gun went off, a window shattering to their left as the bottle slammed into their abductor's forehead, breaking into dozens of pieces. He dropped in a heap and Acton stepped forward, pressing his foot down hard on the man's wrist as Laura rushed past him and grabbed the gun. Reading knelt down and checked for a pulse.

"Dad!"

Acton looked up to see Reading's son rush toward them from the hotel.

"Just stay there!" said Reading, holding up a hand. He searched the pockets, finding only a phone, a second gun confiscated from Laura earlier, and a money roll. Nothing that could identify their assailant. Reading rose, taking the gun from Laura, who appeared reluctant to give it up. "Any idea who he is?"

Acton shook his head, gripping his side as a sharp pain jolted his body. "None, but he works for Pierre Ridefort."

"The son of the man you were supposed to meet."

"Exactly."

"Okay, this guy's a pro, and probably has friends. Let's get the two of you to safety. I've got a car out front."

"I think they've got eyes on the hotel."

Reading frowned for a moment, then reached into his pocket. He tossed a set of keys to his son. "Bring the car around."

Spencer grinned then sprinted back toward the hotel. Reading glanced at his friends. "They don't know who we are, so he's safe." His phone vibrated in his pocket and he fished it out. He held it up so they could see the display.

Milton, Greg.

"Put it on speaker," said Acton as they huddled closer. Reading swiped his thumb then tapped the speaker icon.

"Greg, this is Hugh. I've got them."

Acton grinned at the phone. "Hey, buddy!"

"Hi, Greg!" waved Laura.

A sighed burst of static erupted from the phone. "Oh thank God! You've had us worried sick. Are you guys okay?"

Acton shrugged. "I've got another heroic wound, but we're okay."

"Are you safe? I mean, where are you?"

Reading held the phone closer to his mouth. "We're not secure yet. We're waiting for our car, then will be leaving shortly."

"Okay, where will you be going?"

"I'm not sure. Right now I just want to get out of town, then we'll regroup."

"Well, I have a thought on that. I just talked to a Captain Durand of the French National Police. He's at your chateau, investigating what's going on. He's urged me to have you turn yourselves in."

Laura exchanged a look with Acton then leaned in. "I have no problem with that, but I don't think this town is safe. Our driver was taken out by a sniper, and he's probably still out there. I think we'd be safer to get on a plane for home, then talk to the authorities from there."

Acton held out a hand, gripping Laura's shoulder as an idea took hold. "Wait a minute. You said he's at the chateau?"

"Yes."

He smiled. "That's maybe ten minutes from here. And with the police already there, I'd say it's probably the safest place to be right now."

Reading grunted. "Anything's better than this alleyway." He pointed to the far end, Spencer nudging the nose of the car in, waving. "Let's get our arses out of here and discuss it in the car."

287

Schmidt kept his eyes shut and his breathing steady as he came to, the phone conversation occurring nearby too important to risk ending. Besides, he was outnumbered three to one, and they had all the guns. When he was in the military, he never had any intention of dying for his country, and he certainly had no intention of dying for his client. But these idiots were giving him everything he needed.

A destination.

The chateau. He had to admit, it was probably the best place they could go right now. It had high walls, was defensible from a ground assault, and if he weren't listening to their decision-making process right now, he'd never have guessed to search for them there.

He remained lying in the filth as they passed him, the wounded Acton slowing them down. As their footfalls faded, he risked opening his eyes slightly, and got a good look at the car they climbed in, a mid-sized green Peugeot. The car pulled back onto the road, several horns blaring at them, then disappeared.

Schmidt rolled to his feet and activated his comm. "All units report to rendezvous point Charlie. I want both choppers ready in ten minutes. Prepare for another aerial assault. Out."

Reading slammed his door shut. "This is my son, Spencer. We'll handle the introductions on the way. Let's just get out of here."

Spencer tossed a wave to the back seat as he pulled into traffic. "Hey, Professors, nice to meet you."

Laura reached forward and squeezed Spencer's shoulder. "Nice to finally meet you too, Spencer."

"Where are we headed?" asked the boy, tossing a grin at them over his shoulder.

Reading looked back from the passenger seat, Acton gripping his side. "Are you okay?"

Acton nodded unconvincingly. "I will be. Let's just get to that damned castle. They can call me an ambulance there."

Reading frowned. He wasn't thrilled about the idea of going to the chateau, but it did make sense. There would be a heavy police presence, and in France, that meant guns. There was no pussyfooting around with the police here. They were all armed, quite often to the teeth. And Acton was right. Medical personnel would already be there, or could be summoned quickly.

Acton pulled away his hand, blood visible. "I think I tore my stitches."

Laura leaned over him to look at the bandage. "I think you're right." She turned toward Reading. "Let's get to the chateau, now."

Reading nodded then his eyes narrowed. "How the hell do we get there?"

Laura leaned forward and pointed out the front windshield at a hilltop to the northeast, a castle sitting in plain sight. "Just aim at that."

Spencer grinned. "No problem. I'll have us there in no time."

Ridefort Residence

Saint-Pierre-la-Mer, France

Captain Durand stared at the impressive array of weapons one of his officers had discovered. Dozens upon dozens of machine guns, submachine guns, handguns, grenades, flash-bangs, knives and more, along with body armor, night vision goggles, and every other piece of equipment a modern army required. He shuddered to think what could happen if a cache like this fell into the hands of Islamic terrorists.

He had little doubt these men weren't crazed zealots out to destroy Western civilization, yet that didn't justify them possessing these illegal weapons. They had obviously been acquired on the black market, and from what they were discovering, they had an apparent need for them.

A crypt had been uncovered earlier with half a dozen bodies, including one with a head shot, dressed as a chauffeur. Something had happened here last night, something big, and the residents of this medieval maze of secret chambers and twisting corridors, had done a remarkable job of covering it up.

If they had just left the horses in their stalls.

If it weren't for that one mistake, that one step too far, he never would have thought to look at the floor.

"Captain, those two professors just showed up, along with an Interpol agent."

Durand's eyes narrowed. "Interpol?"

What the hell are they doing here?

"I'll be up in a minute." He stared at a recently discovered lockbox cut open earlier, dozens of fake passports and IDs inside. Whoever lived here had the ability to disappear without a trace, and no matter what they found here over the coming days, it was unlikely any of them would be brought to justice.

Earlier, he had been willing to forgive some of their transgressions, self-defense providing some excuse. But these fake IDs changed everything. Only criminals had fake IDs. Though the weapons cache was illegal, it at least could be explained away as necessary for self-defense—and whatever had happened here certainly suggested they had the need. But the IDs were too much. It redefined who they were.

Yet despite his anger, his rage at their escape, he'd exchange their capture for answers.

Real answers.

What is this all about?

He inhaled deeply, then headed for the courtyard, hoping he might be about to finally get some.

Acton lay on a stretcher, two medical personnel tending to his wound, both again insisting he go to a hospital, and again he refused. "Not until I know everyone is safe."

"You'll be safe at the hospital, I promise you."

Acton shook his head. "No, I won't. These are pros. You don't think they're watching the hospitals? Right now they could have a sniper in position, ready to take any of us out."

Both of them paused their work, glancing about.

"I doubt that, Jim," said Reading as he stepped over. "We're too high, and so are the walls." He raised a finger, cutting off one of the paramedics. "But, leave these walls, and you'll be exposed."

The paramedic frowned, checking Acton's vitals once again as the other finished hooking up an IV.

"I'm Captain Durand, in charge of the investigation. And you are?"

Acton turned his head to see a new arrival, prim and proper as good a description as any to describe the man.

"Agent Hugh Reading, Interpol." Reading stepped forward and extended a hand. "I'm here in an unofficial capacity. These are friends of mine. I understand you're interested in talking to them. Professor James Acton"—Acton raised a hand in a half wave—"and Professor Laura Palmer." Laura leaned forward and shook Durand's hand.

"Well, professors, do you care to explain to me what happened here last night?"

Acton nodded toward Laura, too tired to bother. He just wanted to recover the True Cross and get out of Dodge. And into his own bed back home.

"Well, Captain, we were invited here by Jacques Ridefort, under the pretense that he was going to provide us with information proving who the four Templar Knights were buried under the Vatican."

"That business with the Koran and the Muslims a few years ago?"

"Exactly. On our way here from the airport, we were attacked. Our driver was killed, and we barely escaped with our lives, saved by the men in this very chateau. We then met our host and were shown a room with a relic he claimed had been protected by his family for some time, when they fell under attack. He claimed it was his son. Pierre, I believe he said his name was—"

"Yes, Pierre. I'm familiar with him. A bit of a troublemaker, but harmless."

"Well, last night he graduated from troublemaker to murderer."

Durand frowned. "I must admit I have a hard time believing that. We had reports of helicopters, automatic weapons fire, explosions. Where would Pierre Ridefort get access to such things?"

Laura shrugged. "Money can't buy happiness, but it can buy weapons. We've been pursued by several men all day, and I'm guessing they're not locals. I would assume he hired outside help."

Reading grunted. "Mercenaries."

Durand sighed. "Wonderful. That's all we need. Men with no morals and machine guns, during tourist season." He glanced at Acton, then back at Laura. "So, why do they want you two?"

"They think we have something they want."

"And what is that?"

The thunder of chopper blades suddenly filled the courtyard and gunfire erupted. The police scattered and Reading grabbed his son, shielding him as best he could. Durand ran for the side of the ambulance as Acton struggled to get off the buffet tray he was lying on. Laura shoved him back down and pushed the gurney toward the entrance of the chateau where they had met Jacques Ridefort the night before.

Someone cried out and Acton spun his head to see an officer drop, writhing in agony. Spencer ran toward him and grabbed him, hauling him behind a police vehicle before scrambling back to retrieve the man's weapon. A second chopper appeared over the opposite wall, and Spencer sprinted after his father. Acton heard the crackle of service weapons returning fire, but it was disorganized and ineffective, as two sets of heavy machine guns rained lead on the courtyard.

Laura yelped, jerking the gurney to a halt as the cobblestone was torn apart just in front of them. Acton felt a surge, and tilted his head back to see Reading shoving the gurney toward the doors, Spencer grabbing Laura and shielding her as best he could.

He's his father's son, all right.

As they cleared the doors, he caught a glimpse of Durand, on his radio, crouched behind the ambulance as bullets tore it apart.

"We need backup, now!" shouted Durand into his radio. "And we need air support. *Military* air support. We have two choppers attacking our position!"

The gunfire let up for a moment, at least from one of the choppers, and he took the opportunity to peek out from behind the shredded ambulance. Men were rappelling down, and once on the ground, they didn't stand a chance, not with their weapons.

A thought dawned on him.

He took one glance at the other chopper, still firing, as it banked for another pass. "Get to the weapons cache!" he shouted as he sprinted toward the gaping hole of the secret chamber. Gunfire tore at the ground and he dove, sliding on the hay-strewn floor, gasping as he fell into the pit, slamming hard into the roof of the Maybach then falling unceremoniously onto the floor.

He lay for a moment, groaning in agony, then shoved himself to his feet as two more officers dove into the hole, one crying out, something snapping with the impact. Durand ignored him, instead sprinting down the corridor toward the illegal weapons that might just save their lives.

He entered the room, soon followed by several more of his men, and geared up. He loaded an FN P90 and flicked off the safety, then turned to the others who had made it.

"Kill anything that has a gun and isn't in uniform."

Mario Giasson rolled down the window of their diplomatic vehicle and poked his head outside. "What in the name of God is that?" He pointed, the others in the security detail leaning over to see what had caught his attention. To their left, atop a hill with the chateau the Actons had apparently had their altercation in last night, two helicopters were circling the ramparts, muzzle flashes evident even from this distance, the echoes of gunfire reaching his ears.

He pulled out his phone and dialed Reading's number. The phone went directly to voicemail. He cursed as he stared at the battle raging only a few miles away. He knew the professors too well to know they weren't mixed up in this. His reports had indicated that the police were now in control of the chateau, which meant it was fellow officers that were under attack by what appeared to be overwhelming forces.

They had to help.

It was a matter of duty, of honor.

And it was the right thing to do.

"We need to get in there, now!"

The driver looked back at him in his rearview mirror. "Are you kidding? We're barely armed, and this is a diplomatic mission."

Giasson growled in frustration, the driver correct. This was technically none of their business, yet he was also certain it had everything to do with the business at hand.

And he was powerless to stop it.

They couldn't intervene, and even if they could, what could they possibly do? His security detail had a few handguns with a handful of magazines, and if they were to fire them in anything other than self-defense, it could cause an international incident. And if that castle atop the hill was under attack by two armed helicopters, they wouldn't last a minute in that fight.

He slammed his fist against the headrest in front of him, then tried the new number he had for the Actons, receiving an offline message. He punched the headrest again. "Why is everyone's cellphone turned off when we're in the middle of a crisis!"

Reading covered their escape, turning to watch as half a dozen hostiles hit the ground at the far end of the courtyard, spraying a steady stream of lead as they descended. The second chopper continued to provide cover, most of the remaining police hiding behind columns, or simply cowering behind the handful of police vehicles strewn about the area. He noticed several running toward what appeared to be stables, the ass end of a horse visible. One was mowed down, two others oddly disappearing from sight.

He took aim at the black-clad group systematically making their way through the courtyard, but thought better of it. They had two guns, and only the bullets in them.

And it would draw attention to their position.

He stepped back into the shadows, closing the door, Spencer flipping a large, heavy drawbar in place, something left over from medieval times.

Reading frowned. "I doubt that's going to hold them for long."

"Come on! Hurry!"

Reading turned to see Laura pushing the gurney down a long hallway, dimly lit with ornate sconces at regular intervals, dozens of suits of armor visible. He jogged after her, Spencer following. "Where are you going?"

"There's a secret room. I'm sure they don't know about it."

"And you do?"

She rounded a corner with confidence. "We were shown it last night. There's an escape tunnel in it."

Reading followed her around the corner, urging Spencer to keep up. "Let's hope they don't know where the other end of it is."

Laura glanced over her shoulder, frowning. "Hugh, really? Must we always be the pessimist?"

He scowled. "It's in my nature."

Durand climbed up the ladder, the three officers gathered below, their weapons aimed at the opening overhead. He poked his head above ground level, taking a quick look, then dropped back down. He could see the bodies of several of his men lying in the courtyard, and spotted at least two hostiles heading toward their position.

They must have seen us coming in here.

He readied his weapon, then took two steps up, clearing the lip of the floor. He took aim and squeezed the trigger, a short burst erupting from the machine gun, hammering at his shoulder, the sensation something he hadn't felt since training.

This was not his area of expertise.

Proven by the fact he missed, the wall to the right of his target torn apart as the weapon jerked up and to the right. And, unfortunately, he had revealed his position, gunfire spraying the wall behind him. He ducked as a second ladder slapped against the rim beside him, another officer rushing up, opening fire as he cleared the edge. The bravado delivered a boost of confidence to Durand's system, and he rose, spraying gunfire left to right, unconcerned with his aim, instead providing what he thought the movies called suppression fire. Two hostiles dropped, but one got up moments later, their body armor apparently effective.

"You go, I'll cover you," said the officer.

Durand nodded and the young officer opened fire again. Durand cleared the final few rungs then rolled to the side, putting the thick stone wall of the stable between him and the hostiles. Immediately his position on the ladder was taken by another, and between the two of them, they delivered a sustained barrage, allowing everyone to get clear.

We might just win this thing!

He poked his head out to see another half-dozen hostiles dropping from the second chopper.

Merde.

Giasson pointed at a string of police cars, sirens blaring, lights flashing. "Follow them!"

"But, sir!"

"Follow them, that's an order!"

"Yes, sir."

Giasson motioned to Alfredo Ianuzzi. "Give me your weapon."

Ianuzzi frowned but complied, handing him his handgun and three magazines.

"When we get there, I'll go in. You guys stay outside."

"Sir, we're here to protect *you*. Where you go, we go."

Giasson shook his head then grabbed the handhold as the driver took a hard left onto a winding road that appeared to lead up the hillside and toward the danger. "No, if something goes wrong, I'll be the one to blame, not you guys. I can't ask you to go in there. These are *my* friends, not yours."

Ianuzzi looked at him. "Sir, I know them too, and God knows they've gone above and beyond for us before. It's my duty, as a man of God, to help those in need." He drew a second weapon from an ankle holster. "I'm coming with you."

Giasson shook his head, smiling. "You're an insubordinate bastard. Remind me to fire you when we get back home."

Ianuzzi grinned. "I make no promises."

Schmidt dropped to the ground as part of the second wave, and headed for the main entrance. His targets had disappeared through the doors only moments before, and he had a feeling he knew exactly where they were going. The room with the hidden chamber.

Little do they know, I know exactly where it is.

He raced toward the closed doors, pouring a steady stream of lead at the center of them, shattering any lock that might have been holding them back. He slammed into it hard, the wood splintering but holding. He stepped back and fired some more, two of his men joining in, the other three covering their position. He shoved again, and this time it gave.

Gunfire continued from the stable, the police making an effective stand, his men keeping them pinned down where they were essentially harmless to the mission. He frowned as he spotted another go down. He pointed at the three covering their position. "Go give them a hand. When I give the signal, fall back to this position. We'll egress as planned through their own escape tunnel."

"Yes, sir."

The three men broke off, hugging the wall as they headed toward the only resistance left in the courtyard, both choppers now hammering the stable with heavy fire.

Just a little bit longer.

Acton gripped the sides of the gurney for dear life, as Laura navigated the corridors from memory, finally reaching the outer room leading to the secret treasure room.

"Hugh!"

Reading jumped ahead, opening the doors, and Laura shoved the gurney through. He slammed the doors shut behind them as Laura rushed over to the pedestal they had seen Jacques Ridefort's attendant push the night before. She shoved it toward the window.

And it didn't budge.

Acton pushed up on his elbows. "What the hell?"

Laura tried again, harder this time, and still nothing. She turned to Acton. "This was it, wasn't it?"

He nodded. "Absolutely."

She pushed again, gentler this time, and again nothing. "What the bloody hell is wrong with this thing!"

Reading rushed over and leaned into it to no avail.

"He must have done something else before he pushed it. Try turning the bust or something," suggested Acton.

Laura grabbed the head of Jacques de Molay, and gave it a twist. Nothing. She turned toward Acton. "What are we going to do?"

Acton struggled to his feet. "We fight."

Reading spun, his eyes scanning the room. "Where's Spencer?"

Giasson threw open the door as the car came to a halt behind one of the police vehicles. Gunfire filled the air, the smell of gunpowder

301

distinct and strong. Helicopter rotors pounded the area, and one of them banked toward their position, firing at the new arrivals from a side-mounted machine gun.

Giasson took cover with the others. A hail of gunfire responded from the ground, raining bullets on the helicopter. It banked away to protect those exposed by the open side door, giving Giasson the opportunity to capitalize on the confusion, rushing past the dozens of armed officers and toward the open gates, Ianuzzi on his heels along with the rest of his detail.

He rounded the corner, peering into a large courtyard as other officers rushed past them, their mere presence apparently enough to make the officers think Giasson and his team belonged there.

This is idiotic!

Almost a dozen hostiles were firing at the far end. Bodies riddled the courtyard, mostly police, some alive, most still. Giasson scanned the area for any sign of his friends, but saw nothing, the only thing of interest a set of large doors, shredded by weapons fire.

Somebody wanted in there.

He pointed. "We need to get to those doors." He stepped into the courtyard, then someone grabbed him from behind, hauling him backward.

"Who the hell are you?"

Weapons were aimed at them, and Giasson raised his hands. "Would you believe I'm Inspector General Mario Giasson from the Vatican?"

The officer motioned toward them, and he was grabbed by both arms, along with his detail, and led away from the fight. He glanced over his shoulder at the man. "You need to get through those doors. Something's going on inside!"

The man dismissed his words with the bat of a hand, and Giasson cursed.

God, please take care of them.

Captain Durand hugged the wall, as did the others. The firepower directed at them was overwhelming, and there was no way they would defeat their enemy, not alone. He could hear the sirens outside, reinforcements arriving, but the helicopters pounding the stables had redirected their attention to his comrades outside the gates.

Another horse cried out and collapsed as it was hit by a stray bullet, three of the creatures now dead or dying, each one enraging him even more. He hoped these bastards they were fighting weren't intentionally targeting the animals, because if he thought they were, when his people finally did win the day, he might just walk out of here and place a bullet in each of the bastards' heads.

He stole a quick glance, then stuck his weapon around the corner, firing blindly, a few of the hostiles having closed the distance.

"Why haven't they just used grenades?" asked one of his men.

Durand shook his head. "They're after someone. They must not know where they are."

He frowned.

Once they do know, we're dead.

303

Schmidt reached the door Pierre Ridefort had led him to last night, and tried the handle. Locked. He motioned toward the lock and one of his men placed a small charge. Schmidt turned away and the device detonated, blasting the door open. He tossed a flash-bang inside as a flurry of rounds slammed into the wall behind him. The grenade detonated and several people cried out.

One of his men surged forward and three shots rang out, all nailing him square in the chest. He fell backward, collapsing on the floor, gasping for breath, several ribs probably broken. Schmidt cursed and grabbed him by the vest, hauling him out of the line of fire.

"Professors, I know you're in there. All I want is the cross."

"Go to hell!"

He smiled. It was Acton. He activated his comm. "We have them." He returned his attention to his targets. "Just tell me where it is, and this is all over."

"Forget it. You'll kill us anyway."

Schmidt's mind was racing. Why were they still there? If he were in their situation, he would have used the secret exit from last night. Why would they have stayed in there? He knew that a simple push of the pedestal opened the secret chamber, and from there, an escape tunnel led to the water below. Why sit and wait for him to arrive with far more firepower than they had?

His eyes narrowed. "Professor, can I ask you a question?"

"Sure, I've got time."

Schmidt smiled. "Is your escape not going to plan?"

There was no reply, which confirmed his suspicions. These Templars had sealed off the escape route, which meant he and his men were trapped inside as well.

Not good.

Though he knew there was a secret chamber on the other side of the wall, and he had explosives. Blow the wall, get to the other side and through the tunnel.

Problem solved.

But he had to get through *this* door first.

"I'm assuming your silence means the escape route through the secret room isn't working. That means you're trapped in that room, Professor. Tell me what I want to know, and I promise I'll let you go."

"And why should I believe you?"

"Because I'm not some nutbar, Professor. I'm a contractor. I have a job to do, and that's to recover the True Cross for my client."

"That didn't stop you from trying to kill us yesterday."

Schmidt closed his eyes, leaning his head against the cool stone wall. "That's because we were trying to prevent the meeting. Once the meeting happened, and we knew you had the cross, our mission changed. Now all our client wants is for you to give up its location, and then you're free to go."

There was a laugh. "Right, and leave us as witnesses. Your client, Pierre, knows we know he's behind this."

Schmidt pulled a grenade from his belt. "Professor, I'm not sure if you're aware of what's going on outside, but half the damned French police force is here. They already know Pierre Ridefort is behind this."

Off the coast of Saint-Pierre-la-Mer, France

Pierre sat in the boat, watching the assault unfold through binoculars. It was exhilarating and heartbreaking at the same time. He had just heard the radio transmission that Schmidt had captured the professors, so they would soon know the location of the True Cross, and all of this would be over.

Yet he had to stifle tears at seeing his home attacked so violently. The only comfort he took was that an overheard police report suggested those he had grown up with had escaped before the assault began.

He didn't want them dead, none of them.

When his father finally died, and he had the True Cross in his possession, he would welcome every one of them back into the fold, should they pledge their allegiance to him. He would need them all to carry on the duty handed down for so long.

He sighed, wiping away a stray tear. "Should we head to the rendezvous point?"

Schmidt's man nodded and fired up the engines, turning the boat back toward the hidden dock under the hill the chateau sat atop. Schmidt and his men were supposed to use the escape tunnel, though from the sounds of the battle overhead, he wasn't sure how many they would be actually meeting, the police apparently putting up a good fight.

We may reunite as a family, but we'll definitely need a new home.

Ridefort Residence

Saint-Pierre-la-Mer, France

Acton looked at the others. "If the police are here, then we just need to hold out a little longer until they reach us."

Reading shook his head. "There were two choppers out there providing cover. Until the police take them out of the equation, they're not getting in here. And that assumes they know we're in here. We might not be found until they mop up."

Laura pushed on the pedestal again, Acton smiling at her wishful thinking. She looked at him. "We can't fight them off. I've got three bullets left."

Acton nodded. "I've got four, I think. They're coming in here one way or the other." He glanced at Reading. "I don't think we've got a choice." Something bounced on the floor and Acton gasped as a small black orb rolled toward them. "Grenade!"

He grabbed for Laura but she was already surging forward. She kicked the grenade like Beckham, sending it back through the door as Reading clotheslined Acton to the ground, his free arm reaching for Laura. He caught the back of her shirt as he dropped to the floor, dragging her with him.

The explosion was deafening, cries of agony filling the hall as shrapnel spread in all directions. Laura cried out just as she hit the ground, Acton gasping for breath as he slammed onto the stone, his wound tearing open even more. The pain was overwhelming, but he pushed through it, scrambling around to check on Laura. She was lying on her back, across Reading's, and he breathed a sigh of relief as she looked at him, alive.

Then he saw the blood.

And the jagged piece of stone lodged in her neck.

Durand's eyes widened as a grenade rolled into the room then dropped into the pit, the explosion tearing apart the Maybach below. Something had changed, their lives now forfeit.

They must have found the professors.

Their only hope was the tunnels below. He pointed into the pit. "Everybody down below, now!" He leaned out slightly from the wall, spraying bullets in all directions as his men leaped to safety, one at a time. He saw a grenade sailing through the air and turned his weapon on it, there no time to jump, and no point—it was going where he wanted to go.

He got lucky.

The grenade erupted into a fireball in midair, blasting shrapnel back at his attackers, and toward him. He was blown off his feet, and something tore at his shoulder, but it was something else that held his attention. A massive explosion ripped through the sky, just visible through the doorway, one of the choppers now a ball of flame that seemed to slowly collapse to the ground. A jet engine shook the area as he dragged himself back to the wall he had been hiding behind, risking a look outside and smiling at the sight of the French Air Force arriving on the scene.

We might just get out of this after all.

He glanced at his shoulder then gasped. He was riddled with wounds, the blood rapidly spreading through his clothes.

Maybe not all of us.

Spencer pressed his back against the wall, burying himself in the shadows as two men, all in black, surged past him, machine guns held high as they headed hopefully toward wherever his father and the professors had ended up.

He had been a bloody fool. When he had heard the sounds of the door being shot apart, he had turned back to take a look, hoping to see how many hostiles they were facing so that he could give his dad better information to work with. Part of him had even thought he might play the hero and shoot them before they could get inside, but the heavy, sustained gunfire, and the sight of weapons far bigger than his, had put those thoughts to bed almost immediately.

Though he did get his intel.

There were three.

Yet when he had tried to find his father, he couldn't. But their attackers had no doubt as to where they were heading, running toward him without hesitation. He had spotted an alcove behind a suit of armor, and squeezed inside as they rushed past, his eyes shut as his heart slammed against his ribcage.

And now it was happening all over again. And this time he had to bollocks up and get into the action. He slipped out from behind the statue and followed, praying they didn't hear him, and wondering just what the bloody hell he'd do when he found them.

Schmidt pushed himself with his elbows away from the doorway. His leg was severely wounded, though luckily one of his men had caught the brunt of the blast. He was dead, the other gasping for breath, a football-sized hole in his chest that had him rapidly bleeding out. He'd be done in seconds.

What the hell had just happened, he had no idea, but his grenade had bounced back, which should have been impossible. It was why you didn't whip a grenade inside a room like this—it could hit something and come back at you. A gentle toss was all that was needed.

Someone must have kicked it back.

And my money's on Palmer.

A smile spread across his face as he thought of her.

My kind of woman.

He glanced at his shredded leg.

If you're gonna be taken out, it might as well be by a beautiful woman.

He propped himself up against the wall, the pain subsiding as soon as he stopped dragging the damned thing. "Professor, are you all okay in there?"

"Peachy. You?"

Something was wrong. Acton's voice had changed, his stress level high. "Please tell me your lovely wife is okay."

Acton's voice cracked. "No, you bastard, she's not!"

Schmidt genuinely felt bad at the news, his chest tightening slightly. "Is she dead?"

There was no response. He reached into one of his pockets and pulled out an emergency medical kit. He leaned over and tossed it into the room. "Here, this might help." He heard noises as someone grabbed it. Schmidt's upper body collapsed on the floor, too weak to sit back up.

Lovely.

Footfalls echoed to his right, and he forced himself back to a sitting position, holding his MG4 as high as he could. He dropped it to the ground with relief as two of his men appeared.

"What the hell happened?"

Schmidt was growing weaker. "Grenade." He motioned toward the door. "They're still inside. We're trapped. Need to blow the wall to get to the secret chamber."

"What about them?"

"Kill them."

Spencer clasped a hand over his mouth as he heard the order. He had no choice. He had to act. He checked the weapon the wounded police officer had dropped, confirming the safety was off, then squeezed his eyes shut and took a deep breath, holding it.

What would Dad do?

He smiled.

He'd keep firing until they were dead.

He opened his eyes and slowly exhaled, wishing he had a pint for courage right now. He stepped around the corner, weapon raised, clasped tightly in both hands as he took aim. The two new arrivals were standing with their backs to him, unaware they were about to die.

He squeezed the trigger, and kept squeezing, trying to remember to keep his eyes open. The first bullet hit one of them square in the back, but the next several missed, his aim lost after the first kickback. The second spun toward him as he re-aimed, and a lump formed in his throat as he realized he was about to die. He kept firing, moving his hands slightly to the left and right, then as a muzzle flash from his opponent lit up the dim hallway, one of his bullets finally found its mark, nailing him in the chest. He fell backward into the doorway, still alive.

Acton and Reading both shielded Laura with their bodies, careful to not touch the long sliver of stone embedded under her chin. Someone was firing at the newly arrived hostiles outside the door, and Acton said a silent prayer of thanks to the French police.

Suddenly the gunfire stopped, then one single shot fired, inside the room, causing him to flinch. He searched for where the sound came from and found Laura's right hand gripping a weapon, pointing at the door, the barrel smoking. He looked where she was aiming and saw one of the hostiles lying in the doorway, the upper half of his body inside the room, a fresh hole in the top of his head.

Acton took the gun and jumped to his feet, rushing toward the door as he gripped his side. Another hostile was on the ground, the wind knocked out of him. He reached for his weapon and Acton put a single bullet in his skull. Somebody groaned to his right and he spun, aiming his gun at the man who had captured them at the restaurant.

"Professor Acton?"

Acton spun toward the voice, his weapon raised, then sighed, returning his aim to the lone survivor. "Spencer, thank God! Where have you been?"

"Umm, lost? Is my dad okay?"

"In here, son!"

Spencer grinned at Acton then rushed past him and into the room. A relieved reunion took place inside as Acton disarmed the man then made sure everyone else was dead. He checked the man's wound. "Looks bad."

"It *is* bad."

Acton frowned, then pulled a belt off one of the dead bodies. He wrapped it around the top of the leg and tightened the makeshift tourniquet. "You *might* live."

"Thanks." The man looked at him. "It was never personal."

Acton frowned. "That's what makes it worse. You did it for money. Most people that try to kill me, do it for something they believe in."

The man's eyes narrowed. "Who the hell are you people?"

Acton chuckled. "An American and two Brits who don't take shit from no one."

Giasson sat in the back of a police van with the rest of his detail, unceremoniously handcuffed, two police officers with submachine guns keeping a close eye on them. His discomfort was forgotten as he watched the surviving helicopter bank away, making a run for the water as the two jets turned hard for another pass. A missile streaked from one of their wings, quickly closing the distance with the chopper. It tried to evade the missile uselessly, the rocket slamming into the hot tail rotor, the fuel igniting, the helicopter erupting then dropping into the sea below.

A round of cheers erupted from the police surrounding them, at the mercy of the two craft only minutes before.

"Let's get in there!" cried someone, and the two long lines of men, one on either side of the gates, surged through, weapons blazing revenge on those inside. Giasson closed his eyes and said another silent prayer for his friends, the risk of getting caught in the crossfire increasing with every moment.

Off the coast of Saint-Pierre-la-Mer, France

Bernard Ridefort stood in their boat, the waves gently rocking them, as they all watched the battle rage in their former home. He sighed with relief as the second helicopter was downed by the Air Force, and watched as a stream of police officers cleared the front gates. He bore them no ill will whatsoever, the police having done nothing wrong, even those who had held them at gunpoint earlier.

They were just doing their job.

As was his family.

What had transpired was all Pierre's fault, and he was determined to make the boy pay if they should ever find him. But time was limited. For now, while his brother Jacques was still alive, Pierre was a traitor to the Order, and could be killed for those crimes. Though should his father die first, Pierre automatically inherited, despite his crimes, and it would create a schism within those few who remained, for he had no intention of ever swearing an oath of allegiance to Grand Master Pierre Ridefort.

"Father, look."

He lowered his binoculars and stared toward where his son was pointing, a boat approaching from the southwest.

"Isn't that one of ours?"

Bernard peered through his binoculars and his heart leaped as a smile spread across his face.

Pierre!

Someone he didn't recognize was piloting the craft, but Pierre was sitting in the back, appearing rather smug. Bernard hit the speed dial on his phone, placing it to his ear.

"Allô?"

"Do you see the boat approaching us from the south?"

There was a pause as his lookout on the shore sought the target. "Got it. Is that who I think it is?"

"Yes. Can you make the shot?"

"Yes."

Bernard closed his eyes for a moment as the debate raged within. This was his nephew. He loved the boy. His brother still loved him, despite the hatred displayed by his son over the past several years. But he had betrayed the Order, had betrayed his family, and had betrayed his father.

He opened his eyes and focused on Pierre through the binoculars. "Take the shot."

He ended the call and shoved the phone in his pocket as he continued to watch. Pierre jerked, then slumped in his seat.

And Bernard felt sick.

Ridefort Residence

Saint-Pierre-la-Mer, France

Acton rushed back to Laura's side, Spencer kneeling behind her head, holding it in place. The blood continued to ooze slightly, though there didn't appear to be much, Reading having wiped it clear with some gauze from the med kit.

"Is she okay?"

Reading nodded, staring down at his friend. "She's going to be fine, right?"

Laura's eyes focused on Reading. "Stop asking me questions I have to answer 'yes' to. The temptation to nod is almost overwhelming."

Reading laughed, and a smile spread across Acton's face. "How about we take a closer look at that. I'm a surgeon, you know."

Laura's eyes moved to her husband. "Just because you pulled a piece of wood out of your side against medical advice, doesn't mean you're licensed to operate."

He knelt down beside her, gripping his side, the pain temporarily forgotten with the adrenaline rush of the attack over just moments ago. He leaned in and examined the wound. "I think the shard nicked your neck then embedded itself under your chin as you fell backward. Does it hurt?"

"Not at all, actually."

"And you don't taste any blood?"

"No."

"You're not thinking of doing what I think, are you?"

Acton grinned at Reading. "If it were you, I'd yank the thing out in a heartbeat, but this is the woman I love."

"Glad to know where I stand."

Acton eyed him. "You're a handsome man, but you'll always be at least one rung lower."

Reading grunted, Spencer grinning at the exchange.

"Nooo, what I'm proposing is that it's perfectly safe to move her. I say we get her on the gurney and get her out of here."

Reading looked at Laura. "What do you think?"

"If it stops the bloody questions, then let's do it."

Acton rose then gasped, falling back to one knee. Laura sat up, reaching out for him, and the shard in her neck fell onto her blouse. Reading reached out and pinched it between his fingers, holding it up.

"I guess that settles that."

Laura felt for the hole it had left, now bleeding slowly, and pressed on it. "I guess it does. Let's get him onto the gurney. He needs it a hell of a lot more than me."

Acton was in no position to argue, the pain threatening to overwhelm him as he grew weaker. Reading and Spencer lifted him by the legs and shoulders, as Laura held the gurney in place. They gently lowered him, then Laura grabbed the compression bandage from the med kit, placing it over his wound. "Let's get the hell out of here. He needs medical attention."

Reading cocked an ear, Acton hearing it too. The dull thuds they had been feeling the entire time were fading, though hadn't yet stopped. There was still a battle raging outside, so where they were this very moment might be the safest place to stay.

Acton looked at Spencer then Reading. "It's too dangerous. Let's stay here until that"—he pointed at the doorway—"stops."

Reading frowned, glancing at his son then at Laura, who said nothing, leaving the decision to him. "I'll go see what's happening," he finally said. "You stay here."

Spencer followed him to the door. "I'm coming with you."

Reading shook his head. "No, it's not safe."

"But—!"

Reading put a hand on his shoulder, pointing at the dead piled outside their door. "You already saved us once, now it's time to keep being smart. Take one of their weapons and guard this door."

Spencer nodded. "You can count on me, Dad."

Reading slapped him on the back. "You're going to make a fine copper."

Durand gasped for breath as the life left his body.

"Captain!" cried one of his men from a ladder, those who had made it to safety apparently wondering what had happened to him. The young officer rolled to the floor then crawled rapidly toward him, the bullets no longer focused on the garage, as those outside engaged his fellow officers at the gate, now that both choppers were down.

This battle would soon be over, yet at what cost? His eyes burned as he pictured his wife and three little girls.

"Sir, are you okay?"

He reached up and grabbed the man by the shirt. "Tell my wife…" But he no longer had the strength, his world fading to black as the last of his strength left him, the dull thuds of the firefight dying in the distance.

"Captain!"

He jolted awake, a tremendous pain searing through his body as he gasped, his eyes shooting wide open as light flooded the darkness that had been.

"He's back!" shouted someone, the voice quickly fading as the adrenaline rush he was experiencing faded. His eyes were blurry, but as they focused, he saw people surrounding him, the walls of the chateau moving rapidly, several moments needed before he realized he was on a gurney. He felt himself drop then lift as he was shoved into the back of an ambulance.

"Don't worry, Captain, you're going to be all right. Just hang in there for me, okay?"

He said nothing, instead focusing on the light shining through the open doors of the ambulance, and wondered why he hadn't seen a light when he was dead.

For he was sure he was dead. There were no dreams, no sensations, just nothingness. And the very idea that there was nothing after this life, caused an overwhelming tightness in his chest.

"His BP is spiking."

"Captain, you've gotta calm down. Just take deep, slow breaths."

The giggles of his daughters echoed in his head, a reason to live remembered. He drew in a deep, slow breath, and the monitors he was hooked up to slowed their beeping as the doors slammed shut and the ambulance jerked forward.

"I died."

The paramedic leaning over him smiled. "Just for a couple of minutes, if that."

"I saw nothing."

The woman paused. "What did you expect to see?"

"Heaven."

She laughed. "You weren't finished here."

He nodded, the idea comforting.

My job isn't done.

And right now, the only job he was interested in was being a father and a husband. He sighed, closing his eyes. "I need a vacation."

Giasson watched as the latest of many ambulances blasted past with the wounded bound for the hospital. He had decided to simply remain seated, there still too much adrenaline in the fingers of those guarding them to bother challenging them once again.

"Hey, I need some help over here!"

Hugh?

Officers rushed toward the voice, Giasson leaning as far forward as he could, trying to catch a glimpse of what was going on. He smiled. Reading was standing near the main doors, his hands up.

"I'm Agent Hugh Reading, Interpol. I'm going to reach into my left pocket and get my ID. Everyone remain bloody calm, and somebody please tell me at least one of you lot speaks English."

Somebody said something that Giasson couldn't hear, but it was enough for Reading to produce his ID without getting shot. An officer inspected it, and weapons lowered.

"I've got a wounded man in here. Two actually, but one's the bastard responsible for this, so take your time with him."

Paramedics were called for, two gurneys pushed toward Reading's position. He disappeared through the doors, and Giasson smiled. His friend was too calm for anything serious to have happened to the professors. He closed his eyes.

Thank you, God.

"Someone's coming!" hissed Spencer. Laura headed for the door and peered down the hallway.

"It's me!"

She reached over and pushed Spencer's gun toward the ground. "Better give me that."

He nodded, his entire body trembling as he handed it over. She ejected the magazine and cleared the chamber, tossing the weapon aside as Reading rounded the corner, several armed police behind him.

And four paramedics with gurneys.

She heard their kidnapper groan and smiled as Reading arrived, giving his son a quick thumping hug. She pointed at the wounded man. "Watch him, he's one of the hostiles."

Two of the officers trained their weapons on the man who appeared in no condition to fight, a large pool of blood surrounding his leg. Laura urged the paramedics into the room, and they went to work on her husband as she held back, out of their way.

She chewed on her knuckle as Reading helped sort out the mess in the hallway, Spencer watching him like a proud son. She had hoped that their vacation would draw them closer together, and had hoped perhaps she and James could help in some small way. Never would she have thought that the two of them would charge to their rescue, bonding in the process.

Did he say he'd make a good copper?

Her eyes narrowed as she watched the boy for a moment.

I'll have to ask Hugh about that.

She chuckled.

His mother's going to hate that.

It had been the job that ended Reading's marriage, and Laura was certain his ex wouldn't want to lose her son to the job as well. She knew from Reading it could be a lonely life, an all-consuming one.

"Okay, let's go."

She turned to see the paramedics rolling James toward the door. "Is he going to be okay?"

The paramedic nodded. "He'll be fine. He's got the start of an infection, but he's stable. Some good drugs, lots of fluid and rest, and he'll be back to normal in no time."

James raised a thumb, smiling weakly. "You don't know me very well. I've never been normal."

Laura grinned, taking his hand as they maneuvered around the bodies, their attacker already taken away, his wound far more critical. "You know me, darling, I abhor normal."

She led the paramedics through the winding corridors, and they soon emerged outside, the sun just starting to fade in the west, the shadows from the tall stone walls casting long shadows across the courtyard, hiding some of the carnage. James was loaded into the back of an ambulance, but she was waved off from joining him.

"We have some questions for you," said an officer. "Don't worry, we'll take you to the hospital right away. But first, we need a few things answered."

She nodded as they were led out of the crime scene and through the gates. Then she grinned when she saw four convicts sitting in the grass. "Mario!" She eyed him. "Now, what did you do?"

Giasson smiled. "I tried to save *you*."

She turned to the officer. "Sir, this is Inspector General Mario Giasson from the Vatican. I can assure you he's one of the good guys."

The man's eyebrows shot up. "You mean he was serious about that?"

"Yes, he's a friend of ours."

"Very well." He flicked his hand toward the four prisoners, and their handcuffs were quickly removed. Giasson struggled to his feet, some limbs apparently asleep.

"Where's Jim?" he asked, concern written on his face.

"Heading for the hospital. He was wounded last night."

"Is he going to be okay?"

"Yes." She lowered her voice, giving him a lingering hug. "What are you doing here?"

Giasson held her closer. "We're here for the, umm, item."

Laura nodded, letting go. "Officer, if we could hurry this up, I'd really like to join my husband."

Off the coast of Saint-Pierre-la-Mer, France

Acton sat on the edge of the boat, peering over the side as people far healthier than him worked twenty feet below. It had been two days since the attack, and he was feeling dramatically better. His wound was healing, his new stitches were holding, and his infection was nearly gone. He was healthy enough that when he insisted on leaving the hospital, the frowning and tsking had been kept to a minimum. He had promised no heavy lifting, and to report to the hospital stateside as soon as he landed.

But he had no intention of leaving France without recovering the True Cross from the bottom of the sea.

While stuck in bed, Laura had managed to find where they had come ashore, and Giasson's men had conducted dives, locating the crate. It had been left untouched though guarded until the proper equipment could be arranged, and the moment it had, Acton had insisted on coming along. So much blood had been shed, including his own, that he wouldn't miss this for the world.

History was about to be made.

The motorized winch whined behind him, and he saw bubbles rising to the surface as four divers guided their precious cargo. The first corner of the crate broke the surface, and his heart hammered in anticipation, Laura squeezing his hand with excitement. The rest of the crate, still intact, cleared the water, and he sighed with relief.

"Thank God!"

Reading's eyes narrowed. "What?"

"It's not draining."

"What do you mean?"

"It means it was properly packaged. If it was just a crate with the cross thrown in, it would be filled with water, and it would be draining right now. That's just surface water coming off it."

His biggest concern had been what damage the cross might be suffering after three days on the seafloor. He watched as the crate was swung onto the boat and lowered, the Vatican specialists rushing forward. Giasson held out his hand.

"I think Professors Palmer and Acton should have the honors, don't you?"

Frowns of disappointment spread, though they acquiesced. Reading helped Acton over to the crate, and he lowered himself to his knees. Tools were handed to him but he waved them off, pointing to Laura. "Better let her. I'm liable to pop my innards again."

She smiled, her hands trembling with anticipation. She wedged the crowbar into the top of the crate and gently tapped it, then pushed down. The corner popped, and she quickly continued around the outer edges, Acton's heart pounding as she made quick work of the top. She stood, nodding, and the specialists raised the lid off.

Acton's pulse pounded in his ears, a large plastic wrapped box inside. A box cutter was handed over, and Laura leaned in, slicing the plastic away, the others pulling at it, a case revealed that matched the size of the cross they had seen in the Treasure Room just three days ago. It was surrounded with latches, at least two on each side, and Laura popped the three closest her, the others eagerly following, the top lifted away.

Acton rose to his feet to see the True Cross, finally in the hands of the common man after eight centuries.

And cursed.

"What the hell is that?"

Laura gripped his arm, her jaw dropping as murmurs of surprise turned into outright anger. Inside the case, inside the case so many had died to protect, was nothing but a pile of bricks, neatly filling the cross-shaped indentations.

Jacques Ridefort had lied to them the entire time.

A phone rang, and the ship captain reached into his pocket. "Allô?" He stepped toward his disappointed passengers. "Umm, is there a Professor Acton here?"

Acton held up his hand, still glaring at their betrayal. "Yeah, I'm Acton."

"It's for you."

Acton didn't react, still staring at the stones filling the crate.

"Monsieur?"

He tore his eyes away and looked at the Captain, then his phone. He took it. "Hello?"

"Professor Acton, this is Bernard Ridefort. I have a message from my brother, Jacques."

Acton's heart pounded. "Yes?"

"He asks that you join him at the Vatican at eight PM tonight, at the front gates to St. Peter's Square."

In Front of Saint Peter's Square, Outside Vatican City State
Rome, Italy

Jacques Ridefort sat in the back of the box van, his brother Bernard sitting across from him, Vincent at his side, the True Cross, freed of the packaging used to transport it across the Mediterranean in his boat, looking resplendent between them.

Vincent checked his watch. "Sir, it is time."

Jacques closed his eyes, saying a silent prayer, the pain of losing his son now overwhelmed by the knowledge 800 years of duty and honor were about to come to an end, a pledge made eight centuries ago about to be fulfilled. Three generations of peace had reigned in Rome and the Vatican, and the time had come.

The vehicle came to a halt, and Bernard opened the doors, stepping outside. He helped Jacques down and adjusted his tunic, the red cross emblazoned on a white background, the eternal symbol of the Knights Templar, proudly displayed in public by true Templars for the first time in seven centuries. His only regret was that he was too weak to wear his armor. Bernard and Vincent wore theirs, their tunics fluttering in the gentle breeze, Jacques peering out at the gathered crowds, curious as to what had shut down St. Peter's Square, and the streets surrounding it.

All had been arranged as requested, and tonight, the Poor Fellow-Soldiers of Christ and of the Temple of Solomon, would perform one last ritual before disbanding forever. Bernard and Vincent lifted the cross from inside the truck, lowering it to the ground. The crowd gasped as they realized what it was, rumors having swirled all day at what might be happening, someone leaking the news, though few had believed it.

Unfortunately, the True Cross wasn't returning home. That, Jacques feared, would never happen, peace in the Holy Lands perhaps never to come. But it *was* returning to the Church, where he had been assured it would be displayed publicly for the world to see, and to bring reverence to the man who had died upon it, staked by evil to a slab of wood thought lost forever.

Bernard smiled at him. "Are you ready, Brother?"

Jacques nodded, and Bernard and Vincent lifted the cross, Jacques positioning himself on one side, the beam crossing his shoulders. He had always dreamt that he would carry it alone should this day ever come, though that was not to be. He was too sick. Bernard supported the other side, and Vincent carried the foot so it didn't scrape on the stone.

He looked across the threshold into Vatican territory, Swiss Guards in their colorful uniforms forming two rows from the edge of the tiny city-state, extending to the doors of the basilica, where Jacques could see the Pope himself standing.

The murmurs from the crowds erupted into cheers and prayers as he took his first, painful step. He could feel Bernard reposition himself so he bore more of the weight for his dying brother, and he smiled at him. He didn't blame him for killing his son. It was necessary should this part of his plan have failed. His son could never possess the cross, could never lead the Order, and only his death could have assured both would never come to pass.

The pace was slow, excruciating. His heart hammered, his entire body shaking from the effort, but he forced himself forward. The roar of the crowd behind him gave him strength, and for the first time he felt what it must have been like when the Order was at its height, and the knights were adored by the pilgrims they protected. Pride surged through him, giving him renewed strength, and he pressed on, Bernard, pulling down on his side of the cross with his outer arm, relieving him of more of the weight, to the point he could barely feel it.

Part of him wanted to be burdened with the weight of it, as his Lord Jesus Christ had been so long ago. He wanted to experience what He had, yet he knew that wasn't to be, nor should it be. Nothing could match the burden He had carried that day, the weight of all Man's sins.

Today, Jacques carried eight centuries of sacrifice and secrecy, almost thirty generations of isolation and denial. The Templars had their revenge on their betrayers, yet had continued to pay the price to this day for those events. But finally, after all this time, trust had been restored, mankind and the Church had proven themselves worthy of the return of this precious relic, and the Knights Templar could finally rest in peace, with one last heroic display, proving to the world that they had never gone away, and that duty, and honor, were ideals that hadn't died so long ago.

A wave of weakness washed over him, and he dropped to a knee, the crowd gasping behind him.

"Sir!"

Jacques waved Vincent off, and forced himself to his feet, draping his arms over the cross once again, Bernard now holding almost all the weight without complaint. He stared ahead at the Pope and gathered dignitaries, smiling slightly as he spotted the two professors he had used to draw out his son. He regretted the danger he had put them in, yet it had been necessary. He had to mislead them to deceive his son, and while everyone was focused on the decoy crate, he had managed to sail across the Mediterranean to Italy unscathed. Judging by the smiles of excitement, mixed with looks of concern, he was confident this pair bore him no ill will.

His legs were like lead now, his chest afire with each breath, his shoulders screaming in agony. He had nothing left, nothing more to give. He dropped to the ground, mere feet from his destination, and rolled onto his back. Vincent rushed to his side as Bernard pushed the cross upright, several priests hastening forward to support it, his brother soon at his side.

"Jacques, are you okay?"

Jacques gasped, unable to speak, the pain too great, the pain all he now clung to. And as the sun set in the west, its last rays shone against the gold of the True Cross, and he smiled, the last sight he would see on this earth, that of a promise fulfilled, a duty completed, an honor restored.

Thank you, Lord, for giving me the strength.

And with one last gasp, Grand Master Jacques Ridefort was no more.

Tears streamed down Laura's face as she watched the final moments of an honorable man, and despite her previous anger over what he had done, she couldn't help feel anything but pity for the man, and pride in knowing such dedication still existed in the world today.

She stared at the True Cross, glowing brilliantly in the setting sun, as if it were the only thing of importance in this massive tribute to Christ, built in the center of the former Roman Empire. She watched as the Pope rushed forward, dropping to a knee, Bernard and Jacques' attendant standing respectfully to the side, as the final Grand Master of the Knights Templar was given his Last Rites.

Laura took her husband's arm and rested her head on his shoulder, looking up at him as tears unabashedly rolled down his cheeks. She closed her eyes, feeling his body tremble as he struggled with his own weakness, insisting on standing here with everyone for this moment that would go down as one of the greatest in modern history.

The Pope rose, then shook the hands of the two remaining Templars. "I thank you on behalf of Christians everywhere, for having protected the True Cross from the evils of man for so long, and for fulfilling your promise made centuries ago. You have done your family, and your Order, proud."

Both men bowed, then removed their tunics, carefully folding them, then placing them beside the body of their fallen brother. Bernard faced the Pope, pain etched on his face. "Your Holiness, our Order is no more, but we ask only one thing."

"Anything."

"Your Holiness, we ask that our fallen brother, who sacrificed everything, be buried with his ancestors."

Laura gasped and James gripped her hand tightly, the thought having never occurred to her.

The Pontiff bowed slightly, making the sign of the cross. "It shall be done."

Fontainebleau, France

November 29, 1314

Henry poured the poison provided by his grandfather, Sir Raymond, into the glass of wine, giving it a swirl before darting back into the shadows, an attendant rushing into the room where King Phillip continued his recovery from a hunting accident a few weeks before.

A hunting accident caused by Henry's father, spooking the king's horse with a well-placed stone fired by a slingshot to its hindquarters.

His entourage had claimed a nasty blow to the head resulting from a fall, unwilling to suggest he had been thrown from his horse without evident cause, that simply too embarrassing for a King to have had happened.

Henry and his father and grandfather, had prayed for the king's death, though had to be content with serious injury, one that had him convalescing in bed at his boyhood home where there would be fewer guards than if at the palace. It was decided that his grandfather, Sir Raymond, was simply too old for a mission such as this, and though his father was spry enough, he too wouldn't go unnoticed.

But a boy?

Henry hadn't needed to be asked. He had immediately volunteered. He had watched as the Grand Master died at the stake, had stood dumbstruck as he saw grown men weep openly, then felt the burning rage in the pit of his stomach as the treachery of Pope Clement and King Philip were discussed.

Money and power.

And probably a bit of jealousy.

Those were the reasons the Templars had been brought down.

King Philip held sway over the Pope, and he owed a great deal of money to the Templars. He also had owed an enormous amount to Jewish lenders, but had expelled all Jews from France in 1306, seizing their assets to escape that debt.

A year later, he had ordered the arrest of all Templars. He had seized their assets and properties, took over their bank, wiping his debt clean with the commission of the two atrocities.

He wasn't fit to be king, and wasn't fit to wield so much influence over the papacy.

Clement was dead, the Templar Curse credited for a fortuitous fire that had razed the church in which he was lying in state, a true act of God. Lightning had struck the building, burning much of it to the ground, leaving the diabolical Pope Clement a charred mass of bone and ash, just as he had left Grand Master de Molay only a month before.

It was a fitting end, reinvigorating Henry's faith in God, his father and grandfather both rejoicing at the news.

And now, today, the Templars would have their revenge on the man truly responsible for their downfall. He watched as the attendant helped prop the King up in his bed, then give him the glass of wine Henry had poisoned only moments before. He sipped it, then finished it off with two large gulps, his penchant for drink legendary among his inner circle, lore among his subjects.

Henry pressed against the wall, behind a tapestry depicting a hunting scene, peering out with one eye. The attendant bowed and left the room, and moments later, the king gasped, his entire body spasming.

Henry rushed from his hiding place and raced to the king's bedside.

"Help me, lad!"

Henry leaned over the king so he could see his face. "I bring you a message."

"From who?"

"From the last of the Knights Templar."

King Phillip's eyes widened as he continued to writhe in agony. "Wh-what are you talking a-about?"

"Grand Master de Molay said you would answer for your crimes, and my grandfather, Sir Raymond of Ridefort, swore he would see it through. You will die, today, knowing that the Knights Templar will continue to protect the True Cross from the evil that is your bloodline. And with the fulfillment of our sworn oath to make you answerable to God, my father and grandfather are confident He will deliver you to eternal damnation for the evils you have wrought upon the land."

The king reached for Henry, but the boy jumped back. "C-come here."

Henry shook his head, and the king lunged for him, falling from the bed and tipping over a nightstand. A tray clattered to the stone floor, prompting the attendant's return.

"What are you doing in here, boy?" She gasped. "My lord!"

Henry rushed out of the room as the attendant called for help, but he knew it was too late.

And he knew he had just committed his first act as a member of the greatest order of knights to have ever walked God's earth, knights who now had their revenge.

The Knights Templar.

THE END

ACKNOWLEDGEMENTS

This book was a challenge to write, and oddly enough, was inspired by a mistake. The Templar's Relic is my best selling novel, having made the USA Today list three times, and for some time, I had wanted to do another book featuring the Templars. Many ideas were tossed around, then I remembered a review where a reader asked who the four knights buried under the Vatican were.

And the idea was born. How about a book that explained who they were, and why they were there?

The idea excited me, then when combined with the mystery of the disappearance of the True Cross, the plot for this book was born.

But it was a mistake.

A mistake that pigeonholed me.

For the identity of the four knights *had* been revealed in The Templar's Relic, and they didn't match with what I had been writing. The reviewer had been mistaken.

This is the problem when you have dozens of books—it's hard to remember what you've written!

But I am a writer, and getting myself out of corners I've boxed myself into is something that I thrive on. So the fake nameplates were born. Problem solved. I think it was a clever way to deal with the issue, and I hope you agree.

Another challenge, of course, was that The Templar's Relic was centered around the scroll with the Koranic verse, and not the True

Cross. Weaving those events into this story was also tricky without dwelling on them, and if you haven't read The Templar's Relic, I encourage you to do so, so you can read even more about these characters and the scroll.

As many of you are aware, I like to take things from my life and throw them into my books. This one included the little Spanish town of L'Estartit, where I visited three times as a child, but also a little story from when we were driving down there the first or second time. The Reading anecdote about snorting his allergy medicine while approaching the border is from my own life. Good times!

As usual, there are people to thank. My dad for all the research, Lindy Jones Zywot for choosing Acton's beer (join me on Facebook to participate in these decisions!), Debbie Wilson for some horse equipment info, Brent Richards for some weapons info, Fred Newton for some nautical info, Dee Denton and Lindy Jones Zywot (again!) for some secret passageway help, Isabelle Laprise-Enright for some French translations, Kevin Dawes and Antoinette Ayers for some UK terminology help, and my proofreading team. And, as usual, my wife, daughter, and mother.

To those who have not already done so, please visit my website at www.jrobertkennedy.com then sign up for the Insider's Club to be notified of new book releases. Your email address will never be shared or sold, and you'll only receive the occasional email from me, as I don't have time to spam you!

Thank you once again for reading.

ABOUT THE AUTHOR

 With over 700,000 books in circulation and over 3000 five-star reviews, USA Today bestselling author J. Robert Kennedy has been ranked by Amazon as the #1 Bestselling Action Adventure novelist based upon combined sales. He is the author of over thirty international bestsellers including the smash hit James Acton Thrillers. He lives with his wife and daughter and writes full-time.

Visit Robert's website at www.jrobertkennedy.com for the latest news and contact information, and to join the Insider's Club to be notified when new books are released.

Available James Acton Thrillers

The Protocol (Book #1)
The Final Skull Has Been Found. Now All Hell's Breaking Loose.

Brass Monkey (Book #2)
Will a Forgotten Weapon and an Uncontrollable Hate Unleash the Ultimate War?

Broken Dove (Book #3)
Will a Secret Desperately Hidden for over One Thousand Years by the Roman Catholic Church Finally Be Revealed?

The Templar's Relic (Book #4)
The Church Helped Destroy the Templars. Will a Twist of Fate Let Them Get Their Revenge 700 Years Later?

Flags Of Sin (Book #5)
China is About to Erupt in Chaos!

The Arab Fall (Book #6)
The Greatest Archaeological Discovery Since King Tut's Tomb is About to be Destroyed!

The Circle Of Eight (Book #7)
Abandoned by Their Government, the Delta Force's Bravo Team Fights to Not Only Save Themselves and Their Families, but Humanity as Well.

The Venice Code (Book #8)
A 700-Year-Old Mystery Is about to Be Solved. But How Many Must Die First?

Pompeii's Ghosts (Book #9)

Pompeii is About to Claim Its Final Victims—Two Thousand Years Later!

Amazon Burning (Book #10)

In the Depths of the Amazon, One of Their Own Has Been Taken!

The Riddle (Book #11)

The Russian Prime Minister Has Been Assassinated. The World Stands on the Brink of War.

Blood Relics (Book #12)

A Dying Man. A Desperate Son. Only a Miracle Can Save Them Both.

Sins of the Titanic (Book #13)

The Assembly is Eternal. And They'll Stop at Nothing to Keep it That Way.

Saint Peter's Soldiers (Book #14)

A Missing Da Vinci. A Terrifying Genetic Breakthrough. A past and Future About to Collide!

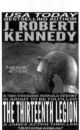

The Thirteenth Legion (Book #15)

A Two-Thousand-Year-Old Destiny Is about to Be Fulfilled!

Raging Sun (Book #16)

Will a Seventy-Year-Old Matter of Honor Trigger the Next Great War?

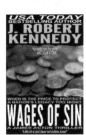

Wages of Sin (Book #17)

When Is the Price to Protect a Nation's Legacy Too High?

Wrath of the Gods (Book #18)

A Thousand Years of History Are about to Be Rewritten!

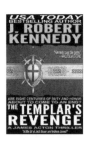

The Templar's Revenge (Book #19)
Are Eight Centuries of Duty and Honor About to Come to an End?

Available Special Agent Dylan Kane Thrillers

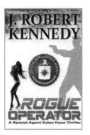

Rogue Operator (Book #1)
In Order to Save the Country he Loves, Dylan Kane Must First Betray It.

Containment Failure (Book #2)
The Black Death Killed Almost Half of Europe's Population. This Time It Will Be Billions.

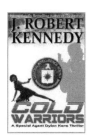

Cold Warriors (Book #3)
The Country's Best Hope in Defeating a Forgotten Soviet Weapon Lies with Dylan Kane and the Cold Warriors Who Originally Discovered It.

Death to America (Book #4)
Who Do You Trust When Your Country Turns against Itself?

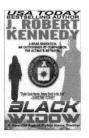

Black Widow (Book #5)
A Mass Migration. An Outpouring of Compassion. The Ultimate Betrayal.

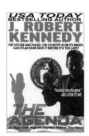

The Agenda (Book #6)
The System Has Failed. The Country Is on Its Knees. Can Dylan Kane Save It before It's Too Late?

Available Delta Force Unleashed Thrillers

 **Payback (Book #1)**

The Vice President's Daughter Is Kidnapped. Delta Is Unleashed on Those Responsible!

 **Infidels (Book #2)**

Islam's Holiest Relic Is Stolen. America Is Blamed. Chaos Erupts.

 **The Lazarus Moment (Book #3)**

Air Force One Is Down. But Their Fight to Survive Has Only Just Begun!

 **Kill Chain (Book #4)**

Will a Desperate President Risk War to Save His Only Child?

 **Forgotten (Book #5)**

One of Their Own Is Dead. Now It's Time for Revenge.

Available Detective Shakespeare Mysteries

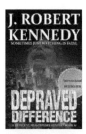

Depraved Difference (Book #1)
Sometimes Just Watching is Fatal.

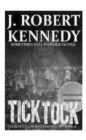

Tick Tock (Book #2)
Sometimes Hell is Other People.

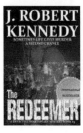

The Redeemer (Book #3)
Sometimes Life Gives Murder a Second Chance.

Zander Varga, Vampire Detective

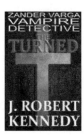

The Turned (Book #1)
Zander has relived his wife's death at the hands of vampires every day for almost three hundred years, his perfect memory a curse of becoming one of The Turned—infecting him their final heinous act after her murder. Nineteen year-old Sydney Winter knows Zander's secret, a secret preserved by the women in her family for four generations. But with her mother in a coma, she's thrust into the frontlines, ahead of her time, to fight side-by-side with Zander.

Made in the USA
Middletown, DE
26 May 2021